Deaths of the Shah

by Donald E. Hough

A new novel by the late Donald Hough, beginning in Persia (Iran) in the 1930s, turning into assassination and violence in suburban and rural America during the Twenty-First Century.

Library of Congress Control Number: 2009920134

ISBN: 978-1-932109-49-8

Printed in the United States of America
Ross & Perry, Inc. Publishers
3 South Haddon Avenue
Suite 4,
Haddonfield, N.J. 08033

Book Cover designed by Just Ink

DEDICATED WITH LOVE

to four fantastic women,
two beautiful granddaughters
and five handsome grandsons:

To Shirley, my wife, who gave me Cynthia, Rebecca and Melissa
To Cynthia, who gave us Logan and Riley
To Rebecca, who gave us Ryan and Zachary
To Melissa, who gave us Sam, McKenna and Dylan
    what more could I ask for.

PERSIA, THE NINETEEN-THIRTIES

PROLOGUE

The weather on the eastern slopes of the Zagros rarely had been hotter and drier this early in the summer. All but a few of the normally full runoff streams were now dry or slowed to a trickle. Sparse vegetation at this elevation offered little resistance to the searing midday sun, with reflected glare burning-out even the shadows cast by the rocky overhang bordering the rutted trail. However primitive, this twisting road through the mountain range was the shortest passage connecting the village of Deheq in the north with the trading center at Najafabad, more than a days journey southeast.

A heavily laden wagon inched its way over a rise, pulled by a lone mule, who at times seemed barely able to maintain headway. Rubble from frequent rockslides further impeded progress and caused the wagon to lurch wildly. The driver spoke continuously to the animal, first cajoling, then rebuking. The severe angle of a rear wheel went unnoticed as the old man concentrated on the treacherous trail ahead.

The wagon driver, Husein el Sadiq, was no stranger to the desolate province of Isfahan, having spent his entire life in these mountains. He had made this journey countless times since first accompanying his father as a small boy more than a half-century ago. He knew every rock formation and every turn in the road between his home, still hours away to the north, and the market where he traded figs, goat cheese and grapes for grain and other supplies. Today he had been on the move since dawn, and had stopped only twice; once to relieve himself, and once to eat his lunch of dried fish, black bread and cheese, in a small glen where he also refilled his waterskin from a stream – the last he knew he would find before home.

The rocky prominence bordering the right side of the road began to flatten as the wagon rounded a long bend. Gradually dropping to road level it revealed a panorama of fertile valley extending to the east as far as the eye could see. Rocky slopes sparsely tufted with green gave way to a stand of broadleaf timber, then rolling pasture and, disappearing in the distant haze, the quilted contrast of planted fields. Passing his favorite lookout, the old man stopped, as had become part of his regular routine, to admire the beauty and stark contrast of his world. Below, in a hillside clearing, he spotted sheep and goats and heard the shouts of two young shepherds as they herded their flock down a steep wash.

   Until now, he had led a very uneventful and colorless life, probably influencing no one. What Husein el Sadiq could not know was that in less than five minutes he would start a chain of events that would forever alter the history of the world.

The two boys were paying little attention to their charges. Achmed leaped over a slab of rock as he darted between two sheep to the far side of the gully. He roared with laughter and then yelled again at his cousin Mohammed, who had stumbled and fallen. It seemed no matter how hard he tried, Mohammed could not master these tricky slopes that were his cousin's playground. More than anything, Mohammed wanted just once to out-jump and out-run Achmed. He may be almost a year older, Mohammed rationalized to himself, but he can outrun me through these rocks only because he's spent most of his life up here with his smelly sheep and goats. Things would be different on the streets of my city. Besides, he smiled, being able to run like a mountain animal isn't as important as other things – his sisters all say I am more handsome, particularly Katarina.

Big for his age at twelve, Achmed outworked most of his father's hired hands, and was proud that his father considered him a man and gave him much responsibility. He loved his family and his home, but, even though he would not admit it to anybody, he was jealous of his visiting cousin. He was envious because Mohammed not only lived in the city in a big house with servants, but his father was the leader of the frontiersmen, the Cossacks, and everybody knew he was the most important and feared man in the province.

Despite his nagging envy, Achmed looked forward each year to early summer when his uncle brought Mohammed to spend the holiday. Even though his uncle stayed only a few hours, he came with gifts for the entire family and, before leaving, would pluck Achmed from the ground and take him for a whirlwind ride through the valley on his giant white stallion.

Besides his veiled resentment of Mohammed, Achmed had another perceived problem; being the youngest of six children. The other five were girls. Since he was after all his father's pet, this bothered Achmed only when his sisters persisted in treating him like a child and, worse, when they doted on Mohammed and told him how cute he was.

But because he could physically intimidate his cousin, envy notwithstanding, he secretly enjoyed having Mohammed around each summer. By taking great pride in showing Mohammed how to gather and drive the sheep, and how to tend the other animals, it enabled Achmed to brag to his sisters that he was certainly somebody special, definitely not their little brother. And because many people said they looked more like brothers than cousins, he also loved to show everybody how he could outwit his little brother and beat him in games such as they were now playing.

Mohammed could not keep up and had disappeared from sight. Probably fell again, thought Achmed, or was he hiding on the other side of the gully? As Achmed scanned the rocky slope his attention was caught by something near the top of the rise; a wagon stopped up on the high trail, the driver apparently watching him. Suddenly, a wheel collapsed, sending the rear of the wagon down over the edge of the rise. The driver jumped to the ground and tried to halt the slide of the wagon with his body. Mesmerized, Achmed watched as the man and his mule strained to stop the wagon's backward motion, only to have the rim of the road crumble and break away. The traces snapped, the animal lurched forward, and the wagon slowly toppled over the edge, the driver disappearing beneath it. In an instant a cloud filled with dirt and rock grew until it seemed the entire upper slope was cascading down the wash directly toward him. Achmed knew he was trapped; his only hope was to get beyond the far crest of the gully. His screamed warning to Mohammed was lost in the thunderous roar.

Mohammed, exhausted and out of breath, had been hiding behind a huge slab of rock when the deafening noise started. The ground began to shake and, before he could react in any way, his feet were swept from under him, causing him to fall beneath a rocky outcropping just before the avalanche roared past. In the lee of the sheltering ledge he escaped the main rockslide, but was caught in the spreading dirt and rubble. Quickly covered, he panicked at the thought of being buried alive and kicked and clawed with all his strength. Finally freeing his arms, he pushed the dirt from his face and gagged as he spit the choking grit from his mouth. Crying, the tears caking the dirt in his eyes, Mohammed kicked even harder to free his legs. His shame at crying quickly turned to anger – anger at himself – when he realized what his father would say, and how he would be teased by Achmed and his uncle, if he was seen crying.

Hearing a cry and thinking it was Achmed, he grabbed at the ledge in front of him and scrambled upright. He heard the cry again, but then realized it wasn't human, it was a half-buried sheep just a few feet away. Thankfully, the deafening roar had stopped and the sun could be seen again through the settling clouds of dust. Squinting through the haze he yelled Achmed's name again and again, but the only sound came from the few surviving animals on the far side of the gully. Mohammed retched when he realized that most of the flock was probably buried under his feet, and his cousin might be with them. His first reaction was to run – run to his uncle's farm, about three kilometers down the valley. But the thought of his father stopped him; *I must at least try to find Achmed. Father must be proud of me!*

Still sobbing, he wiped his face and mouth on his sleeve and stepped carefully through the fallen rock. Moving toward the bottom of the wash he saw some splintered wood and a broken wagon wheel protruding from the rubble. Totally confused and not knowing where to begin, he began pulling at pieces of wood. He stopped when he thought he heard his name being called. Nothing. He screamed Achmed's name again and again, and then listened. From almost below his feet he heard a faint voice, "Mohammed, Mohammed, I'm here...under the wheel. I can't move. Be careful...I'm hurt bad."

"I'll be careful, don't worry. Keep talking so I know where you are."

But silence from beneath his feet led Mohammed to scream his cousin's name repeatedly. Digging with a piece of broken wood, he exposed a cavity below the wheel, in which he saw Achmed's ashen face. Seeing his closed eyes Mohammed yelled over and over, "Oh no, no, don't be dead, don't be dead!" For what seemed an eternity Mohammed dug and pried and pulled. His hands were bloody when he finally made an opening large enough to drag Achmed through. Eyes now partly open, and obviously in great pain, Achmed mumbled that he couldn't move his legs, and then lapsed again into unconsciousness. Mohammed shook Achmed in panic when he realized his cousin might really die before he could get help.

A strange animal noise caused him to look up, and he was surprised to see a large mule angling down the rocky slope toward them. Not having seen the incident that started the avalanche, Mohammed had no idea where the mule came from, but shuddered with relief when he realized that the mule might help him save his cousin. If only he could grab the dangling reins.

Remembering a piece of leftover lunch bread in his pocket, he offered it and found the animal to be quite friendly, and easily led by the broken harness.

Mohammed was drenched with sweat when he finally succeeded in wrestling Achmed's lifeless body onto the mule. He lashed him in place as best he could with part of the reins and, shaking with fear and exhaustion, grabbed the mule's collar and began the long descent to the valley below.

Before reaching the road that led to the farm, the mule and boys were spotted by a farmhand who had been working on a perimeter fence. Having talked with both boys early that morning, the farmhand knew something was wrong when he saw the limp figure on the back of a strange mule. Minutes later he intercepted them in his horse-drawn tool wagon. After a quick look at the unconscious boy, without a word to Mohammed the farmhand untied Achmed from the mule and carefully lifted him into the back of the wagon. With a thankful Mohammed clutching both Achmed and the bouncing wagon, they sped at a full gallop toward the farm.

Achmed's mother became hysterical when she saw her son. His father screamed at the farmhand, "Get the big wagon, and hitch-up my four best horses. Now! Hurry!" He then ran through the house like a madman, tearing a mattress from a bed, gathering blankets, bandages, and canteens of water. Within minutes they were on their way to the hospital at Isfahan. The farmhand drove the team and Mohammed and his uncle rode in the wagon with Achmed, who now lay wrapped in blankets on the mattress, his head cradled in his father's arms. It would be yet another hour before they would arrive at the hospital.

Even though it served the entire province whose name it bore, the hospital at Isfahan was small and poorly staffed. The small oscillating wall fan did little to offset the stifling heat in the room. The lone doctor on duty in the emergency ward was sweating profusely. He and two nurses had just spent more than two hours attending Achmed's injuries, more the result of intimidation than dedication – Achmed's father had not left his side. The boy had sustained a broken leg, a fractured skull, at least three broken ribs, and numerous cuts and bruises. The doctor expressed concern about severe shock, about which he knew very little, and the fact that Achmed had not regained consciousness.

It was now well past sundown. Mohammed and the farmhand, uncomfortable with the heat and sickening odors inside the hospital, had returned to the wagon some time ago. After they both stretched out on the mattress, Mohammed, for at least the third time, was relating his terrifying experience in finding and rescuing his cousin. During their wild ride to the hospital Mohammed had told the story to his uncle, and was disappointed and angry when his uncle seemed too preoccupied with Achmed to listen. He would now be equally upset if he could see the sleeping farmhand. Mohammed's voice trailed off in the darkness as the excitement of the day finally caught up with him and, he too, fell asleep.

Inside the hospital, Achmed's father paced the dimly lighted corridor like a caged animal, impatiently awaiting the arrival of the hospital's director. Outraged when the staff doctor had been reluctant to discuss his son's chances for survival, he had demanded that the director be summoned from his home.

After what seemed like an interminable wait, the door to the outside flew open and the director stormed into the waiting area. He barked a reprimand and slapped an orderly dozing at the front desk. The staff doctor watched through an open doorway and mumbled to himself as he quickly ducked from sight – *tonight's going to be a nightmare, the bastard will make us all pay for having his dinner interrupted.*

Even though he had been furious when told that someone was at his door with a message from the hospital, occurring just as he was slicing the lamb roast, the director's anger quickly turned to fear when told the patient's name and the demands of the patient's father. He had left immediately for the hospital, knowing full well what the conesquences would be should he ignore the summons.

The director apologized effusively to Achmed's father for his delay in arriving, all the while mopping perspiration from his florid face and bald head. He yelled for the absent staff doctor and then directed the orderly to fetch cold drinks for him and his guest. When the staff doctor finally appeared he was greeted with a profane tongue-lashing for not summoning the director sooner and was ordered to immediately produce the boy's chart and x-rays. Twenty minutes later, after scanning the records and examining Achmed himself, the director led Achmed's father into his office. Closing the door behind them, he motioned to a visitor's chair and then retreated behind his cluttered desk, as if it offered him protection. "Sir, your son should survive his ordeal, but the next forty-eight hours will be crucial. I guarantee that he will have the best medical care available, and I, sir, will not leave the hospital until the crisis is past – on this you have my word."

Again mopping perspiration from his face, the director looked like he was about to have a coronary. "I suggest you go home now and return tomorrow..."

"No!" Achmed's father shouted. "I, too, will stay here. He is my only son...everything I have is for him! He cannot be allowed to die. I will stay here until he is out of danger. I will watch over him – and I will watch you!"

Four weeks later, Mohammed's father and mother arrived at the farm to attend a feast in celebration of Achmed's recovery. The only visible evidence of Achmed's injuries were a leg cast and crutches. The entire family was there, together with neighbors and friends from miles around. A pig and a lamb were roasting in an open pit, and tables were piled with mountains of food and sweets. There were dancing and games and singing and toast upon toast. But the highlight of the festivities came when Achmed's father lifted Mohammed to his shoulders and, signaling for everybody's attention, toasted Mohammed as the hero who had saved his son's life. Mohammed flushed with embarrassment when the people applauded. He was even more thrilled when later his father shook his hand, congratulated him, and told him that he never had been as proud as he was that day of his only son.

Even Achmed treated him differently now. And when Mohammed left for his home at the end of the summer, Achmed tearfully told him that he owed him his life, and such a debt could only be repaid in kind.

Little did he know.

THE UNITED STATES

THE NINETEEN-NINETIES

CHAPTER ONE

I didn't mind picking up David at the airport. What ticked me off was driving in a blinding rainstorm in my day-old car, a car that twenty minutes ago turned into an instant sauna when the air conditioner suddenly blew hot air. So much for technology and cars with automatic everything.

The Philly International terminal wasn't much more comfortable, but at least the rain had slowed some as I was parking the car. According to the arrival's board his flight was on time, which was the first thing to go right today. As I approached the gate the British Air passengers were just starting to file through.

His long flight and our heat and humidity aside, David Nesbitt looked like most people picture an affluent London banker, which he is; mid-sixties, steel gray hair and van-dyke beard, well over six feet tall without an ounce of fat and, as always, impeccably tailored. Walking ram-rod straight he obviously takes great pride in his appearance.

I haven't seen David in almost a year. We've worked together a number of times during the past dozen or so years, whenever his employer would retain my company to help spend their money – or more accurately, the money of one of their deep-pocketed clients. Over the years my company has found and bought things for them; things like ranches for raising cattle and thoroughbred horses, resort hotels, factories, farms, and land to build things on. All kinds of things. It was an intriguing relationship.

I'd guess that over the years we've spent about a half-billion of somebody's money, plus or minus a few mil. And from what we could piece together, it was all for the same buyer. We knew David, and we knew his bank – one of the oldest and most prestigious in England – yet we hadn't a clue as to the identity of old moneybags. It was a screwy business relationship, almost bizarre.

"David, good to see you again."

"Likewise, Cole. Looks like you're having a bit of weather."

"We've had sweltering heat and humidity for almost two weeks; one of those damned Bermuda highs. It's typical Delaware Valley August, but if we're lucky the storm will cool things off some. I sure hope so, because we won't have air conditioning until we get to my office. I took delivery of my new car yesterday, and on the way here the air conditioning died."

"Pity. Had I known you were shopping for a new automobile I would have sent you literature on one or two of our superior British motorcars," David chuckled, knowing his dry humor wasn't wasted on me.

After claiming his luggage, we returned to my car and headed for my office in Jersey, with the windows down. The rain had stopped, but it was still warm and sticky.

"Is our property settlement still scheduled for the day after tomorrow?" David asked.

"Yes, four o'clock on Wednesday. Before we have dinner tonight I'd like to review the survey and settlement papers with you. Tomorrow morning we can drive out and look at the land. We've completed a preliminary site plan and there are a few problems, mostly with drainage and a buffer zone, but after my last meeting with the township engineer I think we have solutions he'll accept."

"That's good. I am anxious to see the land, particularly the surrounding area, but tomorrow morning presents a problem. Before I left London I had my secretary change my hotel reservations here. I'm spending tonight at the Taj in Atlantic City; I thought I'd give the wheel a try – but I can be back in your office by mid-afternoon tomorrow. That should give us ample time to visit the site, that is if it's convenient for you. And by the way, you are more than welcome to come with me to the casino."

"No thanks, as close as AC is, I try to stay away; I never seem to know when to walk away from the table. But please go and enjoy yourself – it's not the least bit inconvenient. How are you getting there and back?"

"I've arranged for their limousine to pick me up at your office at ten o'clock tonight. That should give us sufficient time for dinner, wouldn't you say? They'll return me to your office tomorrow afternoon."

"Ten should be fine," I replied. "I have a great little Italian restaurant in mind for dinner. I think you'll enjoy it."

The wet roads made the commute traffic worse than normal, whatever the hell normal is these days. By the time we arrived at my office the staff had left for the day but, as usual, my partner Suzy was still there. Suzanne Hammel – I'm the only one allowed to call her Suzy – is the better half of Hammel & McQuaid, Incorporated. I'm the other half. We're primarily builders and developers, and we do most of our own engineering and design. Over the years we've also acquired a number of investment properties, most as settlement on bad debts. This led us into real estate management, which in turn brought us more business from David's bank; management of a few of old moneybag's properties. Truth is, we'll do just about anything in our field as long as it's legal and will make money.

Suzy is the widow of Walter Hammel, the founder of our company, who died six years ago in an automobile accident. Walter hired Suzy as his secretary when she came east from San Francisco with her young daughter about twelve years ago, running away from a bad first marriage. Walter had hired me fresh out of engineering school about four years before Suzy showed up. When I interviewed for the job he told me he had a sixty-year old body with ninety-year old knees, and he was looking for an engineer with a strong pair of legs who wanted to learn the construction business. I qualified on both counts and he hired me.

He was a widower, and even though considerably older than Suzy, he obviously also had an eye for a great-looking pair of legs. I always felt that she was somewhat on the rebound, and seemed to crave the kindness and affection that Walter freely gave – not only to her, but to her daughter Julia as well. But the chemistry must have been right, because less than three years later Suzy and Walter were married.

Walter had no children from his first marriage and, from the beginning, treated me more like a son than an employee. We quickly developed a bond that was even closer than I enjoy with my own father; partly, I guess, because I've lived about twelve-hundred miles from my parents since finishing high school. When Walter died so tragically I felt as though my whole world had ended as well; the future I had so carefully planned revolved around Walter and the business. I really enjoy engineering and design, and spent the first few years in the company rotating between board work and field assignments, but the last nine or ten years I've had precious little time on the drawing board; mostly chasing around from one construction project to another, or bird-dogging something for David's client.

Walter's estate was divided between Suzy, Julia and myself. I inherited a nice little nest egg plus about thirty acres of prime land near Hilton Head, Julia had her college education secured with a fantastic trust fund, and Suzy was left everything else, including the business.

In the weeks following Walter's death Suzy received and promptly rejected two very lucrative offers for the business. She said Walter left it to her and, by God, she was going to either run it successfully, or run it into the ground. And, much to my surprise, she offered me a full partnership to help her run it. She became Ms. Inside, while I as Mr. Outside. Not only does she do a great job managing the office, but she can wrap a tough client around her little finger in nothing flat, combining a no-bullshit approach with a rare mix of high-society class and sensual charm. Better yet, she uses the same approach to keep our accounts receivable on time. Our aging schedule has to be one of the best in the industry.

On the subject of age, I know she tops my thirty-eight years by at least three or four; Suzy jealously guards her age, and can get really testy whenever anyone is stupid enough to ask her about it. But, not so amazingly, her age is rarely the subject of male conversation. What is, is her long-legged blond good looks, and the way she fills-out her clothes. And it appears the heritage will continue for a long time; Suzy's fifteen-year old daughter Julia is a clone of her mother.

After David washed-up, he joined Suzy and me in my office. As he usually does when he visits, he produced two small wrapped boxes from his attaché case. Ever the gentleman, he bowed slightly as he handed both to Suzy. "Suzanne, you look lovelier then ever. This is another sterling owl for Julia's collection, and a small piece of Victorian jewelry I thought you might enjoy."

"Thank you, David, you're a dear," she said, "Julia will be pleased, and you know how I love Victorian jewelry. Julia's coming here directly from her tennis lesson – she's been looking forward to seeing you. She should be here any minute now."

"Suzy, bring Julia in when she arrives. David and I have a lot to do before dinner, and I'd like to get started. David's going to the casino later, so we have to be back here before ten. If you'd like, why don't you and Julia join us for dinner?"

"Thank you Cole, but tonight will be difficult. Julia won't be dressed for dinner, and I stayed late to catch-up on some paperwork; today has been absolutely impossible. Besides, I'm sure we can all get together before David returns home, possibly dinner tomorrow evening."

"Sounds excellent to me," David said with a grin, "as long as you all join me as my guests."

Dinner was exceptional. It's a small place where you bring your own wine. David and I shared an antipasto and then each had a great filet of blackened salmon, accompanied with sides of salad and linguine, warm, crusty bread and a bottle of my best Chianti. We finished with creamy cannoli and espresso. I've always had difficulty deciding which is more satisfying; good food or good women. I can live very happily with an excess of women. Luckily, good metabolism and exercise help offset my indulgence in the other.

We made it back to my office with half an hour to spare. My car's air conditioning still didn't work and, since it was a warm, steamy evening, I invited David in to wait for his limo. I decided to use the time to quiz him again about our mysterious client. Past attempts at this had produced almost nothing, so I decided to try a different approach.

"David," I started, after we settled into the two most comfortable chairs in my office, "Suzy and I consider you a good friend, in addition to being a great client. I'm sure I don't have to tell you what you and your bank have meant to Hammel & McQuaid. In the years we have worked together I don't think you and I have had one serious disagreement. But, unfortunately, the issue of your client's identity is beginning to cause real dissension between my brother Ben, Suzy and myself. I know you and I have gone in circles over this more than once – I've even tried making an inside joke out of it with Ben and Suzy – but Ben is dead serious and refuses to see any humor in it. And, common sense tells Suzy and we that we can't disagree with him.

"As our company attorney, Ben has badgered us for years to find out who we're involved with. It may seem ridiculous to you, but Ben's concern is that we're unknowingly aiding in the laundering of mob or drug money. He believes that if somebody were to come down on you or your client, Hammel & McQuaid would be in a very precarious position. Just yesterday, Ben told me he intends sending you a letter formally requesting identification of your client. He said he should have done it years ago. His pessimism and concern have started to rub off on Suzy, and, I admit, I'm getting..."

"Pardon me," David interrupted, an edge to his voice, "sending the letter will accomplish nothing, except to agitate my directors, and possibly jeopardize our relationship. Believe me when I tell you that we have been as concerned about this issue as your brother – and we have been for quite a few years. Not too long ago it resulted in the resignation of three of our directors. This happened when they panicked after discovering that over the years we had received a number of inquiries from Scotland Yard, Interpol, and even your own CIA, about the client's identity."

David got out of his chair and began pacing my office. His face was expressionless as he continued, "You must believe me when I say that no one in my organization knows who the client is. Also, other than myself and Alexander Trimble, our CEO, no one even has access to any of the key account records. With those records an investigation might uncover the name or names, but, with the mind-boggling paper trail and red herrings created by the client we're convinced it would take years of digging – and with no guarantee of success. Some years ago we did attempt an investigation, thorough but very discreet. It quickly ended in a blind alley and we backed off. To conduct such an investigation today presents a risk we just cannot take. It is not an exaggeration to say that if an investigation succeeded in identifying the client, and they in turn exercised their threat to terminate our relationship, it would most likely destroy the bank. At best, the financial impact would be staggering.

"Off the record, I can give you the reason for our dilemma, and how the whole bloody mess started." David's gaze drifted around the room. He seemed to be searching for words, almost stalling – totally out of character. He also was avoiding my eyes, and this bothered me even more. I'm pretty good at flushing-out a snow-job, so maybe I was hearing what he thought I wanted to hear.

"The account was first opened in 1953," he continued. "and by the way, the age of the account is what still convinces most of our directors that we are not handling drug money, either then or now. Likewise, the international dimensions of the account quells their fears about mob ties. Personally, I have disagreed all along with their rationalization – drugs and world-wide organized crime existed long before 1953 – but it satisfies them, so I keep my opinion to myself.

"To get back to my story, it all started when the bank received a detailed letter of instructions followed by a wire transfer from a Milan bank. The transaction was to cover the purchase of ten-thousand shares of our bank's stock – a relatively small purchase, and a bit out of the ordinary, but properly structured. What was odd were the instructions. They were brief, but very explicit. They stated that future investment activity would occur on a regular, but unscheduled basis, and would always be either by wire transfer or private courier. They also told us to retain all shares, unless notified otherwise, and to pay any administrative fees and taxes incurred by the account. Finally, they warned that outside accountants would conduct unannounced, periodic audits of their portfolio and, the kicker; that any attempt on our part to trace transactions, or otherwise meddle, would result in immediate loss of the total account.

"I've been told that Peter Willard, the bank officer who was assigned to handle the initial transaction, and later the full account, wasn't overly concerned about the unusual conditions. The bank was prospering in the post-war economy; our stock had appreciated more than twenty percent during the previous year, and Peter apparently thought the investor was some eccentric old coot trying to capitalize. At the time he also assumed that future investments would be in additional bank stock. He was wrong."

David sat down and loosened his tie. He was more up-tight than I had ever seen him and it was making me uncomfortable. "For the first year or so," he continued after a deep breath, "there was little activity, and the investments were limited to bank shares. But then we started receiving very large deposits, with specific instructions as to what other things we were to purchase or invest in. This type of investment management in the banking industry is fairly common today, but in the mid-fifties it was somewhat unique, particularly at our bank. Willard and the other bank officials at that time had, at best, little experience in such matters. In a matter of a few short years they placed the bank in an inextricable position. Alex Trimble and I agree they must have been blinded by optimistic dreams of unlimited bank growth, possibly fueled by personal greed.

"When I took over the account in 1967, after Peter's death, the bank had grown considerably, most of the growth attributable to the value of the account. It had mushroomed to the point where a majority of our directors finally began expressing concern about the phantom ownership. There was considerable talk about the situation – all behind closed boardroom doors – but they couldn't agree on a course of action. The issue was repeatedly tabled. By the mid-eighties, when Walter Hammel turned our projects over to you, the account represented a considerable percentage of our total assets. Today its value is staggering, probably more than the combined national budgets of two or three small countries I could name."

"David, I hear what you're saying. Most of it is news to me, but I seriously doubt it will change my brother's mind. And it'll add fuel to his argument when he hears your personal feelings about the possibility of drug and mob ties. You have to admit, it's a classic money laundering scenario."

"I agree, up to a point..."

"Look David, for now the best I can offer is to set up a meeting between you and Ben, maybe tomorrow afternoon after you return from Atlantic City. I think Suzy and I should sit in as well. Would that be acceptable with you?"

"Yes. I don't know what more I can add, but I'm willing to talk to Ben and try to convince him not to do anything rash."

"One other thing," I continued, "your statement that the bank's financial security would be jeopardized if the client's identity is disclosed puzzles me. How? What the hell David, if I know anything I know how much of the client's money Hammel & McQuaid has invested in hard, real property. No stocks, no bonds, no pork bellies or commodity futures. Just hotels, resorts, land, mineral rights, industrials – all rock-solid deals. We've never been permitted to buy into anything; it has always been *buy it all – or buy nothing*! The client wouldn't be a partner to anybody. I'm sure most, if not all, of our deals have appreciated ten-fold. I mean what the hell David, how can that hurt your bank?"

"Cole, your involvement usually ends when the investment is in place, so you probably don't know what frequently happens at the other end. You are correct about the present worth of most of the investments. Other than their early purchase of shares in our bank, no stocks, no bonds. And they have prohibited investment in any publicly owned entities. We can only guess that this is caused by their obvious desire for complete control, and concern for their anonymity."

David again got out of his chair and walked to the window where he gazed out at the darkness, his face expressionless. "We very closely monitor the performance of all account holdings. Early on, we were ordered by the client to liquidate anything that didn't appreciate at least seven percent each year. I can recall only one exception to that rule. And, regardless of performance, it applies to anything in which they feel a killing can be made with a quick turnover. So, and this is where the wicket gets sticky, with a percentage of the total account constantly being turned over, we're forced to retain considerable working capital, usually the proceeds of liquidated assets. However, to maintain a good bottom line, we invest most of this capital in short-term paper, usually at the highest current rate of interest. Good banking practice demands we do this. But this also forces us to outguess the client; we base our strategy on short-term market projections, plotted against what we think the client will order us to buy – massaging the crystal ball if you will – and creates the situation that can seriously hurt us. At any given time we're holding between four-hundred-fifty and six-hundred million in deposits for the client, only a small portion of which is liquid. Loss of the account would therefore cause a colossal cash flow pinch. If you understand the domino effect this might create, you can certainly appreciate our concern. It could even bring down the bank."

On a few occasions in the past I had actually felt guilty about some of the fees – large but legitimate – we had invoiced David's bank for our services. It now struck me that the effect of those fees was as significant as spitting in the ocean. The account was big all right; I never realized just how big. "I'm trying to understand, David, but it's hard to reconcile all of what you've said. How can so much money be handled for so many years without some direct contact, without a screw-up by somebody?"

"There have been a few, but fortunately they've been at our end and have been easily resolved. The basic procedure hasn't varied one iota since the first transaction." David looked at his reflection in the window and buttoned his collar and adjusted his tie. "All withdrawals requested by the client and account earnings are wire transfers to a number of banks in your country, South America and Switzerland, or are paid out as cash transactions, picked-up at our bank by courier, usually with about five days notice. They use a number of courier services, but never the same one twice running. Traceable, you ask? Probably. And I'm sure without too much effort; if it weren't for the confounded risk! All instructions and correspondence from their end arrive by messenger or, believe it or not, by regular mail. Mail comes with various postmarks, mostly from the continent, and always without a return address.

"Due to the paper balances on hand, actual deposits by the client are now much more infrequent, usually occurring only when they have ordered a major acquisition. When they do occur, it's by wire transfer from the same Milan bank. Speaking of Milan; in addition to the usual identification number, shortly after the account was opened it was labeled 'The Milan Portfolio' by Peter Willard. It is still known by the same name. And Cole, to put things in perspective, in 1953 all account records were kept in a single manila folder in Peter's desk. Today the account has a dedicated file room, with an integral vault, and is administered by myself and a staff of five."

I was about to ask another question when a honking horn broke the silence. His limo had arrived. We agreed to continue the discussion tomorrow afternoon and I gathered-up his luggage and headed for the parking lot. After wishing him luck in the casino, I watched the taillights of the white Lincoln disappear down the drive, then set the security alarm, locked the office and headed for home. The Phillies were playing in St. Louis and I could probably catch the last few innings on the tube.

On the drive home I thought about what I had heard tonight. It was mind-boggling. Whoever our oddball client was, he or she – or maybe it – had been around a long time, and was very, very rich. Too rich for my tired brain to comprehend. It had been a long day.

When I awoke the next morning the sun was shining and a light breeze was fluttering the birch tree outside my window. Mrs. Tomasello, my housekeeper, would undoubtedly suggest we turn off the air conditioning, as she usually did whenever there was more than a breath of air.

She didn't disappoint me. After I showered, shaved and dressed, I was pouring myself a cup of coffee when she came in from the rear yard, a bunch of fresh picked flowers in her hand. "Buon giorno," she said, "it's a beautiful day. The weather has changed, it's much cooler than yesterday and there's no humidity. Please turn off the air conditioning so I can open the windows. I love a breeze through the house."

"Consider it done," I said, smiling to myself. "By the way, I won't be home until late tonight, so please don't fix dinner for me."

"*Mi scusi*, you don't eat enough, and you're getting too thin," she said, scolding me with a wagging finger. "I'll fix something and leave it in the refrigerator for you. Something easy for you to heat-up when you get home."

"That won't be necessary because I'll already have eaten. Besides, I'm not losing weight, with you constantly feeding me I have to work like hell to keep my weight where it's been for the last ten years." As always, I knew this was a debate I'd never win, so I finished my coffee and headed for the door. After stopping to turn off the air conditioning.

"You won't let me cook breakfast for you either," she said, in her best wounded-dove voice, "so at least have some fruit on your way to the office, per piacere, and don't swear at me." She grabbed my arm as I opened the door and jammed an orange in my hand. Like I said, why argue.

Mrs. Tomasello is sixty-three years old, has two grown daughters, and buried two husbands before she was fifty-five. She's been my housekeeper ever since I got fed up with apartment living eight years ago and bought myself an old three-story Victorian money-pit in historic Haddonfield. She comes in three days a week to clean and do my laundry; no cooking – or at least that was the deal when I hired her. As it turned out, she cooks whenever I'm home to eat – sometimes when I'm not – and does whatever else she feels needs doing; everything from food shopping to watering the garden.

Angelina Tomasello is the traditional Italian momma; small in stature, strong as an ox, capable of totally intimidating you in her native tongue when she's frustrated or trying to impose her will, then wrapping you in a tender hug to show her affection. She treats me like a son, so I guess I shouldn't complain. And I'm sure she knows how much I care for her. When my parents came to visit from Florida, shortly after she came to work for me, I overheard part of a conversation between my mother and her. Mom gave her a complete set of instructions on my care and upbringing. I guess I'm now one of the few men accused of ignoring two mothers.

There was a stack of telephone messages from yesterday awaiting me on my desk. Nancy, my secretary, had also left a few letters for my signature. I knew I had about thirty minutes of peace and quiet before the staff arrived and the phones started, so I spent the time reviewing revised estimate sheets for a project we're bidding. It's a complex estimate; a new middle school and high school, plus heavy renovation of two old schools – lots of margin for costly error – and bids are due day after tomorrow. I'm due to meet again with our estimator at eight this morning to see how much we can sharpen some of our numbers.

Our meeting ended shortly after ten. I had just poured my second cup of coffee of the day when Nancy buzzed me. She said a Lieutenant Ronko of the Atlantic City police department was on my line and that he insisted on speaking with no one but me. Before picking up the receiver it flashed through my head that David had gotten into some kind of trouble, although I couldn't imagine him breaking the law. I didn't know anybody else in Atlantic City, and certainly not in their police department. "Hello, Cole McQuaid," I said.

"Mr. McQuaid, my name is Ronko, Lieutenant Ronko, with the Atlantic City police. I'm calling in regard to a David Nesbitt, from London, England. Do you know him?"

"Yes I do. He's one of our clients. What's the problem?"

"There is a problem, Mr. McQuaid, and it's serious. I can't discuss it on the phone, so I'm afraid I have to ask you to come to my office. If you don't have transportation I'll send a car for you. I'm sorry for the inconvenience, but it's important that you get here quickly."

"I have a car, and I can leave almost immediately, but can't you give me some clue as to what this is all about? Is David in jail?"

"I'm sorry, but I can't discuss it further on the phone. When you get here ask for me at the front desk – Lieutenant Al Ronko." He then gave me directions to his station from the expressway.

"I'll be there in about an hour," I responded, and hung up the phone. All kinds of crazy thoughts were racing through my head. What the hell was going on? It must be serious, but why hadn't David called me if he had a problem – why Ronko? I didn't like the answer to that question. I stopped at Nancy's desk on my way out and told her what Ronko had told me, and that I would call her as soon as I knew what was wrong.

I made it to Ronko's office in just under an hour, and found him on the second floor of the building. His office was small and cluttered, and reeked of cigarette smoke. He stuffed out a cigarette in an overflowing ashtray on his desk as he arose to shake my hand. He was on the short side, bald on top, with a fat face and bushy mustache. The mustache did nothing to hide his veined, bulbous nose. It looked like Al Ronko enjoyed his booze. "Please sit down, Mr. McQuaid, thanks for getting here so quickly." He produced a pack of cigarettes from his shirt pocket, shook one out, lit it and blew a cloud of smoke in my direction. "I'm sorry to have to tell you this, but there's been a homicide. David Nesbitt is dead."

Damn! My worst fear had just come true. I had pushed this reality from my mind a dozen times on my way here. I felt like I'd been kicked in the gut. "God, no! What happened...are you sure it's David?"

"I'll tell you what I can at this point, but first I need answers to a few questions. Also, when we finish here I'd like you to come with me to the morgue. The description of Nesbitt given to us by the hotel staff fits, but we need a positive ID. Now, when and where did you last see him?"

Cold sweat trickled down my spine as I recalled my conversation with David last night, and of the plans we had made for the next few days. I told Ronko about having dinner with David, and of seeing him off in the limo. I also mentioned David's plans for last night and today at the casino. "I'm curious Lieutenant, just how did you locate me so quickly?"

Ronko leaned across his desk and handed me a business card. "Recognize this?" he asked.

"Yes, it's my card. Where did you get it?"

"It was in Nesbitt's pocket when he was found. Just before you arrived I spoke with a girl in the limo service office. Your name came up there, too."

"Please, Lieutenant," I asked, "tell me what happened. This whole situation is unbelievable."

"Well, we're still piecing bits of information together, but apparently Nesbitt returned to his room from the casino around three this morning. He phoned room service and ordered breakfast for seven-thirty. We don't think he ever made it to bed. When the waiter arrived with breakfast he found the door partly open, badly sprung. When he pushed the door open he saw Nesbitt on the floor in the bathroom. The waiter called security; they called us. Everything so far indicates Nesbitt had been dead for a couple hours before he was found. Those hotel doors are tough. By the looks of things, whoever broke in had some heavy-duty equipment and knew what they were doing. And Nesbitt must have been taken by complete surprise; there were no signs of a major struggle, no calls to the desk, and nobody in other rooms on the floor heard a thing."

"How was he killed?"

"Two shots through the temple, one on either side. We know the shots were fired at very close range, probably with a silencer since nobody heard anything."

"Is it possible he was killed resisting a robbery? He could have been carrying a lot of cash; after all he came here to gamble. Have you checked with the casino to see whether..."

"Hold it," Ronko interrupted. "We don't think it was robbery, there are too many inconsistencies. And we have talked to some of the casino people. But before I go any further with this I need you to come with me to the morgue. We've got to have a positive ID, just to be sure. I'm sorry to put you through it, but you can save us a lot of time and trouble, particularly since he's from out of the country. After you confirm the ID we'll have to come back here, 'cause we'll need a statement from you, too."

On top of the foul smell, Ronko's office was hot as hell. My stomach needed this whole bad dream to end; I felt like I was going to lose my breakfast and I really didn't need any more upset – I needed to get outside. The morgue was probably in another building, and maybe on the way there I'd get lucky and find some fresh air. Besides, even though my heart still held out some hope, my head told me it was David.

The trip to the morgue did nothing to relieve my queasiness. Once inside, things got worse. When the attendant pulled back the sheet I knew it was David, not so much by the facial features as by the hair and beard. Unfortunately, there wasn't a doubt. I've always considered myself physically and emotionally tough, but I had never seen what gunshot wounds can do to a human face. The attendant offered to uncover more of the body if I had any doubts, but cautioned me that there were other wounds. I said no thanks, I had seen enough.

On the way back to the station Ronko questioned me about David's personal life, what little I knew of it, and his relationship with my company. He admitted that they had no suspects, but that the lab crew was still in the casino hotel room doing their thing, and that maybe they would turn up something his people could run with. He didn't sound the least bit optimistic.

I again questioned the possibility of robbery. "Anything's possible," he responded, "but I still don't think so. I admit, we have a lot more in-house casino robberies than the public ever hears about, but they rarely result in murder. Usually the victim gets mugged by some low-life trying to cover his losses, or by a doper desperate for a fix. We're waiting to talk to the roulette dealer from Nesbitt's table when he comes on duty today. One of the pit bosses remembers Nesbitt and said he thought he dropped about six or seven hundred at that one wheel, but he didn't flash around any big money. To further spoil your robbery theory, Nesbitt's wallet and credit cards were scattered on the bed in his room, along with traveler's checks and more than seventeen hundred bucks in cash. Why would thieves or druggies leave that kind of loot behind? It just doesn't happen, particularly when it appears they weren't scared off. The only thing that appears to be missing is his luggage. There was none in his room and the bellhop can't remember for sure, but he said he took up two or three bags when Nesbitt checked in. He said Nesbitt also gave him a nice tip."

"He had a carry-on bag and a two-suiter when he left my office last night," I said. "I know because I carried them out to the limo. But why in hell would somebody leave behind that much cash and steal two suitcases? It's crazy."

"Exactly," Ronko answered, pulling into the station parking lot. "There are a lot of things that don't add up. When he was found, your friend was gagged and his hands and feet were bound with duct tape. He also had what looked like burns – maybe from a cigarette or cigar – on his hands and the soles of both feet. It was almost as though he was being tortured. Maybe we'll know more after the autopsy. It's scheduled to be started within the hour."

I still couldn't believe any of this, it was crazy. I followed Ronko back upstairs and gave my statement to a police stenographer. I told Ronko I'd take care of notifying London about David, and that I would call him as soon as possible with instructions for the body. Ronko knew how to reach me, and I asked him to call me immediately if the autopsy turned up anything or if there were any other developments. He said he would.

Walking back to my car I felt totally wiped out, and I felt even worse knowing I had a couple of tough phone calls to make. My car was parked in the sun and was stifling. After putting down the windows, I called Nancy on my car phone and, as directly as I could, told her of David's death – leaving out the grisly details. She was stunned. She probably had had more frequent involvement with David than anybody in our office, including Suzy and myself. She usually talked with David or his secretary at least once a week. She liked him, and enjoyed mimicking his clipped British accent. I asked her not to say anything to Suzy; I'd take care of that myself, and I wanted to do it in person. I also told Nancy to cancel everything on my schedule for the next few days, since I had no idea what'll happen when I call London. I sensed, rather than heard, Nancy crying on the other end of the line. After I ended the call I fiddled again with the air conditioning controls, to no avail.

So I left the windows down and drove home with the wind whistling through the car, trying to get the stink of death and cigarette smoke out of my nose and off my body.

Suzy and Nancy were sitting in my office with the door closed when I arrived. They were quietly talking and trying to console each other. Nancy saw the unasked question on my face and apologized. "I'm sorry, Cole. I came in here to be alone and Suzy came in and found me crying. I had to tell her."

An apology certainly wasn't necessary and I said so. They both asked the expected questions, and I told them what I had found out in Atlantic City, leaving out the details I didn't even want to think about, much less discuss. When I mentioned David's missing luggage, Nancy said that shortly after I left for Atlantic City she had found his attaché case standing on the floor next to the sofa here in my office. She had put it in my closet for safekeeping. She said she knew it was David's because of the hunter green color; he had had it custom made some years ago. I guess he and I were so preoccupied with our discussion last night, the attaché was overlooked when we walked to the limo.

It was now almost nine-thirty in the evening, London time, and I couldn't chance waiting any later to call. I asked Nancy to get me David's home phone number, but had second thoughts as I started to dial. *Damn!* I just hated delivering this kind of news by phone, even though I knew I had no choice. On top of that it seemed almost cruel for me to call his wife when I had never met the woman. Then I remembered that because of the time difference, David had also given Nancy other phone numbers where he might be reached after banking hours. I asked her to check and was relieved when she found a home telephone listing for Alexander Trimble, David's boss. I don't know why, but I felt a lot more comfortable calling him. I couldn't delay any longer so I dialed Trimble's number.

A woman answered the phone. I asked for Trimble by name, and after a long wait he came on the line. "Mr. Trimble, we've never met. My name is Cole McQuaid, of Hammel & McQuaid in the States. We've worked with David Nesbitt and your bank for a number of years..."

"Yes," he interrupted. "I know exactly who you are, Mr. McQuaid, David has told me quite a bit about you personally. And I'm certainly familiar with your company, including your latest endeavor. The parcel of land you procured for us seems to meet all of our client's specifications. But why are you calling, isn't David there with you?"

"Mr. Trimble, I'm sorry to have to tell you this, but I have very bad news...David is dead. He was killed early this morning." I heard a gasp at the other end and then a deep sigh. I waited, not knowing what to say next. Finally, Trimble spoke, his voice quivering, "McQuaid, oh god, this is terrible. He and I have been close friends for over forty years. This is unbelievable...you say he was killed – was it an accident?"

"No, I'm afraid he was murdered. The police say they have no suspects, and apparently they're not even sure what happened." I then told Trimble about David's side trip to the casino, and what I knew about his death. I also mentioned that David's family had not been notified. When I finished he said that he and Mrs. Trimble would immediate visit Mrs. Nesbitt to inform her of what had happened; the Nesbitt home was apparently just a short distance away. We then discussed arrangements for sending David's body home.

"Mr. McQuaid, if you'll be so kind as to contact British Air and arrange for shipment of David's body, I'll take care of everything on this end. Just let my office know which flight he'll be on. I believe they have a flight out of Philadelphia every evening. And please, call me if your police uncover any further information...anything. Do you feel the police are competent? Should we hire our own investigator?"

"Mr. Trimble, I'll take care of everything here. I think we should be patient and let the police handle things, at least for a few days. I don't even know the results of the autopsy yet. But I promise you, if I feel they're not doing enough, I'll call you. At this point I don't think a private investigator can do any more than the police."

"All right, I trust your judgment. At the moment I'm finding it very difficult to think straight. This news is so shocking to me I'm not sure what I should do, but there is one thing of which I'm certain; I think it very important that you and I meet in the immediate future. David's death is going to be devastating to my Board, and they're going to have many questions that I probably cannot answer. On the other hand, if his death was not the result of random violence, there are some things that may have a bearing on what has happened. At least you should know what they are. I apologize for the imposition, but how soon could you come to London? Of course we'll pay all expenses."

I was more than a little confused by what I'd just heard. David's death was scary enough, but what the hell was Trimble talking about? I'm not sure, but I knew I'd have to find out. "Can't we discuss this by phone, maybe in a day or so? It would certainly simplify things."

"No! I'm sorry, but that is out of the question – it is too risky. After we talk you'll understand why. I would greatly appreciate your cooperation in this." Trimble may not realize it, but he really knows how to sink the hook. Now I'm really puzzled and frustrated. And if the situation wasn't so somber I'd probably be ticked-off. All my life I've hated waiting for things; particularly things that directly affect my life or my business. Things like waiting for a phone call you know is coming; tomorrow's answers to today's crossword puzzle; waiting for people to make a decision, when you know they've already made one – like bankers and clients; and waiting for people to share important information they admittedly have – like now. Maybe I'm just impatient, or maybe it's a flaw in my personality, but it annoys the hell out of me. Under the circumstances I guess I have to bite my tongue and cooperate.

"Well, today is Tuesday, Mr. Trimble, I'll have to cancel or reschedule some things to come this week, but that shouldn't be a major problem. There's also the question of how soon David's body will be released, and what you want us to do about settlement on the new property. It's still scheduled for tomorrow afternoon at two."

"Have the settlement postponed for thirty days. That certainly is not an unreasonable request, considering what has happened. If they refuse to cooperate let me know and I'll call them and threaten to cancel the entire deal.

"If David's body is released tomorrow or Thursday, you might possibly accompany it home. I'm sure services could not be held before next Monday, and that would allow us to meet on Friday or Saturday. I do think we should talk as soon as possible."

"Postponing settlement shouldn't be a problem, I'll call them first thing in the morning. I'll also call the police about David's body. And please assure Mrs. Nesbitt that we'll handle all arrangements here. I should be able to call your office by four tomorrow afternoon, your time, and give you the details. There is a British Air flight out of Philly for Heathrow every evening; at least there was the last time I flew to London. I don't know if everything can be done in time for the Thursday flight, but we'll certainly try. Friday is probably more realistic."

"Just do your best, Mr. McQuaid. I'm sorry you had to get caught up in this tragedy, but on behalf of all of us here I do thank you for your kind assistance. David and his wife Anne just celebrated their fortieth wedding anniversary – they were very close. I really dread calling on her tonight with such terrible news."

It was shortly after five when I walked into Suzy's office. She was curled up in a chair, looking out the window, and holding a cup of tea. Her eyes were still red and puffy. I told her about my conversation with Trimble, and asked why she hadn't gone home, considering how upset she was.

"I waited because I hate the thought of facing Julia alone with the news about David. She thinks the world of him. He has been the closest thing to an uncle she has ever had. I'd be grateful if you'll come home with me and help break the news to her."

"Sure, I understand how you feel. I'm sorry that both of you have to go through this. I can't help but think back to when Walter was killed. I was worried about how you would come through it, but I was totally convinced it would destroy Julia – she had become his pet, and other than you probably the center of his world. But we both know she handled it well, and seemed to get her life back on track faster than either of us. So don't underestimate her ability to cope. She's tough Suzy, and she's a survivor. Maybe it's just another blessing of youth."

"You may be right, Cole, but she's much older now and I just don't know how she's going to react. She baby-sat for a neighbor this afternoon, but was supposed to be home about half an hour ago. I haven't called because I'm afraid my voice will give me away if she answers the phone. She's probably getting dressed for dinner now, as you know we were supposed to be David's guests for dinner this evening. I hate to impose, but if you don't mind I think we should leave right away. I certainly don't want her hearing about David on the radio or TV."

Julia was coming down the stairs as we came into the living room. She was dressed for dinner, and her big smile told us that she hadn't heard the news. I got my usual high-five, low-five greeting from her, followed by a solid punch to my shoulder, to which I responded by pinching the tip of her nose. Julia is an unbelievably competitive athlete. A high school sophomore last year, she beat-out a junior and a senior to advance to first-singles tennis. She also played soccer, passed-up basketball because she thinks it's a stupid game, and, at third base was the leading hitter on the varsity softball team. But with all of that, Julia is a very beautiful young lady, and probably the nicest, most level-headed teenager I've ever known. To my knowledge, she has never given her mother a moment of grief. The only problem I've heard Suzy mention was the issue of Julia's dating; Suzy absolutely forbids lone dates until Julia is sixteen. Given the number of young stallions I've heard about, if she were my daughter I'd probably never let her out of my sight. At five-seven she is only an inch shorter than her mother. Her light blond hair is long but curly; it balances her height and beautifully frames her wide, full mouth and striking blue eyes. She and her mother have the most vivid blue eyes I have ever seen.

It upset me to think about what I had to do. It saddened me even more when my mind raced back in time six years, *dejavu; I had stood in this same room, fumbling for words, trying to tell Suzy as painlessly as I knew how that Walter had just died in an automobile accident.* A few minutes ago, on the way home from the office with Suzy, I was searching again for words to use with Julia. As I stared at her, I knew there were no right words, and that any further delay on my part would not make the telling any easier. Suzy's face was white as a sheet, and I guess mine reflected my thoughts; as I looked at Julia the smile left her face and she asked me what was wrong. Instead of answering, I took her by the hand and led her to the sunporch, with her mother following behind.

When I finished talking, Julia stared at me in silence for what seemed an eternity. Suddenly, she threw her arms around my neck and began sobbing. "It's not fair," she cried, her tears wetting my cheek. "First I lost my daddy, now uncle David. Why does it always happen to my family, to me...it's not fair. It's just not fair, dammit...it's not!"

The three of us sat on the sun porch until well past sundown. I held Julia in my arms until the tears stopped and she finally began to calm down.

She then began asking questions about how David had been killed. I told her he had been shot, but was determined not to tell her any more. So I lied, and told her I had no further information or details, but that we probably will know more after the police finish their investigation. We hadn't eaten dinner, so I went to the kitchen and found the ingredients for a batch of McQuaid's famous country scrambled eggs. With muffins, jam, and lots of hot coffee, it makes for a decent meal, even though it's a much better Sunday breakfast. The three of us kind of picked at the food and wasted more than we ate. I cleaned up the kitchen while Suzy helped Julia get ready for bed, and finished just as she walked through the kitchen door and said that Julia was already asleep. The sedative she had given her earlier had apparently worked. "I'm glad," I said. "it's been a long, tough day for all of us. The next few aren't going to be much better either, I'm afraid. I'm going home and hit the sack."

She took both my hands in hers and looked up at me. "I couldn't have gotten through this tonight without you," she said softly, tears glistening in her eyes. "Thank you for being so kind to Julia, and to me." With that, she kissed me tenderly on the mouth. In the years I have known Suzy, that was the first personal contact we have ever had, other than the usual Christmas and birthday pecks on the cheek. Even though we have been partners for some time, I have always considered her the boss's wife. Untouchable. And she has never indicated that she wanted it any other way. I guess old habits are hard to break.

By nine-thirty the following morning I had contacted Ben and the property owner's agent and their attorney, and agreed on a new settlement date. The agent and his lawyer both bitched about the eleventh-hour postponement, but when I explained what had happened they reluctantly went along. It also didn't hurt that we threatened to walk away from the deal if they refused. I knew they needed our cash much more than we needed their land.

I then called Ronko. He told me the autopsy hadn't produced any surprises; the cause of death was the gunshot wounds. But David had been tortured before he died. Aside from the burns Ronko had mentioned yesterday, David's lower abdomen and groin areas had been pierced numerous times with something sharp, maybe an ice pick. Ronko said the wounds weren't deep, but had occurred before he died. There was a lot of blood. *God, David must have gone through hell!*

"Look Lieutenant, David was big and strong, and in good shape. There is no way one person could have done this without a helluva fight, and you said there was no sign of that in the room. It just doesn't add up – something's wrong. The only way it could have happened is if there was more than one attacker. Even then they would have had a fight on their hands. Maybe they drugged him."

Ronko mumbled something I couldn't understand, then responded in a voice so low I could hardly hear him, "We know he had a few drinks, but drug results were inconclusive. The lab boys still have some more tests to run. And we haven't ruled out the possibility that more than one person was involved."

There was a long pause. I was about to say something when he continued, again almost whispering, "Mr. McQuaid, I'm sorry, but I've said too much already. I'm not even supposed to be talking to you. I'll tell you part of it, but only because I think you should know that something screwy is going on with our investigation. Maybe you know something I don't. First thing this morning Captain Murphy called me into his office and chewed my ass – but good. Murphy's my boss. He said he doesn't like the way I've handled Nesbitt's homicide; supposedly sloppy procedure on my part, too many loose ends. So he ordered me not to discuss the case with anybody, including you. It's goddamn ridiculous, the case isn't two days old and *everything's* been done by the book. Murphy's had nothing to do with the investigation until now – he was off yesterday and hasn't even read my reports – so I told him it looked like somebody was squeezing him to muzzle me, but

I sure as hell can't figure out why. He denied it; said I was overreacting. Truth is, other than the casino people you're the only outsider I've talked to, and the killing has gotten hardly any media coverage. After my session with Murphy, I had my men do a quick check through the department. As far as we can tell there have been no calls about Nesbitt, other than yours, and no sign of anybody snooping around. I don't know who or why but somebody got to Murphy; he knows who you are, and knows you were here yesterday, and that we talked. I told him I didn't discuss the investigation with you, that in fact you could be considered a suspect, and I only answered some of your questions because you i.d.'d the body. That's when he said no, you're a civilian, and could compromise our investigation; you'd just have to keep your nose out of police business. His words exactly. It's bullshit, you never stuck your nose in our business – I think he's the one overreacting. Just understand that Nesbitt's homicide still has top priority with my squad, and I'm not the one stonewalling you – I'm only following orders. Oh, one more question before we end this; you said Nesbitt was a London banker, do you know anything more about his background that might explain Murphy's action – was he some kind of big shot?"

"David was *just* a banker, and a hell of a nice guy. He was one of the top two or three executives in his bank, but certainly no 'big shot'. I've already told you all I know about him. I have no idea why anybody would pressure your boss or interfere with your investigation, certainly nobody I know of. And I have no intention of meddling in your case; all I want is for you to catch the bastards who killed him. I talked with David's boss last night, and believe me, he feels as I do about this, and he expects results. I can promise you that he has the resources to back up his demands and, if you don't come up with something in the next few days, you're going to have his private investigators all over your case like ants at a picnic – whether your boss likes it or not. That's the way David's boss wants it, and I can assure you that's the way it's going to be. Understood?"

I knew I was going well beyond what Trimble and I had discussed last night, but since I didn't have a clue about where this guy Murphy was coming from, I felt it was a bluff worth running.

"Yeah, I do." He started to say something else, but stopped. Again there was a long pause before he continued. "I really can't talk any more now, but I'll tell Murphy what you said about Nesbitt's boss. In fact, it'll give me great pleasure. One other thing before I hang up – Nesbitt's body can be picked-up anytime this afternoon or tomorrow morning. We're finished with it. Are you handling the arrangements?"

"Yes, in fact that's the main reason I called. I'll call the funeral director now and see if I can have the body picked up this afternoon. I'm going to fly to England with the body, and I probably won't be back before next Tuesday or Wednesday. So, if anything important develops, tell your boss to call Nancy Todd, my secretary. She can get in touch with me, *if she thinks it's necessary.*" I hope my sarcasm was obvious. "And before you hang up, I have one question for you: what the hell do you mean by saying 'I could be considered a suspect'? How the hell can that be?"

"Come on, Mr. McQuaid," he said with no humor in his voice, "unless we find evidence to the contrary, anybody who had contact with Nesbitt is a suspect."

I resented it, but he was right.

After I hung up, I called an old college buddy who manages a local funeral home. I explained what had to be done, and he agreed to have everything ready for a Thursday evening flight; all he needed was the airline and flight number. I turned that chore over to Nancy and made my promised call to London just before eleven – four o'clock their time.

When Trimble came on the line he said he and his wife had spent most of the night with Anne Nesbitt. She had taken the news of David's death very hard. At first, she insisted on immediately flying here to be with him. Trimble had talked her out of it, but was relieved to hear that I would be arriving Friday morning with the body. He asked if I had checked other airlines for an earlier flight; I said no, I'd be coming British Air. I do a fair amount of flying, but unfortunately not as much as I'd like to Britain. Some of our domestic lines are O.K. but when I fly to England or Scotland I use British Air. I'm just impressed with the way they run their airline: smooth takeoff, drinks, close the shades, drinks, dinner, drinks, nap, breakfast, open the shades, smooth landing. Very orderly, good drinks, decent airline food, very professional.

"There's only one British Air flight each day from Philadelphia," I said. "It arrives at Heathrow about seven-thirty in the morning, your time. You mentioned that the funeral service probably won't be until Monday. I'd like to attend. You and I could meet any time before Monday that's convenient for you."

"That's fine. I'll take care of arrangements here for the body, and I'll have a car pick you up at the terminal. The funeral service has been tentatively scheduled for eleven Monday morning, pending your call. I'll firm that up now. Services will be held at the family church just outside London, with burial in the church cemetery. If you'd like, we can meet in my office late Friday afternoon – that will give you time to check into your hotel and freshen up. We can conduct our business and then I'd like you to be my guest for dinner Friday evening. Can we arrange hotel accommodations for you?"

"No thanks, Mr. Trimble, that's not necessary. I've been to London a few times and know a number of good hotels. I'll have my secretary find out what's available and make a reservation. As far as our meeting is concerned, Friday afternoon sounds fine."

I no sooner finished talking with Trimble when Suzy walked into my office. A good nights sleep had done her a world of good; she looked great, and had the familiar sparkle back in her eyes. "Cole," she said, "If you have no serious objections, I'd like to go to London with you. I feel I owe it to David and his widow; I've never met her, but given the circumstances it must be doubly difficult for her. Besides, I've never been to England and I haven't had a vacation in three years. With all that's happened I think it would do me good to get away for a few days."

"I agree... it's kind of a somber occasion for a vacation, but I certainly have no objections. In fact, I'll enjoy your company – I hate traveling alone. But what about Julia, you can't leave her home alone."

"I wouldn't, I'm still concerned about her. I hadn't thought about going with you until Becky Seifert called before breakfast this morning. Becky invited Julia to spend the next ten days with her family and her at their cabin in the Poconos. The Seiferts' live just down the street, they're really lovely people. Becky and Julia are classmates. At first, Julia said she couldn't go; she told Becky she had to stay home to take care of me, can you imagine? I knew it would do her good to get away too, so I lied. I told her you had asked me to go to England with you, but I couldn't leave her home alone. Within a minute she had called Becky back and agreed to go. They'll be leaving this evening right after dinner. If you had said no I'd be in deep trouble."

"Good," I said, trying to keep a straight face. "I just changed my mind – you can't go. It'll be worth going alone just to see how you wiggle off the hook with Julia."

"That's not fair. Besides, I can invoke executive privilege. After all, we are equal partners – I have as much right to go as you – so there!" Problem was, she couldn't keep a straight face, so we both had a good laugh, our first in some time.

"O.K.," I said, "We both go. We'll be leaving tomorrow evening; I'll have Nancy make the arrangements. Trimble wants to meet with me Friday afternoon, and have dinner Friday evening. I don't recommend that you attend my meeting with him; my gut feeling is that we'll be rehashing everything that's happened, but maybe you could join us for dinner."

"I think you're right, but I'd also rather not attend dinner either. It'll give you an opportunity to get all of the talk over with. I'll do some shopping, or maybe just relax at the hotel."

"One other thing, Suzy, Trimble said they will pay all of my trip expenses. I have no intention of letting him do that, but I don't want to offend him. Having you along will make it easier to decline; we're there to pay our respects to David's family, but we're also taking a little vacation."

After lunch I had Nancy make the travel arrangements. In deference to Suzy's desire to shop, I told Nancy to try for two rooms at Dukes Hotel, just off St. James Place. It's in a great part of London, but is relatively small and quiet. It's also within walking distance of some of London's best stores, and is only a short taxi ride from Trimble's bank on Queen Victoria Street.

When Nancy buzzed me a short time later she said everything was confirmed. She reminded me to pick up traveler's checks and to dig out my passport. She said she had also reminded Suzy about her passport. Suzy had gotten a passport about a month before Walter was killed – he was going to take her to Paris – but she never got to use it.

I spent most of the afternoon closeted with Joe Mancuso, our estimator, going over the final figures for tomorrow's school bid. Joe had squeezed a number of our subs for better prices, and was still waiting to hear from two. Other than that our bid was ready and the numbers looked good, but you never know in this crazy business. You spend countless hours putting together what you think is a tight bid and then somebody hungrier, or dumber, than you decides to literally buy the job. He's in, you're out.

Even though I had a lot of unfinished work on my desk, I left the office at five. I had some errands to do on the way home, and there wouldn't be any time tomorrow. I also wanted to get home early, fix myself some dinner and hit the sack. I wanted to get to the office by six tomorrow morning to get a jump on things, and I knew I wouldn't be getting any real sleep on the plane tomorrow night.

I was pulling out of the dry cleaner's parking lot, my third stop on the way home, when something caught my eye in the rear view mirror.

It was a dark blue Ford, with two men in the front seat, and I realized this was the third time I had noticed them since leaving the office. Oh, shit, with what's happened during the last two days it's damn spooky to think somebody is following me. Or is my imagination playing games? On the other hand, it's ridiculous. Why would anybody be tailing me? To put my mind at ease I decided to find out. I pulled out of line, hit the gas and passed a few cars. At the next side road I ducked back in line, braked hard and made a fast right turn, with horns honking behind me. Two blocks later I looked in the mirror and there they were. They stayed about a block behind me all the way home. At least I answered my question, but with all my bobbing and weaving of a few minutes ago, they have to realize that I know. When I pulled into my driveway they drove past without slowing and continued out of sight. It dawned on me that these guys were either rank amateurs or they don't really care that I know I'm being followed. If they know who I am they sure didn't have to follow me to find out where I live – my number's in the book. Then I thought about what Ronko said, and my concern was replaced with curiosity; they did nothing but follow me. Maybe they're cops.

CHAPTER FOUR

Between juggling my schedule, the bid opening, and last minute preparations for the trip, Thursday turned into a two-day marathon. As far as I could tell there were no more tailing incidents, although I admit to looking over my shoulder more than once. Every dark blue Ford on the road got my attention. I decided against telling anybody about what happened yesterday on the way home; nothing came of it, so there was really no point. Besides, who could I tell?

The funeral director called late in the afternoon and said that delivery had been made; the casket was at the airport awaiting placement on the plane. As usual, whenever I'm leaving on a trip the last hour in the office was bedlam – the phones never stopped. Always something off the wall, and everybody needs an answer. So, I did what I usually do: call Nancy and delegate, or totally ignore – about a sixty-forty split.

We made it to the airport with about ten minutes to spare, and our flight left on time. The 747 was crowded, but Suzy and I lucked-out and had a window row all to ourselves. The drink cart came down the aisle after we were in the air about fifteen minutes. While handing Suzy her vodka and tonic it struck me that this is the first time she and I have ever been alone together, outside the office, and also the first time we could sit and make small talk, without phone interruptions or an office crisis dominating the conversation. After that first drink, Suzy kicked off her shoes, pushed down the arm rest and rearranged herself in the seat, then told me she wanted a complete rundown on today's bid opening. I had forgotten that she was home packing when Joe and I got back to the office.

"All right," I said, "I'll give you the meat of it, but then no more shop talk until we get home. You're supposed to be on vacation, remember?"

"So are you," she smiled. "Just tell me how things went and I won't mention the office again until we get home. Promise."

"O.K., but I'm going to hold you to that." The attendant came down the isle with the food cart and we both selected the poached salmon. I also ordered wine for each of us. "Most important, we're the apparent low bidder on the combined package. I was also relieved to hear that we left only about eleven grand on the table, on a bid of just over forty-one million. You can't get much closer than that. Joe and the guys did one helluva job. What's even better is we know we're right on the mark; our three big competitors were all bunched together, with a spread of less than eighty-five thousand. Everybody wanted the job bad."

"That's great. With those two jobs we picked up last month, this gives us more work on the books than we've had in over two years. What's the completion date?"

"The school board rep said they want to award within a month and break ground by early October. We'll have about twenty-three months to complete the job, which shouldn't be a problem. I plotted it against our other schedules and I think we can do it without hiring any more inside people."

"That's great, and it's also going to look great on our statement," she said, patting me on the arm. "Now I'll keep my promise – tell me all about London, and all the fabulous things you're going to show me. Remember, I've never been there before."

Through the rest of dinner, and for an hour afterward, I talked. I get really wound up when I start talking about London; I think it's the most fascinating city on earth. I love the place. I told her about my favorite pubs and restaurants; about Soho and Mayfair and Piccadilly Circus; the museums; shopping on Oxford and Regent Streets; and walks along the Thames. I had been rambling on for some time about the bombing of London and how the city had been rebuilt after the war, when I felt the weight of her head on my arm. I looked down and saw she was sound asleep. So much for my scintillating conversation.

I turned out the overhead lights and closed my eyes. Sitting there, being lulled by the almost hypnotic harmonics of the jet engines, it suddenly dawned on me that I had forgotten something; I had left David's attaché case back at the office. The day after his death I had locked it in our fire file for safekeeping, intending to bring it with me tonight. I'll call the office from London and have them ship it to his widow.

My body craved sleep, but my churning brain wouldn't cooperate. I tried making a mental list of all the things Suzy and I should do and see in London. It didn't work. My thoughts kept drifting back over the tragedy of the past few days – the loss suffered by David's family and friends; how so many lives can be drastically altered so quickly, and in David's case so permanently.

It also bothered me that I had no idea what to expect from Alex Trimble. The reality of this is: what the hell can I do to make this trip even resemble a vacation for Suzy? Maybe I should have insisted she stay home. After half an hour I gave up on sleep, grabbed my newspaper and started working the crossword puzzle, squinting in the semi-darkness. Suzy stirred and gave me a big sigh. *O.K., I thought, whatever happens we'll try to minimize the nasty stuff and do our damnedest to have a little fun.*

London was warm and dry. As promised, a car was waiting at Terminal 4, and, even with the commute traffic, we were at the Dukes in just under an hour. The Dukes is a comparatively small hotel, situated in a quiet courtyard off St. James Place. It's right in the middle of everything, yet seems private and low-key. Outside, gas lanterns and an abundance of potted flowers lend a lot of charm.

Inside, the polished mahogany in the lobby and the crisp British service raised my concern that maybe it wasn't to Suzy's liking, but she seemed impressed. After registering, she insisted on peeking into the hotel restaurant to look at the luncheon menu. She came out a few minutes later raving about the murals and the Roland Batchelor watercolors on display. I knew she was hooked on the place. I told her the restaurant was good, but asked her to bear with me; I wanted to have lunch in one of my favorite pubs. We agreed to meet in the lobby at one, which gave me time for a couple hours of badly needed sleep and a hot shower.

Lunch at Watling's was as good as I remembered. I convinced Suzy to try the 'Ploughman's Plate' with me. I love English Stilton and cheddar, with their course bread and hot mustard. Wash it down with a pint of lager and I'm set – at least until dinner. During lunch I bored Suzy with some of Ye Olde Watling's history. I knew it when she reached across the table and pressed the tip of her finger against my lips. I guess I never learn. She laughed and said the history lesson was very interesting, but we were wasting a lot of quality shopping time.

After spending the next hour or so in a couple of very pricey boutiques, I hailed a taxi and dropped Suzy at the Dukes on my way to meet with Trimble. She said not to worry; she was going to explore some of the stores near the hotel, have dinner in her room, and go to bed early. I knew by the expression on her face that she was like a kid in a candy store. These London shops may never recover. We agreed to meet at nine the next morning for breakfast.

Trimble's bank is in an area known as *The City*, London's answer to Wall Street. Only a few blocks from the Bank of England, the bank was clustered in a group of classic nineteenth-century buildings – somewhat as I had imagined. The massive entrance, containing huge bronze doors, was flanked by ornate marble columns, and imposing polished brass lanterns. Quite a contrast to the cookie-cutter drive-ins we have back home.

Trimble was expecting me, but I was asked to wait in the lobby. After a few pointed questions and some terse answers from a receptionist I concluded that as the bank's executive vice-president Trimble ran the show; the president was apparently a figure-head who spent most of his time in Bermuda. It was also obvious that at least the receptionist was totally intimidated by Trimble and considered him a pompous ass. After a short wait his secretary, a very unattractive pinched-face woman named Nickleby, Miss Nickleby, she informed me in a very acid tone, came out to escort me up in the elevator and into his office.

Trimble came from behind his desk to shake hands and invited me to sit in a narrow wingback chair opposite his desk. He didn't look like I imagined he would. On the short side, he was heavy, well past sixty, and wore his jet-black hair combed straight back. The hair looked like it came right out of a bottle, which I guess is preferable to coming off a wig stand. His clean shaven face and mottled pink complexion brought one thought to mind: if there was such a character, this was Mr. Piggy. He wore half-glasses low on his broad nose, and carried his head down to look over them. Trimble told Miss Nickleby to bring tea – I guess coffee wasn't an option – and when she did he snapped at her to close the door on her way out; we were not to be disturbed, and absolutely no calls. Maybe this explains the reaction to Trimble I had encountered in the lobby. He certainly doesn't come across as Mr. Nice Guy.

Without any small talk Trimble immediately asked about the details of David's death and the investigation, and then sat with his hands clasped on his ample stomach while I told him everything I knew about it. I didn't withhold anything, including the details of the torture and what Ronko had told me about somebody suppressing information. When I finished, he removed some papers from a desk drawer, placed them in front of himself, and looked at me with an obviously forced smile. "Cole," he said, "if you have no objections I'd like to eliminate the formality of last names. Under the circumstances I think it's important that we communicate freely, and in my opinion first names will help – please call me Alex."

"That's fine with me." Maybe the receptionist was wrong.

"I do apologize for dragging you to London on such short notice, but David's death not only shocked me, it frightened the hell out of me! I'm not usually this blunt, but since you called with the news about

David I've found it increasingly difficult to function. I'm frightened because I suspect his killing was not coincidence, or a random act of violence. If I'm right, there's no telling where this bloody business will end. I could be in danger...and so might you! If I'm wrong, I can only apologize for alarming you needlessly."

Alex picked up his cup and spilled tea on the papers lying on the desk. He nervously dabbed at the wet spots with his handkerchief, and then stuffed it back in the breast pocket of his jacket. As he continued, his face colored an even brighter pink and he looked annoyed, apparently embarrassed about what he had just done. "Because of your unfortunate involvement in David's death, and your relationship with us over the years, I feel I can be frank in discussing my suspicions with you. After you hear me out I would like your opinion; whether you agree with me, or possibly think my imagination is running wild. And please... be totally honest with me.

"David and I have worried about this situation for many years, and had more than a few discussions about what to do. We agreed that we could not go to the authorities, it would have been very risky and we had absolutely no proof. And, even though our board of directors know about the account, and our mysterious client, they know nothing of what I'm about to tell you. To involve them was also out of the question ...there are two or three directors who might panic and run to the authorities, or worse, the media. Such a knee-jerk reaction could destroy the bank – or maybe bring about even more tragedy! With David gone I just didn't know where to turn, other than you. That's why I asked you here."

Based on what I had heard so far, my imagination was definitely running wild. I certainly knew which client Alex was talking about but I had no idea how much Alex thought I knew. I thought I had better find out. "I'm anxious to hear about what's bothering you, but if you're talking about the client we have mutually worked for, please understand that I know damned little."

"That is exactly who I am referring to. It might save time if you tell me what you do know."

This isn't what I had in mind, but I decided to go along. "Precious little, Alex. I don't know how many times I questioned David about this over the years. Both my partner and brother have been up tight about legal entanglements with you and your client, and I told David so. Until the night before he was killed David always refused to discuss your client, except in very general terms. We had a lengthy discussion in my office just before he left for the casino. He didn't say much that I didn't already know, other than to explain how the account was started, and how it prospered over the years. He insisted for the hundredth time that no one in your bank knows the client's identity, and the reasons you haven't tried to find out."

"David mentioned your questions to me more than once. Your curiosity is certainly not without justification. The very same issue caused David and me to be at odds with our board for many years. In retrospect, given the strong feelings expressed about it by some board members, I'm surprised they didn't replace both of us. On the other hand, I'm sure they were as concerned as David and I about survival of the bank."

Alex shuffled the papers in front of him and looked at me, his face without expression and his forehead beaded with perspiration. "I may regret this, but it's time to clear the air. I think it best that I start at the beginning and tell you what I do know...and also what I suspect. You can then form your own conclusions. Based on what you just said, David apparently didn't tell you about the many strange things that have happened over the years. Tragic, inexplicable things that happened to people; all of whom were tied in some fashion to the client – or the client's business ventures. The client may have been directly responsible for these happenings, maybe not – we just never knew for sure.

Certainly no definitive proof. I do know that if the client has not been involved, the laws of probability and coincidence are stretched beyond belief. And now this business with David...I really can't ignore what has happened any longer."

Alex picked up the papers and scanned the top page. "I made some notes, I don't want to overlook anything important. There's too much to trust to memory.

"You see, for David and me this all began in 1954, when he and I joined the bank within a week of each other, fresh out of university. The client had opened the account a year earlier, and Peter Willard was assigned to handle the transactions. Willard was a senior teller at the time. My first involvement occurred in 1957. I had just been put in charge of international business development, a new department, when the client instructed Willard to purchase property in the United States, the first time that had occurred. Peter and I worked together researching real estate brokers in your country and settled, unfortunately as it turned out, on a firm in New York City. We retained their services and the first deal went very smoothly. Over the next few years they represented us a number of times, apparently without incident. Willard handled all transactions with them until his death in 1967.

"David was then appointed to replace Willard, and very quickly expressed dissatisfaction the way the New York broker was handling our projects. After reviewing Willard's records, David was convinced the broker had been padding expenses and gouging us with excessive or bogus fees. He decided to visit them, unannounced, to audit their records. It didn't take long to confirm his suspicions. He confronted them, and of course they denied his allegations. Before contacting me, David was invited out for drinks and dinner by one of their principals. After a few drinks, the chap tried to buy David off by offering him kickbacks. When that failed he got downright nasty and said if we didn't back off he would start an investigation to uncover the client's identity – and make sure the media heard about it; pure blackmail. Apparently Willard had let slip enough about the strange nature of the account and the client's insistence on anonymity, at least enough to give the broker big ideas. David then called me and we decided to counter with a threat of a formal audit of their books and criminal prosecution. The next day, after a conference call with their officers, we compromised: we don't prosecute, and they cease and desist, and accept a termination of services. The letter of agreement is still in our file. Shortly after, we offered our business in your country to Walter Hammel."

"So that's how we got your business. How did you happen to pick Walter?"

"He had built a manufacturing plant and office facility for one of your large pharmaceutical firms in Bolton, up near Manchester, about two years before. Our bank had handled the financing. While working together, Walter and I became friends. He was amazing. Not only was he expert at construction, but his business and political connections throughout the United States never failed to surprise us. Nothing was ever impossible for Walter."

I started to say something about Walter when Alex extended a hand in the air and continued scanning his notes; he obviously didn't want to be interrupted.

"We didn't have much business for Walter during the first few years. There were a few relatively small deals; mostly land acquisition, and a resort hotel in Florida. But in 1972 the client ordered us to find a ranch for them. It was totally unlike anything we had ever done for them. We thought it particularly odd when they advised us what they intended doing with it, and their criteria for the purchase. They wanted to raise cattle and horses; experimental breeding stock and thorough-breds. They required at least six-thousand acres of undeveloped grazing land somewhere in your mid-west. It had to be remote, but with paved access to a rail connection, and with good water.

"Walter came through admirably. He found a site in less than a month; seventy-two hundred acres in eastern Montana, with the Powder River running through the property, and rail service less than five miles away. The purchase of that land was the beginning of a great number of acquisitions in the States for the client – first by Walter and later by you. It was also when and where the first of the strange events occurred."

"So, what happened?"

Alex again scanned his notes before continuing. "We had an ironclad agreement of sale for the purchase. About a week before settlement Walter was contacted by the seller's agent, a man by the name of Stiebris, who announced that the seller wanted additional contingencies placed in the agreement, mostly dealing with development restrictions. Walter refused, and David and I supported him fully. The long and short of it was the new contingencies were ridiculous – absolutely without merit and totally unacceptable. They would have prevented use of the property as our client apparently intended. With a signed agreement already in place we knew we could win in court, but were concerned about the possible delay; we knew the client wanted to move quickly. Stiebris and the seller knew we intended paying cash, so in our opinion the eleventh-hour ploy was pure extortion. They were squeezing us for more money. Walter was irate. We gave him the authority to do what he felt was necessary, so he ran a bluff and told them the deal was off.

"Well, two days before settlement Walter called and told David to catch his flight after all; the original deal was back on. As it turned out, Stiebris had suggested more money as the remedy. But, as you're fond of saying in your country, Walter told him to stick it! Walter had already pulled some strings; he discovered the seller was a speculator, but on a grand scale. The seller was deep in the pockets of a half-dozen banks. With Walter's prodding, two of the banks suddenly discovered that the speculator's methods of financing were a bit too creative. Two of his major loans were called, and within hours he became desperate. He needed our cash. End of problem. Incidentally, this was the first of many instances where Walter's connections and resourcefulness saved the day for us. Settlement was held in Billings, as scheduled, without any further glitches."

"I don't see anything strange in what I just heard, it happens all the time."

"So far I agree, but hear me out. Less than a month later our client brought in contractors to clear land and start construction of the main residence and remaining complex. There were no problems except for Stiebris. He persisted in snooping around the property, taking photographs, badgering the workmen, and generally making a pest of himself. He was escorted from the site a number of times by security guards. One morning, a few weeks later, Stiebris told his secretary he was going to the site to take more pictures, left in his car, and has never been seen or heard from since."

"Did he ever show up at the site that morning. His disappearance may have been totally unrelated. A girlfriend, money problems – maybe he was a head case."

"No one saw Stiebris after he left his office that morning," Alex continued. "His car was found about a half mile from the site, with the keys in the ignition and no sign of foul play. His empty camera and briefcase were on the back seat. The police investigated but turned up nothing. Absolutely not a trace. His wife even hired a private investigator. The consensus was: Stiebris had no girlfriend, no major enemies, no money problems, no family problems, no reason to disappear. But he did.

"No one ever determined why he persisted in visiting the site after settlement. Logically it made no sense whatsoever. The authorities could find no involvement on the part of the land speculator, the former owner. The only rationalization we could make was that Stiebris was being vindictive; he wanted to stick his finger in Walter's eye. He believed Walter had deprived him of an even larger commission and soiled his reputation with the local banks. He very nastily said so and created quite a scene with Walter and David as they were leaving settlement."

"If your suspicions were correct," I said, "Stiebris must have been unbalanced. It makes no sense at all – how could making a pest of himself at the site in any way embarrass Walter? Was there any evidence implicating your client, or for that matter any possible reason why the client would want Stiebris eliminated? Certainly your bank and Walter had no reason to be involved."

"No, certainly not Walter or ourselves. But it happened, and as I said, it was the first of many similar incidents. I know we had nothing to do with any of them, nor did your company. That leaves either coincidence or the client, and I am firmly convinced the events were not coincidence. I believe you'll feel the same... after you hear me out."

"Alex, I'm curious about something; you said the client brought in contractors to build the ranch. How did the client do that without some kind of personal involvement?"

"It was really quite simple. At about the same time that we started buying property in your country the client formed a real estate management and holding company. They're headquartered in Tampa, Florida. As we found out later, the client recruited a few key real estate and insurance people, and then proceeded to build the company around them – again, all by remote control. We had them investigated as soon as we were informed of the role they were to play. We found a very convoluted corporate structure, but absolutely no discernible link to the client.

"David and the rest of his staff have always referred to them simply as 'Tampa', and David personally handled the coordination with them. Typically, Tampa steps in and takes control of most of the properties we acquire for the client, at least those that require development or long-term management. The exceptions are the quick turn-around deals we handle ourselves and the few properties managed by your company. So, to answer your question; as in our case, the client apparently issues the orders and Tampa carries them out. They obtain the architects and engineers, the builders, and whatever else is needed. Their operation apparently runs very smoothly."

"Maybe too smoothly. The links of the chain have to connect somewhere. What makes you so sure Tampa doesn't know the client – or maybe is the client? How can you be sure that's not the case?"

"That's part of my concern, Cole, I am not sure! Aside from investigating them, we've asked Tampa a lot of very specific questions, and on more than one occasion. David and I have talked with their top executive, a chap by the name of Alvarez, a number of times since our first transaction together, all to no avail. About a year ago Alvarez came to London to discuss a pending deal. At the urging of our bank's solicitor, David and I used the opportunity to subject Alvarez to a real third-degree. We asked many questions that I would have refused to answer, had our roles been reversed. We were impressed with his candor and apparent veracity, but he told us nothing we didn't already know. They seem to exist in the same vacuum the bank has operated in all these years; just different functions and a different setting."

I was becoming impatient and more than a little annoyed with this whole crazy situation. *God, what have I gotten myself involved in!* For days now it's been nothing but questions, foreign intrigue, and the thickest smoke screen since Oliver North. But dammit to hell, nobody ever has even one answer – just more lousy questions!

I snapped at Alex, "How can you possibly tie the disappearance of this guy Stiebris with David's death more than two decades later?"

Alex's face was devoid of expression, but his coloring was deepening from pink to red. He fidgeted and again shuffled the notes in his hands. He also avoided my stare as he answered. "Again, Cole, I'm not sure, but during those twenty odd years, starting with Stiebris and ending with David, there have been a total of seven disappearances or deaths. Seven! And in my opinion, all were tied in some fashion to the client."

"Seven! My God, that's incredible. How come we haven't heard about any of this before?" Now I was really upset, and Alex knew it. I got out of my chair and began pacing in front of his desk. I was tempted to walk away from this whole mess. The bank's business accounted for about ten percent of our total yearly gross. Did we really need this kind of aggravation and risk? Then my brother Ben flashed into mind. How is he going to react to this news? One thing I did know for sure – he'd want all the crazy details, verbatim – so I guess I'd better listen to the rest of it. *Damn!*

I can understand your reaction," Alex said, his face now glistening with perspiration. "But please consider this: not one of these mysteries has ever been solved. And more importantly, as far as I know the authorities have never tied any of them together, or to any of us. You weren't told because – with the exception of David's death – each occurred well after your participation in the transaction had ended. We felt there was no point. You're hearing this now only because David's death has hit too close to home... I'm really concerned for both you and myself. Other than asking you to come here, I didn't know what else to do. I'm at my wit's end, and we've got to decide what to do before something happens to one of us... or our families. We have to find some way to stop this craziness once and for all!

His hands were shaking and he was really losing it. "Alex, we'll figure out something, you've got to get a grip on yourself! You said the authorities have never tied any of these incidents together. Has Hammel & McQuaid's name ever surfaced, or yours?"

"No, at least not yours. As I said, in each case you were no longer in the picture, so we made the decision not to involve you. David and I were questioned a few times, usually as a follow-up to an inquiry with Tampa. Nothing came of any of it, and no single event was ever tied to any of the others. I can only attribute that to the time spans between them and the fact they all occurred in different parts of the country."

I flopped back in my chair again. Alex was again blotting his face and looked like he was about to have a coronary. "I still don't understand why you or David didn't tell us what was going on. Hell, didn't it ever occur to you that we may have been at some risk, I mean we had a lot of exposure in every one of your deals."

"You're right," he said, his voice somewhat subdued. "But we avoided telling you for what we thought was a very valid reason: we were convinced you would insist on conducting your own investigation. Such action could have placed you in real jeopardy...and may have created the impact with the client we have tried to avoid since the beginning. Maybe not sound or ethical reasoning on our part, but after the second and third deaths I felt we were in a real predicament. And you can rightfully blame me for our silence; after the Chicago incident David wanted to tell you, but I ordered him not to. I truly did not know what to do but sit back and keep quiet."

"O.K., I still don't agree with your logic, but it's too late to argue about it now. You said the authorities never turned up any leads – so what makes you think the client has been involved in all this?"

"What else could we think. The client has been the only common denominator."

"Well, so much for Mr. Stiebris. Why don't you tell me about the rest." I knew this was going to take a while, and the rumbling in my stomach told me it had been a long time since lunch. At the rate we were going it would be a couple hours minimum until dinner – I hope Alex hadn't forgotten.

"I had planned to do just that," Alex said. He had started to calm down some; his coloring was returning to mottled pink. "Incidentally, to save time I'll try to stick to the main points, but I will give you a copy of my notes – they are fairly comprehensive. They're hand written, but they should provide you with most of the details. The only other person to see them was David – I keep them here in my personal safe – so please maintain them as confidential."

"Understood," I said. But I can't speak for Ben.

"The next incident occurred in 1977, about five years after the disappearance of Stiebris. Walter had negotiated the purchase of about three hundred acres outside Houston. It was another property that Tampa took over and developed – an industrial park venture. An attorney by the name of Matthews represented the seller at settlement. Shortly after settlement he approached Tampa and tried to shake them down for a considerable sum. Matthews was apparently connected politically and threatened serious zoning problems unless Tampa went along. Alvarez called David and David reminded him that all approvals had been obtained prior to settlement, thanks to Walter. They then agreed to ignore Matthews and continue the site work. A few days later, before anything further developed, Matthews stopped at a bar on his way home from his office. As he was leaving the bar later that night a small lorry – I believe you refer to it as a pickup truck – jumped the curb at high speed and ran him down, killing him instantly. There were two witnesses who both said they thought it wasn't an accident. The lorry had it's lights off and had no license plates. There were two men inside. After hitting Matthews it never slowed down, but veered back into the street and sped off. The lorry and men were never found.

"Four years later, in 1981, there was a woman who allegedly killed herself in Chicago. Her name was Joanne Myers, a very wealthy forty-one year old widow. We had purchased a hotel from her near O'Hare International, which netted her another ten million after taxes. After the purchase, Tampa took over the renovation and management of the property. They had barely started the renovation work when our client ordered them to sell the hotel to an anxious cash buyer, which naturally they did. The buyer was supposedly a front man for the Chicago mob. The deal went through, and the client made a fast six million clear profit in less than three months, all of which wound up back in our bank.

"The widow got wind of the resale and made a real stink. She said she would not stand by and see the mob take over the hotel her husband had built and left to her. She also owned a local TV station and threatened to turn investigative reporters loose on Tampa. Before she could do anything she died from an overdose of bourbon and barbiturates, or at least that was the listed cause of death. Problem was, she reportedly had an aversion to alcohol, and wouldn't even take aspirin for a headache. Everybody who knew her refused to believe she killed herself. There also was no suicide note.

"The next incident was another disappearance. You may remember the St. Louis shopping mall Walter found for us in '83; I believe you did the initial inspection of the property. It was owned by the McNaughton brothers, Lawrence and George. Both were going to retire after the sale. Lawrence apparently did, but George decided there was still more money to be made in shopping centers. About three months after our settlement he announced that he was going to build a new, bigger mall about ten miles from ours. Tampa told us later that the client instructed them to find a legal way of stopping McNaughton, but they could not. We had erred by not including any such restrictions in the settlement documents. McNaughton proceeded with his development plans and was negotiating with two major department stores to come in as anchors when he failed to show up for a meeting with one of them. He has never been seen or heard from since."

Alex now seemed to be performing like an actor reading for a part. He hardly took his eyes from his notes. I was interested, but I also wanted to get this over with, so I hated to interrupt. But there was a question I had to ask. "You said the authorities have never tied you or us to any of this. Unless you had your own pipeline, I don't understand how you came up with all this information."

"Actually, some information did come from official sources, but most came from David. A lot he dug up on his own, but a fair amount came from a...ah, relationship he established a few years ago with somebody in the Tampa organization; a woman by the name of Maria Sippano. The rest came from my meeting last year with the Tampa CEO."

So, David had a 'relationship'. I wonder what kind? The usual kind would be somewhat out of character, I thought, but interesting. I decided not to comment on it yet.

"O.K.," I said. "What happened next?"

"Almost seven years went by before the next event occurred in 1990. And then another happened in 1991. In many respects those two were similar to David's death – all were cold-blooded, brutal murders. To me, they don't seem to fit the earlier pattern; almost as though they were unrelated. The 1990 killing involved the marina and restaurant complex you located for us in Rhode Island in the fall of 1989. You may recall the place was deeply in debt and about ready to declare bankruptcy. After we bought it, Tampa completely renovated the entire property and imported a top-notch executive chef. They also hired a chap by the name of Ray Durwood to run the whole operation as general manager. Durwood had been with a big marina in Florida and had a reputation as a money-maker. He revamped their dockage and service facilities, brought in two new lines of boats, and within a year had them in the black.

"One morning Durwood failed to show up for work. The next day, after repeated unanswered phone calls, his secretary found him in his apartment. He was gagged and trussed to a kitchen chair, and had been shot twice in the head at point-blank range. No motive, no weapon, no clues. There was no sign of a break-in, and they ruled out robbery; there was quite a bit of cash in his wallet. As in all the rest, no one was ever apprehended.

"The 1991 incident was equally chilling. What set it apart from the others was the timing. You and David purchased the beach resort north of Santa Barbara in 1985. Again, Tampa was running the operation. Shortly after they took over, they installed a woman by the name of Phyllis Byrnes as executive director. As you may recall, it was a very posh hideaway to begin with, but she installed a make-over spa and a nine-hole golf course and made it even more exclusive. It became the in place for super-rich women.

"One evening in June of 1991, Byrnes was relaxing at home with her husband when she received a late phone call. She quickly dressed and left the house, telling her husband only that there was a serious problem she had to attend to at the office. Early the next morning her car was found in her parking space at the resort. She was slumped over the wheel – dead, shot twice in the head at point-blank range. Her unopened purse was on the seat next to her, intact. No evidence, no weapon, no leads. The case is still open."

I again got out of my chair and tried to walk off the stiffness in my legs – and my mounting frustration. Alex put his notes in a pile on his desk and sat back in his chair, looking more at ease than he had since I arrived. Recollection of things I had experienced or heard during the past few days – not to mention the past few hours – began rolling through my mind like chasing lights on a marquee. David's body in the morgue... the similar way he and Durwood and Byrnes had been killed... my being followed, maybe, by God knows who or why. Am I next on somebody's list? Questions. A string of deaths and only one common denominator. Questions. And then something hit me.

"Wait a minute, Alex. Something you said earlier about the client being the only common denominator – that's not true. What about Tampa? Based on what you've said, they've been part of this puzzle since day one. They could even have been involved in David's death. Am I right?"

Alex hesitated a long time before answering. "Yes, technically you are. But I'm still convinced that Tampa is no more involved in any of this than we are. I firmly believe that."

"I don't know what makes you so sure – I'm certainly not convinced, but for now I'll accept what you say. At least until I have a chance to sort out this whole mess. Another thing I find unbelievable is the time span. God, Alex, these incidents have occurred over a twenty-five year period. Could one person or a group of people be responsible for carrying this out over such a long period of time – they'd have to be pretty old by now? I just don't..."

"Excuse me for interrupting, but please understand that I don't expect you to have any immediate answers. And I never thought we could conclude this today; we haven't yet begun to consider how we should proceed with this. I know you need time to think this through – Lord knows I'm pushing you unfairly as it is – and I don't wish to intrude on your time here any more than is absolutely necessary. You were very gracious to come here on such short notice. I hope you might find time to meet with me again Monday afternoon, after the funeral, if that would be convenient. Maybe we can reach some conclusions then. Meantime, I haven't forgotten that I promised you dinner tonight. If we leave now we can make our eight o'clock reservation at my club."

"Monday afternoon will be fine, and dinner sounds excellent." Actually, dinner was the best thing I had heard since I got here.

Alex's club was exactly as I imagined it would be. Very proper. Dark wood paneling, crimson carpet, large gilt-framed oils, glittering chandeliers, bone china, cut crystal, and very heavy silver flatware. There were ornate trays of scotch and bourbon being toted by waiters in tails – not a waitress in sight. Unfortunately, neither the cigar smoking nor the menu were to my liking. Carcinogen and cholesterol were obviously not part of their vocabulary. There were multiple choices of beef, mutton, and veal, a shepherd's pie and a mixed grill. I had the one fish dish on the menu, a rather mediocre fillet of pollock, but I was so hungry it didn't really matter.

During dinner we thankfully didn't talk about the issue at hand. We did talk football – American style, baseball, and some of the problems common to the construction industries in Great Britain and the United States. This led me to a dissertation on the role each country's banking community must play when the economy turns stagnant. I knew by the expression on his face that I had pushed the wrong button; he was a banker and I was a builder. So I switched back to baseball. After some very good brandy, Alex signed the chit and we left. We agreed to share a taxi home, and before dropping me at my hotel, Alex gave me the address of the church where the funeral would be held on Monday.

It was a little past ten when I arrived back in my room. I decided not to knock on Suzy's door. She was probably asleep, and I didn't really feel like talking. Besides, two hours sleep out of the last forty is stretching my limit to the breaking point. I was exhausted. I left a wake-up for seven, peeled off my clothes, and slid between the cool sheets. I don't even remember turning out the lights.

CHAPTER FIVE

I'm an extremely heavy sleeper. I'm also not a morning person. Years ago I discovered that I had to get started an hour or so ahead of morning people just to stay even. I also found I could catch up faster if I started my day with about thirty minutes of body torture – five minutes of stretching, followed by twenty five of exercise. I can think of only one or two things I enjoy less, but I feel guilty if I don't do it. By the time I shower, shave, and have my first cup of coffee, I'm usually ready for the starting gate.

Saturday morning was no different. I managed to call Suzy by eight to tell her that the uniform of the day was jeans and sneakers; we were going to do a lot of walking. I was on my second cup of coffee in the coffee shop when she walked in, looking very cute with her hair pulled up. She refused to sit down, knowing we were going elsewhere for breakfast, and told me to finish off my coffee; she was suffering from world-class hunger.

We wound up at a place that had good food, but the atmosphere of a farmers' market butcher shop; sawdust on the floor, huge display cases, and noise. Lots of good natured yelling and tray clanging. We each had the Brit's version of a healthy way to start the day; eggs, tomatoes, mushrooms, bacon, rounded out with scones, fruit preserves and coffee. I cautioned Suzy about the bacon. You asked for it American style, or you got it almost raw – having seen heat for about thirty seconds. They also offer an alternative to coffee – *wasser*. Not tea with whiskey, but whiskey with tea. We stayed with coffee. Instead of taking a taxi to the Thames to begin our stroll, we decided to walk off our leaden breakfast. Heading south on Farringdon Street to Blackfriars Bridge, we turned west on Victoria Embankment along the river. We passed Big Ben, New Scotland Yard, the Houses of Parliament and, doubling back in the direction of our hotel, spent some time in Westminster Abbey.

By three o'clock, everything was still in good working order except Suzy's right heel and my stomach. Stopping at the next pub, a friendly barmaid found a Band-Aid for Suzy's heel, and a hot meat pastie took care of my stomach. Suzy gave in to the aroma and ordered one too. We each washed them down with a pint of cold lager, while trying to figure out how far it was back to the Dukes. Suzy was stubborn; she refused my offer of a taxi. Blister or not, we'd finish on foot. I agreed, with one condition: everything I had in mind for tomorrow would be by taxi.

Before reaching the hotel we walked past 10 Downing Street. Well, not exactly past – the closest you can get is the mouth of Downing Street, and gaze through the cast iron gates. Aside from the gates, access is prevented by Bobbies armed with Uzis. About all you can see of Number 10 is the black limo parked in front and the armed Bobby at the door. Suzy remarked that it's a shame that such an historic landmark has to be taken from the public because of the threat of terrorism. Sad, but true.

We straggled into the Dukes a few minutes before five, both of us disheveled and footsore. It had been one helluva walk! Suzy said she wouldn't even consider dinner until she soaked for at least an hour in a hot tub. I had suggested fish and chips, so we agreed to meet in the lobby at eight. I didn't admit it, but nothing sounded better than a long hot shower and an even longer nap.

At eight-thirty there was still a short line outside the Sea Shell in Lisson Grove. They sell take-out fish and chips from the ground floor of a corner store, with an old-fashioned but comfortable restaurant upstairs. We were seated after a short wait, and Suzy grinned at me as she scanned the menu. "This looks really different," she remarked. "I'm not much for French fries, but I've never seen so many kinds of fish on one menu. Is it all fresh?"

"As far as I know it is. My favorite is the haddock, I've had it here three or four times and it's always been excellent."

Suzy said it sounded good to her, so we each settled for the haddock, chips and iced tea. The portions were huge and, as usual, everything was delicious. I convinced Suzy to try the cider vinegar on her fish and she loved it. She even raved about the chips.

It was dark when we left the restaurant. Suzy agreed to a nightcap, so I asked the taxi driver to drop us at a pub I knew of about two blocks from our hotel. I knew Suzy would like it. It's a walk-up, located on the second floor above a row of small shops, and has a long, open-air balcony with small tables and clusters of potted flowers. When we arrived an elderly black man was playing good Gershwin on a baby grand. We seated ourselves at a secluded table overlooking the street below, and a waitress came for our drink order.

The night was warm, but a light breeze was blending the fragrance of fresh flowers with the muted piano coming from inside. It created a soft, relaxing mood, conducive to good conversation. I was determined not to talk about my meeting with Trimble unless Suzy asked, and I was relieved when she didn't. We did talk about many other things; our lives as kids, teenage romances, our parents, and her first marriage.

Suzy had always been reluctant to talk about her early life in California. What little I did know about her past were bits and pieces I had picked up from office talk. Tonight she told me her first husband had been a musician. He was also a drunk who couldn't keep a job, and who constantly abused her, both emotionally and physically. When she became pregnant with Julia, he straightened out for about six months. But then the abuse started all over again. One night after a particularly violent episode, she thought she was losing the baby. She grabbed a few belongings and spent six hours on a bus to San Francisco, where she moved in with her older sister and her sister's family. Suzy filed for divorce, found a job, and worked part-time until Julia was born. Her sister convinced her to stay with them, so she went back to work as a secretary while her sister took care of Julia.

A few weeks before Julia's third birthday, Suzy's ex showed up at her sister's front door, nasty drunk, demanding to see his daughter. When Suzy refused, he got really obnoxious and threatened everybody. Suzy's brother-in-law called the cops and had him arrested. Suzy was terrified. She packed their few belongings and left the next morning with Julia, not knowing exactly where they were headed. But she knew it had to be far away. They wound up in Philadelphia where, a week later, she answered Walter's ad for a secretary.

Suzy put Julia in day-care and devoted herself to her new job. Her goal was to be independent and totally free of her past life. But she was terrified that her husband would trace them to Philly, and was also concerned about the safety of her sister's family. About six weeks after coming to work for us she decided to tell Walter everything, and to ask his advice. Within hours he hired a private investigator in Frisco to track down her former husband and determine what he was up to. The PI found him in less than two days – in the city morgue. He had died of pneumonia in a cheap hotel. End of ex husband. The rest of the story I did know.

After the waitress delivered our second drinks, Suzy reached across the table and took my hand. She had a very melancholy look as she spoke, almost in a whisper. "Walter was the greatest thing that had ever happened to me – or Julia. When he proposed to me he said he wouldn't marry me unless I permitted him to adopt Julia. Almost like a pre-nuptial condition, really. As you know, he did adopt her, and she quickly grew to love him.

"And as much as she did love Walter, in the six years since his death Julia has formed an equally strong attachment to you. At first I thought it was nothing more than a schoolgirl crush, because you had been so kind and helpful to her after Walter was killed. I guess in the beginning it was, but over the years it has grown into much more than that. She really loves and respects you, Cole -now you're her father figure. You may not have realized it but she frequently asks me to get your opinion on something or other. But as much as I'm sure she would like you to know, she'd die of embarrassment if she knew I was telling you this."

I looked at Suzy in disbelief. "I honestly didn't realize her feelings ran that deep. I've told you many times what a great job you've done raising her, and how everybody thinks she is one fantastic young lady. I certainly think the world of her, and I know she likes me, just from the way we kid around with each other. But I never thought of it as a father-daughter relationship; more like big brother and kid sister. Do you understand?"

"Completely, I know exactly how you feel about her. But please don't be frightened off by what I've just told you – you're too good to her, and she needs you now more than ever. What I don't understand – and if this bothers you, please tell me to mind my own business – is why you haven't married and had kids of your own. It certainly hasn't been for lack of opportunity; I can recall two or three gals who everybody thought you were really serious about. I'm sorry, I guess I should mind my own business – I feel foolish. I hope you're not angry with me."

She was smiling at me, but even in the reduced light I could see the color rise in her face. "Not at all. I guess I've seen too many friends marry – people I thought were well suited to each other – and then a year or two later they split. That's not for me. It may be old fashioned, but I want the kind of relationship and marriage my parents have. Maybe I'm too damn particular – maybe it's the other way around...I don't know. I hope Miss Right is out there somewhere – looking like hell for me."

I sipped my drink, whistled, and waved to an imaginary girl down on the street. I guess I was trying to lighten the conversation.

Suzy squeezed my hand hard and laughed. "Cole," she said softly, "I understand why Julia feels about you as she does. Other than Walter, you are the kindest, most gentle and caring man I have ever known. We've been friends and partners for a long time now, but do you really know how much I care for you as a person?"

What the hell was I hearing? "You're really stirring some old feelings, Suzy...feelings I thought I buried years ago. Talk about crushes; I had one on you from the day you set foot in the office. I did my damnedest to hide it because I knew from the start how Walter felt about you. He told me more than once. And then he married you. I must have moped around the office for months feeling sorry for myself. I finally forced you out of my head by convincing myself that you were the boss's wife...untouchable, and besides, you didn't indicate any interest in me. Now...I don't know what to say. You've got my head spinning."

"I didn't know you had any old feelings for me. I also didn't mean to upset you with what I just told you. This is very difficult for me – I know how much the business means to both of us, and I don't want to complicate our professional relationship...please understand that. But I've been thinking about this for a very long time, and I had to tell you how I feel. I just haven't had the opportunity until now."

She leaned across the table and kissed me. New emotions were blending with past memories; what the hell was happening? I wanted to speak but I couldn't find the right words. I got up and led her to the balcony rail, where I took her in my arms and kissed her. I felt her tremble as she whispered in my ear, "I've felt untouchable for too long. Take me back to the hotel and let's have some fun."

I awoke the next morning to a colorless dawn; the sun still well below the horizon. The room was dark, with only the early gray filtering through the gap in the draperies. I didn't know where I was, but it was very warm and I couldn't move my left arm.

The perfume of her hair stirred my senses, and as I opened my eyes fully I realized my left arm was under Suzy, with her soft body curled tightly against mine. Her left leg was splayed across both of mine. We were both naked. I knew from her shallow breathing that she was still sound asleep. She sighed, and moved enough to pull the sheet a little lower, exposing a soft, white breast.

Thoughts of last night flooded my consciousness; Suzy unbuttoning my shirt and fighting my belt buckle; the long zipper down the back of what seemed like a fall-away dress; our clothes on the floor; the fireworks when our anxious bodies touched for the first time. She was unlike any women I had ever known. I had always thought of Suzy as beautiful, and very sexy – but sort of quiet and reserved, almost cool. Not anymore. She had been anything but quiet and reserved – absolutely tireless...*almost insatiable!* It was almost eleven o'clock when we got to her room. The last time I remember looking at the clock it was a little past three-thirty. *Time flies.*

As I lay looking at the dark ceiling, vague thoughts of what had brought us to London – not to mention Trimble's bizarre story – began to intermingle with the more vivid intimacy of last night. But the intrusion strangely didn't bother me. It didn't because I suddenly realized that I hadn't felt this happy in a long time, or felt this comfortable with a woman. *Suzy and I seemed to fit.* I drifted off to sleep again.

Bright sun was streaming through the open drapes when I awoke the second time. Suzy was gone, but I heard the shower running and knew where she was. A few minutes later she padded into the room, wrapped in a towel, her hair dripping. When she saw I was awake, she yanked the sheet down and shook her wet hair over me. It was like getting hit with a spray of frozen needles. She laughed as I grabbed a wrist and pulled her on top of me. The towel fell away and she rolled to the bed along side me, propping herself on one elbow. She looked down at me with a devilish grin on her face and began tracing a pattern on my bare stomach with a fingertip. It bothered me and she knew it. "Do you realize," she said, "how very little I know about you or your life outside the office? Last night at the pub you gave me brief glimpse, but that was mostly childhood stuff. For example, I know you're over six feet, but just how big are you? Uh oh!" She laughed, and jabbed me with her finger. "I mean how tall – I know how big."

"O.K. Put that damn finger away and I'll give you 'McQuaid's Famous Personal History, Capsulated Version'." "Fair enough, but I want to know everything." She covered me with the sheet and leaned down and kissed me.

"I'm thirty-eight, a shade over six-one, keep my weight around one-ninety, get my black hair and blue eyes from good Anglo-Saxon stock – Irish and English. My father's name is Ansell, my mother is Martha. Dad's a retired real estate broker. He and mom are both healthy and live in Florida. I'm the youngest of three. My sister Abigail is the oldest, then Ben, then me – about three years between each of us. I don't think you've met Abby; she's married to a doctor in Boston, and doesn't come down to visit too often. By the way, the names are no accident; Abigail, Benjamin and Cole. Mom says she was just following alphabetical progression, but three was as far as she wanted to go. She marked us in another unusual way; Abby, Ben and I all have the same middle name – Catlett – mom's maiden name. I stopped using it in grade school when a girl I didn't like made fun of it and nicknamed me 'cowboy'. Speaking of school, I have a mechanical engineering degree and a master's in business. Walter hired me right out of college, sixteen years ago – four years before you showed up – and here I am in bed with you, the luckiest guy in all of England."

"Only England? I must be slipping." She laughed and kissed me on the nose, pulling the sheet down and starting again with the fingertip. It took all of five seconds to have the same effect as before. "You have two choices, Cole Catlett McQuaid: either make love to me again, or I get to watch you take a cold shower." The choice was easy. I hate cold showers.

It was almost ten o'clock before we made it to the Dukes lobby. We had coffee and scones in the coffee shop and planned the rest of our day. A half-hour later we were on one of the famous red double-decker tour busses doing the London tourist thing. This wasn't my idea of how to see things, but it was easy on the feet and Suzy said she was satisfied. After almost an hour of our driver-guide's monologue she said she had seen enough, and, besides, she needed more retail therapy – she had shopping to do. So we got of the bus at Harrods, after which we did Fortnum & Mason's and Laura Ashley's. Three hours and two taxi's later we made it back to the Dukes, where the doorman took pity on me and helped with some of the packages I was balancing.

Sunday evening we decided to have dinner in the hotel and relax. By nine o'clock Suzy was yawning and rubbing her eyes. I also knew I had to spend some time this evening sorting out everything Trimble had told me. Other than having to meet with him tomorrow afternoon, I still hadn't told Suzy anything about my earlier meeting with him – and she still hadn't asked. I knew it would spoil her trip. But before I could say anything about calling it a day, she said she was tired and was going to bed. "I think," she added, with a big grin, "that if either of us wants to sleep tonight we had better stay in our own rooms." I faked a hurt look, but then she wiggled that talented finger at me – the one I remembered so well. I laughed and kissed her goodnight.

I spent the next two hours sitting in the dark in my room, thinking. I went over everything Trimble had told me, plus what had happened this past week. I could comprehend everything, but yet didn't understand anything. Everything seemed so unrelated, so disjointed. And where was the motive? One minute I was agreeing with Trimble, and the next minute I thought he was nuts. I turned on the light and tried scratching out a time-line on a piece of paper. It didn't help. Frustrated, I crawled into bed. There were no answers, but I was sure of one thing: I had to do something to get to the bottom of this...before I wound up like David! Lying there with my eyes shut and a myriad of thoughts and ideas flashing through my head, it was like a curtain suddenly rose – everything gelled and I knew what I had to do, and what I would tell Trimble tomorrow. As I again looked up at the ceiling, I touched the empty pillow next to me and realized I had another problem. I missed her.

The infamous London weather finally caught up with us on Monday morning; fog and a soaking drizzle. When I gave the taxi driver the location of the church he politely cautioned me about the distance: it was well north of Regent's Park, in a rural area about forty minutes away. I was concerned we might have trouble getting a return taxi, so I made a deal with the driver. For little more than a round-trip fare he agreed to take us both ways, and wait for us during the service. This couldn't be Philly or New York.

The fog had lifted by the time we arrived, but the drizzle had turned into a steady downpour. Alex was waiting for us in the church narthex with his wife. She looked to be about the same age as Alex, was rather mousy and non-descript, but seemed sociable and pleasant enough. After introductions, Alex suggested we find seats, the church was small and was filling up quickly. It didn't escape me that Alex couldn't keep his eyes off Suzy. The service was short but impressive. Alex had mentioned that David and his wife had no children, and between them only a handful of relatives. From the size of the crowd it was obvious they had a lot of friends. As we moved to the cemetery behind the church, Alex introduced us to David's widow. She broke down when she heard my name, quietly mentioning that I was the last friend to see David alive. She thanked us for coming. I never know what to say in situations like this, and always say something that I later consider stupid. But I do try to be sincere.

Mrs. Nesbitt dabbed her eyes and reached in her handbag for a pen and paper. She quickly jotted a number and handed it to me, asking that I call her before leaving for home. She said she had questions about David.

At the grave site we stayed reasonably dry under a canopy. Suzy gripped my hand tightly while the minister intoned standard passages from the bible, concluding with a personal prayer for Mrs. Nesbitt. The rain slackened as the casket was lowered into the ground, and the gathering began to disperse. On the way back to the road, Alex and I agreed to meet in his office at two o'clock.

It was almost one by the time we arrived back at the Dukes. The rain was steady again, so Suzy and I decided to have lunch in the coffee shop. During lunch we discussed the rest of our stay in London and agreed to catch tomorrow's late morning flight out of Heathrow. Finishing her iced tea, Suzy said she was going back to her room when I left to meet with Alex.

"I'll confirm our plane reservations," she said, "then I'm going to sort out everything I've bought so it'll fit in my luggage."

"It won't happen," I laughed, "even if you use my luggage, too. Besides, our plane'll probably never get off the ground. Why don't you call UPS? Maybe they can get all of it on one plane. If it's a big one."

She pouted and then reached across and slapped my arm. "That's not fair. I didn't really buy that much. And I won't need any help – everything will fit in my luggage, thank you. I guarantee it!"

"A dollar says you're wrong."

"You're on! But let's make it interesting – five bucks."

Alex was waiting for me in his office. Before I could say anything he told me that he wanted to proceed with settlement on the Burlington County property, the settlement that had brought David to the States just a week ago today. He then slid an envelope across the desk to me and said it contained a letter authorizing me to represent the bank on all matters pertaining to the property.

"One other point regarding the Burlington deal," he continued. "I want you to finish the site engineering as quickly as possible. David mentioned that he had sent you preliminary drawings for the new plant. The problem is, we have to be ready to move ahead as soon as settlement takes place, and I'm sure you're more familiar with local politics and code requirements than the architect – he's located in Tokyo. Are there any problems at your end?"

"A few, but none we can't resolve."

"Good. You should also know that Tampa will be taking over from you after settlement, but not until you finish your work. Tampa has an agreement to fast-track the plant's construction – you probably already know it's for a Japanese computer manufacturer. It should be a first for your country; not only are they going to assemble computer components shipped from their main plant in Japan, they also hope to crack the American software market, something they haven't been successful at in the past. They plan to employ about eight hundred people, including, I would imagine, a fair percentage of your American software brain trust. I'm sure that won't sit well with many of your 'Buy

American' union people, but it will help your future local economy, not to mention all the immediate construction jobs."

I don't know if it was professional jealousy or what, but what I just heard really ticked me off. "You know Alex," I snapped, "it may sound ungrateful after all the business you've given us over the years, but what the hell, Hammel & McQuaid aren't bankers or private detectives – were builders! And we're damned good at what we do. Why don't we ever get a crack at these construction projects?"

"Two reasons, Cole. First, we don't control the decision making. We're told who is going to do what; sometimes by Milan, other times by Tampa. Second, after all the years I've dealt with this crazy client, I'm convinced they don't want any one of us – Tampa, you, or my bank – to see too many pieces of the puzzle. They want to keep all of us in the dark as much as possible. You should hear some of the idiotic questions asked of us by Tampa. It's another reason why I believe Tampa doesn't know any more about the client than we do."

"But with all their other crazy restraints, they've got to be interested in controlling construction cost. Don't they ever put these jobs out for competitive bidding?"

"As far as I know, never. And I know it's not because they don't care – believe me, they control everything. From what Tampa tells me, bids are by invitation only. It's a very small fraternity, and it changes with project location. But if you're not on the list, you don't get to bid. It's that simple."

Alex got out of his chair and began pacing behind the desk. Without stopping or looking at me he continued talking, but his voice suddenly lost its authority. "Before we stray too far from the main issue, I'd like to say one more thing and then ask you a question. As I hope I conveyed to you on Friday, I'm at a loss trying to decide what to do about this frightening mess. I know I cannot sit idly by any longer and do nothing, but I also cannot do anything that will harm the bank or any of us. And, for the record, my concern for the bank has nothing to do with personal greed – I fear for the institution and the people here. I intend to retire in less than two years; my wife and I have a beautiful little place along the coast near St. Austell, in Cornwall. But I can't leave here until this business is resolved...it would absolutely kill me to see the bank destroyed because of a bad decision on my part."

He stopped pacing and rested his hands on the back of his chair, staring down at me. "And that leads to my question – actually two; have you considered what we discussed earlier, and do you have any suggestions as to what we should do?"

"Yes to both questions. I've blocked out a rough plan that I hope you'll agree with, although I'll tell you up front that some of what I'm going to suggest will happen whether you agree or not – it's too late to do otherwise. It's also a safe bet that my plan will expose us to a certain amount of risk. I really don't care, because it appears we've been at risk all along. We just didn't know it. I know what I'm going to suggest isn't foolproof, but at least it gives us the initiative, so we don't sit on our hands waiting for whatever they want to dish out."

Alex sat down. "I dread what I think I'm about to hear, but please get on with it. I just hope you've considered what I said about the bank."

I don't know why, but I wasn't completely sold on Alex's stated reason for protecting the bank. Was it pride, compassion, or pure greed?

"Yes, I have. Based on what David told me just before his death, I understand your predicament, or what you perceive as a predicament. But, regardless, your first priority should be to liquidate as much as possible of the client's working capital. Everything you have invested in short-term loans...I believe something in excess of two-hundred fifty million. You've got to quickly build as much cash reserve as you can. If the..."

"My god," he interrupted, "if the client gets wind of it – and I'm sure they will – they'll terminate us immediately. Why risk such a drastic result?"

"It's a risk I believe you have to take. You have to prepare for the worst. As I said, some things are going to happen whether we like it or not. Think about what's already happened. Look at the crazy situation in Atlantic City; there is no logical reason why somebody should have meddled with the investigation into David's death, but according to Ronko somebody did. Another thing I haven't told you about; the day before coming here I was followed home by two men in a car. I have no idea who they were – good or bad – or why they followed me. But I know they did. And then add in what you told me last Friday. *Somebody has been stirring this pot for twenty-five years, and I don't like it one bit!* I don't like feeling threatened, and I don't like looking over my shoulder – particularly when I don't know which way to look. If you do as I suggest and the client doesn't like it...and decides to pull the account, it may be a bitter pill to swallow, but if you have the liquid assets your bank should survive. And, consider this, if your earlier suspicion is correct and the client is the bad guy, losing the account may be the least of our worries."

Alex looked defeated, his complexion almost gray. "You're right. Things have gotten out of hand and I've refused to face up to it. In fact, I should have done something about this years ago...maybe David would still be alive. Now I feel everybody is threatened. Even my wife – who knew nothing of this until David was killed – is badgering me to increase security at our home and here in the bank. Maybe I should. But, more to the point, your suggestion about converting the loans is going to be difficult to do quickly; it may take some time, maybe as long as two weeks. I don't know what else you have in mind doing, but I am convinced the client will find out – it's just a question of how quickly."

"That's going to depend on how good their grapevine is, and whether they have a mole in the bank. As far as your part is concerned, you should do as much as possible within the privacy of this office – the less people in your bank who know what's happening the better."

"I'll have to get started immediately." Alex punched a button on his phone. "Miss Nickleby, call Rogers and tell him I want a printout of the latest Milan loan portfolio, and I need it within the hour. When he delivers it bring it to me immediately. Oh, and call my wife and tell her I'll be late tonight – not to hold dinner." Alex turned to me and continued. "Unfortunately, we'll probable have to discount most of the paper. I'm sure we'll take a pretty hard hit on some of it. The best we can hope for is to break even."

"Breaking even is better than belly-up. I still think it's a smart move."

"I hope you're right. With all that's happened I can't disagree with your logic, but once I start this action my directors are going to demand answers...some of them think the bank can't exist without the damned account, and I'm not sure I can – or should – answer their questions. I may be looking at termination instead of retirement, but I guess at this point it really doesn't matter. Other than my reputation and pride. I would feel a lot more confident if I knew what you intend doing next. You obviously have something in mind."

"I do, at least to a point, and I'll gladly tell you as much as I've worked out. But I recommend telling your directors absolutely nothing; stall and try to buy us as much time as possible. And, unless it's absolutely necessary, I wouldn't say a word about this to anybody else, in or out of the bank.

"As far as what I'm going to do, first, I have to convince my brother to help me find out what the hell is going on in Atlantic City. Before he opened his own office Ben was an assistant county prosecutor. He has a lot of connections in South Jersey, both legal and political. On top of that, a college buddy of his is now in the FBI hierarchy in Washington. So with Ben's help I'm sure I can get some answers; maybe even more details than you have.

"Next, I'm going to do some snooping in Tampa – and as soon as possible. Initially I'll try to be as discreet as possible. But, if I fail to turn up anything useful, I won't hesitate to let the Tampa people know who I am and what I'm doing, particularly this Marie Sippano. If you're assessment of their involvement in this is wrong, that's when all hell will break loose, and the client cancels the account. If nothing else, we'll at least know what triggered it."

"Cole, wait a minute, you said it yourself a few minutes ago; you're a builder – not a detective. Why should you get involved in this further? It seems to me it would be a lot safer to hire a private investigator. The bank can do that, and I certainly have the authority to order it."

"No, if we bring somebody else into the loop it'll just delay the inevitable. Besides, I'm already in this up to my eyeballs, and I'll feel a lot better if I'm moving around and taking some initiative...I don't like being a sitting duck. I guess after what happened to David we both should feel a little spooked, but I'm also concerned for our friends and families. I can't sit around waiting for something to happen, I've got to do something – anything. Do you understand?"

"Yes I do, and I share your concern for the others. Things have gone far enough. But, please promise me that you'll be careful; what you plan on doing really frightens me. And I'd also like to reimburse you for whatever expenses you incur, after all, you're doing this for both of us."

"Maybe we'll split them, but let's see what happens first."

When I arrived back at the hotel I found Suzy in her room sitting on an overstuffed suitcase, a big grin on her face. "If you'll snap these latches for me I'll be happy to relieve you of five dollars," she said jokingly.

"You've got everything packed?" I asked. "*Everything?*"

"All but my things for tonight and the trip home, and I have room in my carry-on for all that's left. Oh, that extra bundle over their also has to go in the overhead with my carry-on. But see, I did it without needing any space in your luggage. I won!"

I laughed and handed her five bucks. "O.K. my packing specialist, but with that bundle in the overhead I hope the pilot can keep us flying level."

We decided to have an early dinner at an Italian restaurant we had spotted a few blocks from the hotel. Before we left I found the slip of paper in my pocket and remembered that Mrs. Nesbitt had asked me to call her. The phone rang a number of times and I was about to hang up when she answered. She spoke in a very subdued voice and began crying when I gave my name. She sounded terrible and I apologized for intruding.

"Mr. McQuaid, please don't feel you have to apologize...I appreciate you taking time to call me. There wasn't an opportunity to talk privately at the church this morning and there are so many questions... so much I don't understand about what has happened. I also wanted to thank you for your kind assistance with David's arrangements. It would have been very difficult for me, with his death being so far away. I really don't know how to thank you..."

"Please, Mrs. Nesbitt, I interrupted, it is not necessary. Suzanne and I are deeply saddened by what happened. We're leaving for home tomorrow morning. I will be in contact with Alex Trimble on a regular basis and will keep him informed about the investigation in Atlantic City. I'm sure he'll call you as soon as we know more. Is there anything else we can do before we leave?"

"No, there isn't, except to answer one or two questions."

She wanted to know everything David had said and done during the time we were together before his death. I answered as best I could about the few hours David and I had spent together, without mentioning the mysterious client or Alex Trimble's suspicions; she apparently knew nothing about any of it. Before hanging up I again expressed my sorrow and promised to pursue the investigation into David's death as soon as I got home.

After Suzy and I returned from dinner I decided to tell her of my conversations with Trimble; there was really no point in delaying further. She was shocked to hear about the earlier deaths, and said she couldn't understand how this went on year after year without Walter or me being told. I told her the reasons given to me by Trimble, but she just sat in her chair shaking her head. When I explained what actions Trimble and I were going to take she jumped up and grabbed my hands.

"No, Cole, no! I don't want you involved in this any further. I can't bear the thought of losing you now. My god, this could be dangerous for all of us. And what do you think Ben is going to say?"

I had no good answers. I knew Suzy was right – there will be a lot of risk, and the danger could extend well beyond our families and friends.

"Suzy, I share your concern about the danger...to everybody, but what's the alternative? Do nothing and let the police handle it? Hell, they haven't solved one of these crimes going back to 1972, and they probably won't find David's killer or killers either. And David's murder hit pretty close to home – who's next, you, me, one of our employees?

"Doing nothing hasn't solved or stopped one of these crimes and, as I told Trimble, I don't like being a sitting duck...and I refuse to live looking over my shoulder. I've got to do something! Can you understand that?"

"Yes, Cole, I do, but I'm still terrified for all of us. And what about Ben? I just know he'll want us to bail out of the whole mess."

"You're probable right, but, like it or not, Ben's going to have to understand. He better, because I'm going to need his help and a few of his connections once we get home. Bottom line; it may take some arm twisting, but he is my brother. I think I can convince him."

CHAPTER SIX

Our flight arrived on time in Philly. The weather was still hot and sticky; a thunder storm rumbling on the western horizon. After the usual delays in retrieving our luggage, getting out of long-term parking, and fighting late afternoon commute traffic, it was almost five o'clock when I dropped Suzy at her home. She was tired and wanted a hot bath. Even though it was late I had to find out what was happening at the office, and I arrived there just as most of the staff was leaving. When I walked in, Nancy was stacking opened mail and phone messages on my desk. She looked upset.

"Cole, I'm glad you're back. I didn't know if you'd stop by the office today, so I left a message on your machine at home. Things here are really hectic; today has been a nightmare."

"What's wrong? What happened?"

"Somebody broke into the office last night. They did a pretty thorough job of searching and trashing the place. I don't think they missed a drawer or a closet in the building – everything was really a mess. It took all of us the entire day to straighten things out. The police were here for more than an hour this morning, but I don't think they found anything useful."

"Didn't the alarm system work?"

"Joe was the first one in this morning. He noticed the alarm wasn't working when he tried to disarm it at the keypad. Then he saw the mess and called the police. The detective who came later said the alarm had been disabled by someone who knew exactly how to do it. He said they got in by prying out an air vent in the Blueprint Room."

"Was anything taken? Were the computers damaged?"

"That's what's odd. We can't find anything missing. And the computers and our other equipment appear to be untouched. Even the petty cash box was left intact with the money still in it. All they apparently did was rummage through closets, drawers and files, and make a terrible mess in the process. It's crazy."

Then it hit me. David's attaché case! Before leaving for England I had put his case in our fire file. The fire file is actually a small fireproof concrete room in the basement. "Was anything disturbed in the basement?"

"Joe checked and said everything looked O.K. Apparently they didn't go down there."

I did, and when I told Nancy why, she was right on my heels. Maybe whoever broke in didn't realize we had a basement, or maybe they just missed the door to the fire file. The room is difficult to spot because the only door is set flush in the wall and is painted to match. It can't be seen at all from the bottom of the stairs because it's located off a narrow aisle behind rows of file cabinets. Regardless, I breathed a sigh of relief when I unlocked the door and found David's case standing just where I had left it.

I sent Nancy home and sat at my desk to look at my mail and check the phone messages. Nothing from Atlantic City. Even though it was late I decided to call Ronko to find out if anything new had developed – if he would talk to me. He was in, but all he would tell me was the case was still open and he had nothing new to report. The unspoken message I got was that regardless of what he knew he wasn't talking to me. Frustrated, I hung up and called my brother.

His secretary answered and said he was on another line. She recognized my voice and asked me to hold. She was on her way out the door, but said she would tell Ben I was waiting. Before he came on the line it dawned on me that I had better watch what I say. Maybe the bastards who broke in here last night also bugged our phones.

"Hey little brother, how was London?," he said when he came on the line. His phone greeting to me rarely varies. It isn't just because I'm younger, it's his way of tweaking me because he's five inches shorter. We've always had a close relationship, and love to needle each other. I can always set him off with one of my latest bad lawyer joke. Particularly since he has yet to come up with any bad engineer jokes.

"London was great, Ben, although I didn't like some of the news I heard. On top of that, when I got home I heard my building was broken into last night. I need to talk to you as soon as possible – how about tomorrow morning?"

"The morning's O.K., but it'll have to be early. I've got two late morning meetings and a one-thirty deposition in Philly. What happened last night at your office?"

I told him what I knew about the break-in, without mentioning David's attaché case. We agreed to meet for breakfast at a diner in Cherry Hill at seven-thirty the next morning.

After I hung up I spent the next half-hour wandering from room to room looking for anything missing or out of the ordinary; something that would prove me wrong about David's attaché case being the target. I found nothing other than the remains of what used to be our security system. It may have been the frustration of not finding what they wanted, but after electronically disarming the system, our friends screwed-up the main panel and ripped out just about every motion sensor in the building. Nancy said our alarm company had looked at the damage and told her the system couldn't be put back in service until tomorrow at the earliest.

I then called our local police headquarters to find out what they were doing about the break-in. All they could tell me was that the detective handling the case had gone home for the day. I said I would call back in the morning and also asked that they check our building during the night because of the alarm being off.

It seemed like two days since I had my shower this morning at the Dukes. On top of that I was hungry and tired, so I grabbed David's attaché case, locked the door and headed for home.

With a hundred thoughts spinning around in my head I was about half way home when I suddenly remembered the earlier incident of being followed. I glanced in the rear view mirror and, sure enough, there was a dark blue car behind me. I couldn't tell if it was the same car, so I slowed down until it was about fifty yards back. It looked familiar but I couldn't be sure. For the next mile they stayed right on my tail; speed up, slow down, it didn't make any difference. I weighed the risk and decided to try something. The road was fairly straight with a decent shoulder and traffic in my direction was light. I hit the accelerator and moved up to about seventy. Then I angled off onto the shoulder and slammed on the brakes; they had choices, either stop behind me, ram me, or pass me. They got two wheels on the shoulder but realized they weren't going to stop without hitting me, so the driver veered back on the road and went past; which was exactly what I had hoped for. He was accelerating fast but I was able to make the tag; it was Pennsy registration. And it was the same dark blue Ford that tailed me last week, and the same two guys in the front seat. Why was I not surprised?

I called Ben from my car phone and told him what had happened and gave him the tag number. I knew he had enough contacts to get the tag traced quickly. He said he would, and might have the information for me when we met in the morning. "But tell me, Cole," he continued, "what do you plan doing with the information after you get it – except maybe get yourself killed? God, why the hell are these guys tailing you – have you got any idea what you're involved in? I think before anything else happens you should go to the police and get yourself some protection.

"And what the hell do I tell them? Come on Ben, you know as well as I that they can't protect me any better than I can protect myself.

Besides, I'm pretty sure I do know what this is all about. I think you'll agree when I tell you the rest of it tomorrow morning."

"O.K., but why don't you at least spend the next few days with us? Maybe we can sort this out together."

"Thanks, but no. There's no point involving you and your family anymore than you are now. Believe me, if I could walk away from this I'd do it in a heartbeat. I'm damn well not trying to play hero, but, like it or not, it looks like the mess has been dumped in my lap. And I've got to keep the focus on me – it would kill me if I did nothing and one of my family or friends got hurt. You may understand better after we talk in the morning."

There was no further sign of the blue car the rest of the way home. I did check the streets around my house – no sign of the car; and I went through the house checking doors and windows. No bogeymen.

Mrs. Tomasello had gone home but had left a note for me on the kitchen table. It said dinner was in the ice box – it would always be an ice box, never a refrigerator – and "make sure you eat every bit". God bless her, I was starved. In two plastic containers I found a huge helping of lasagna and a salad of tomato, cucumber and onion, in vinegar. With the help of my microwave, a couple of warm rolls, and some iced tea I had a great meal. While I ate I went through the mail she also had left on the kitchen table; the usual bills, ads and junk mail. I checked my phone messages. Nothing, other than the call from Nancy about the break-in. After cleaning up the kitchen I unpacked my luggage, took a shower and went to bed. It was earlier than usual, but I suspected tomorrow was going to be a long day. Before I fell asleep the phone rang. It was Suzy. She wanted to make sure I was O.K. and to say goodnight. I told her I missed her.

Ben was already having coffee at the counter when I got to the diner the next morning. We moved to a booth where Ben told me he had already managed to get a run-down on the Pennsy license – but it wasn't going to be much help. The tag belonged to a rental picked up at the Philly airport about two weeks ago. Ben's contact was told the car had been charged to a credit card that later was identified as stolen. The car was supposed to be returned in seven days, and when it wasn't it was reported to the police as stolen. It was still missing.

We ordered breakfast, or rather Ben did; I had my usual juice and coffee. For the next thirty minutes or so I went through everything Trimble had told me in London. All the deaths -everything. I also gave him the details of David's death and told him what I knew about the stonewalling I was getting from Ronko in Atlantic City. About half way through his bacon and eggs Ben put down his fork and just sat and glared at me, his chin leaning on clenched fists. I knew he was pissed.

I finished by relating what I had asked Trimble to do and what I intended doing, at least as much as I had worked out in my mind. When I finished he leaned across the table, almost in my face. "Goddamn it Cole," he said in an angry whisper, "this is even worse than I imagined. What the hell were Trimble and his people thinking – how could they have their heads up their asses all those years? They've waited way too long to find out what's going on... what you suggested to Trimble should have been done fifteen or twenty years ago. It serves them right if they go belly up, I couldn't care less. What I do care about is your end of this; with David's death they've got you involved right up to your baby blues. Maybe all of us. And severing ties with them now isn't going to change that, although I strongly recommend you do it, and do it quickly. I know I can protect your business interest from here on – if Trimble cooperates – and hopefully mitigate any liability you have from past dealings, but I can't do a thing about the personal risk. And I don't know if what you propose doing will accomplish anything – other than get more people hurt or killed. I just don't know..."

"Ben," I interrupted, "I know there's risk, and I don't like it either, but do you have any better ideas?"

"No, other than close up shop and move everybody to Tahiti," he answered with a forced grin.

"Good, because I don't either, but I don't know if Tahiti is far enough...this crazy client seems to have awfully long arms. Go ahead and call Trimble and do whatever you think is legally necessary. But beyond that, just don't sell yourself short; there are things you can do to help me with my end. I'm going to need help getting information, and cutting through the bullshit – like you did tracing that license plate. You can probably do with one phone call what would take me days to accomplish – maybe never. For starters, how about calling your friend Brian whatshisname in Washington.

See if he can shed some light on what's happening in Atlantic City. I can't imagine why, but maybe the feds are involved with the investigation into David's death. Maybe they're the reason Ronko's not talking to me."

"You must mean Brian Hamilton. I think what you're suggesting is a little far-fetched, but I'll call him – although I doubt he'll tell me anything. I see him once or twice a year when he comes up for

Princeton games, but since he started moving up in the F.B.I. hierarchy he rarely ever talks shop. We're really not that close anymore, but I'll try."

"O.K., but failing that, do you know any of the powers that be in Atlantic City, particularly in the police department? I can understand the cops not talking about an on-going investigation, except what little they leak to the newspapers and TV. What annoys the hell out of me is the one-eighty flip that Ronko did in less than twenty-four hours. First, he damn near talks my ear off – tells me everything about David's death except who did it – and the next day tells me he can't talk to me at all. Was he running off at the mouth the first time... and his boss didn't like, or did somebody get to his boss?"

"You may be overreacting, Cole, it could be pure coincidence. I don't have any contacts in their department, but I do have a friend in the Atlantic County prosecutors office. We used to work together. I'll ask him to snoop around and see what he can dig up."

"Good. Just let me know what you find out. I'll be in my office all day."

Ben pushed away his half-eaten breakfast. He agreed to call or beep me as soon as he made some phone calls.

As I walked back to my car a thought popped into my head; something one of my college professors used to drill into us: the best and quickest way to solve a problem is to surround it with as much information as you can throw at it. It made me smile. I'm sure my present dilemma is no different.

When I got to the office the alarm company serviceman was busy putting our security system back together. I started attacking the mess on my desk when Suzy came into my office and shut the door – something she rarely ever does. I knew something was wrong.

"Cole, why didn't you tell me last night about the break-in. Nancy just told me about it, and said you mentioned that David's attaché case was apparently what they were after. Do you have any idea why his case is that important? Did the police find anything? What can..."

"Whoa, Suzy, one question at a time. I didn't tell you because you were tired and I felt there was no reason to upset you. Regardless, there wasn't anything either of us could do about the break-in last night. His attaché case spent the night under my bed, and right now it's on the floor here behind my desk. It's locked; I don't have a key, so I have no idea what's in it. I am going to try picking the locks as soon as I convince a very sexy blonde to go back to her office and stop destroying my concentration. But seriously, there is one thing you can do right away; call the police, I tried last night but the detective handling the case had gone home. See if they have any leads and what they're doing to follow-up. Let them know that we're really upset about the whole episode."

"Do you really think I should call," Suzy said, a coy grin on her face, "I wouldn't want to destroy their concentration?"

"Shouldn't be a problem...as long as they can't see you. Oh, by the way, I didn't see any reason to delay, so I met with Ben this morning and told him about my meetings with Trimble. I didn't withhold anything. He was mad as hell, particularly after I told him what I plan doing. After admitting he had no better suggestions he calmed down, and agreed to help anyway he can. He's working now to dig up some information for me – I hope to hear from him later today. Also, he's going to contact Trimble and insist on a agreement outlining our limited involvement in this whole mess from day one, and absolving us from any future liability. Bottom line: after we get through this I don't think we'll be doing any more business with Alex Trimble's bank. But for now, right or wrong, I'm still proceeding with Plan A."

"And I am still terrified for you. Please, Cole, whatever you do be careful. I'd also appreciate it if you would have dinner tonight with Julia and me at my place. A good home cooked meal for a change, and I hope we can talk about just what it is you plan doing next. Maybe I'll feel better after if I know."

"I'll look forward to dinner. And please try not to worry. The more I think this through the more I'm convinced it's the right thing to do." I purposely didn't mention being followed last night.

At noon Nancy sent out for sandwiches and I ate mine at my desk, all the while playing with the locks on David's case. I had learned how to pick a lock back in college when I persisted in losing my locker keys. A friend showed me how to do it with two bent paperclips. I thought I was still good at it, but the locks on David's case proved to be tough; it took me about half an hour to open both. I guess I'm out of practice.

There were a number of things in the case, including the usual pens, pencils, a few ruled tablets and a calculator. It also contained an assortment of maps, an address book, three manila file folders, and a small, well worn leather loose-leaf binder, with David's name embossed in gold on the front. I removed everything and spread the items on my desk. Nothing struck me as out of the ordinary, so I then checked the case for a possible hidden compartment. Nothing. At least nothing my untrained eye could find.

The first manila folder contained computer generated spreadsheets of financial data. There were twenty-five or thirty pages in all, and a glance at some of the mind-boggling numbers told me they related to the client. The second folder held typed lists of properties acquired by David's bank. I recognized the ones we had been involved with. Each contained a date, the full name and location, and in the right-hand margin a series of hand written letters and numbers; I guess some kind of code or cross reference. The last folder was apparently David's expense account records: airline, hotel, restaurant and rental car receipts, and slips for a lot of miscellaneous stuff.

The loose-leaf binder really piqued my interest. It was about two inches thick and had a tab for each year, starting with 1967 and ending with 1997. Behind each tab were dog-eared ruled pages containing hand-written entries, some in pencil, most in ink. Flipping through, I noticed some of the writing was faded and almost illegible. I scanned through a few of the years when I had been involved and saw a lot of familiar names and locations. I also saw notes pertaining to some of the disappearances and deaths Trimble told me about. What really grabbed me were the combinations of letters and numbers written along side each name and location. They were similar to what I had seen in the other folder. I hadn't a clue as to whether anything I was looking at was important or had any bearing on David's death. But something must be – why else would somebody go to so much trouble to steal it. I buzzed Nancy.

"Nancy, all of this stuff came out of David's attaché case. I'd like you to drop what you're doing and run two copies of everything. Put the copies in separate folders and mark each to agree with David's. Oh, and be careful handling the originals in the leather binder, some are really fragile. There's a lot to copy, but I'd like you to finish before you leave today. Can do?"

"Sure. What should I do with everything when I finish?"

"Bring it all back here. I'm going to put the originals and David's attaché case back in our fire file. I guess it's as safe there as anywhere. Tomorrow morning I'm going to put one copy in my safe deposit box at the bank. The other copy I'll keep with me to look over; I still have no idea what some of it means."

Suzy buzzed me around three to tell me that she had finally caught up with the police detective investigating our break-in. He told her they had no real leads; the prints they had lifted from the air vent couldn't be matched and there was no other physical evidence. They would maintain it as an open case, and hopefully something would develop. I knew they were up a blind alley.

Ben called around four and said he had reached Hamilton in Washington. Hamilton claimed he knew nothing of the situation in Atlantic City, but reluctantly agreed to check into it and get back to Ben. Ben had also placed a call to Trimble in London but he wasn't in his office. He had left a message with the officious Miss Nickleby. Ben said he wasn't going to call his friend in the Atlantic County prosecutor's office until he heard from Hamilton. Not a very productive day so far.

Dinner at Suzy's relieved some of my frustration. As always, Julia made me feel like I didn't have a care in the world. Suzy had fixed a great crab salad, with corn on the cob, fresh peas and cole slaw. Julia had her usual iced tea, while Suzy and I shared a good California Merlot that I had picked up on my way from the office. We're both red wine freaks. After dinner Julia went to her room to call a friend. While Suzy and I cleaned up the kitchen we talked about my plans.

I admitted that I was still trying to sort out everything that had happened, and how it fit together... if it fit at all. Was there really a common thread as Trimble suggested... and what about motive? If Trimble's client was responsible for everything that has happened, was guarding their identity the sole reason for all the violence? I don't think so. If what Trimble told me was accurate, some of the deaths may have been pure retaliation, particularly the more recent killings. But David's death still puzzles me – it doesn't seem to fit either pattern. With all this rattling around in my head, one thing was crystal clear; I knew I had to start in Tampa. I wanted to meet the Tampa people, particularly Maria Sippano, the woman identified by Trimble as having some sort of relationship with David Nesbitt. Regardless of what Trimble had said about Tampa's role, I wanted to meet these people face to face and decide for myself whether they were playing some kind of deadly game.

"What I find in Tampa will determine what I do next. If I draw a blank I'll probably come back here and concentrate on the Atlantic City investigation, or maybe follow-up on the death of that Byrnes woman in Santa Barbara in '91. But, if I suspect that Tampa is involved I'll play it by ear and do what I think necessary. Either way, I shouldn't be gone more than a few days."

"Please, Cole," she said, her voice trembling, "promise me two things; that you won't take foolish risks, and that you call me here at home every night to let me know where you are and that you're safe. As I told you, I can't bear the thought of anything happening to you. If you do suspect that Tampa is involved in some way, can you go to the police down there and let them handle it?"

"That depends, Suzy. If all I have are hunches, with nothing to back them up, I can't go to the police as an out-of-town stranger and expect them to do anything. After all, this Tampa outfit has been in business there for forty years. Guilty or not, if they're half as smart as I think they are, they have a rock-solid reputation in the business community. I'll just have to wait and see what develops. As far as your request is concerned, if it makes you feel better I'll do what you ask. How about if I call you around ten each evening?"

"That'll be fine...and it will make me feel better."

I left Suzy's place around ten and headed home. It was a beautiful night, so I decided to take the road along the river through the park. My car's air conditioning was still not working – I've got to take it back to the dealer tomorrow – so I had the windows down, enjoying the cool breeze. The road is poorly lighted, and before I realized what was happening a car with no lights was passing on my left. As it pulled slightly ahead the driver veered right and cut me off. I reacted by slamming on the brakes and skidding onto the adjoining grass, narrowly missing a huge tree. The other car also stopped and quickly backed-up until it was directly in front of me. It was the blue Ford, and as soon as they jumped from the car I recognized the two goons, coming at me fast from left and right. It all happened so quickly I hardly had time to react. I tried putting my car in reverse, but before I could do it Righty reached through the open passenger side window and yanked my keys from the ignition. Then Lefty blindsided me by slamming his fist into the side of my face. I knew he really nailed me – first I had trouble focusing my eyes, and then everything went from fuzzy to black nothing. I don't know how long I was out, but when I started crawling out of my black hole they had me outside the car, spread-eagled, with my chin and arms on the roof.

Lefty did the talking, his voice guttural, with a definite foreign accent. "We will go to your office now and get Nesbitt's briefcase. I don't know where you hid it but I know it is there...it has to be. Your actions have caused us much trouble and I will not tolerate further delay. Come, we will go in my car. My friend here will close and lock your car. If you cooperate you will not be harmed."

His pressing hand had my body pinned so tightly against the car I had difficulty twisting my head around to talk, and I was still having trouble getting my eyes to work. "You're wrong," I mumbled with some difficulty, "I have no idea where Nesbitt's briefcase is... he took it with him to Atlantic City."

"Do not lie to me, McQuaid, I know he didn't take it with him to the casino. He had it at the airport, so it can only be at your office. I warn you, any more stalling and I'll let my friend here use you to practice his knife skills. Believe me when I tell you that you don't want that to happen."

What helped clear my head was the realization that these were David's killers...*they had to be* – they knew about the casino! From the corner of my eye I saw Righty standing about six feet away, a wild-eyed stare on his face and a nasty looking long-bladed knife in his right hand. I didn't doubt he knew how to use it, remembering how David had been worked over with a knife before he died. Even if I give them the damn briefcase I'll probably end up as carving practice for this nut, unless I do something fast. I didn't move, trying to buy time to think. Lefty wasn't going to wait. My chance came when he reached up to grab my arm from the car roof. I knew I had less than a second to act, so I spun around fast, and with as much force as I could muster drove the back of my elbow into his exposed side, just below his armpit. I heard ribs crack and he doubled over, gasping for air. My head felt like it was going to explode. I grabbed one of Lefty's dangling arms by the wrist and twisted it up behind his back. I held on and with a hard shove drove him forward into Righty, who obviously couldn't think fast enough to get out of the way. When they hit I felt something give in Lefty's arm. They both went down in a heap, Righty landing on his back. He dropped his knife and my car keys – and there were also some loose papers on the ground, apparently from one of their pockets. Lefty was moaning and having trouble breathing, his dead weight pinning Righty to the ground. I grabbed the knife, my keys and the papers and quickly got back in my car. I started the engine and threw the shift selector in reverse; Lefty was out of commission, but Righty was on his feet again and he worried me. He might be slow witted, but he had about two inches and forty or fifty pounds on me. I couldn't believe it when he didn't come after me. Instead, he was struggling to get Lefty into their car. Headlights in my rear view mirror told me why.

The lights were moving slowly, but I was thankful for the distraction. Righty finally got Lefty in the car, started the engine and sped off. Before I could do anything the approaching car pulled in ahead of me and stopped. It was a Park Police patrol car. I shoved the knife and papers under my seat, but I knew I couldn't hide the side of my face – I hope it didn't look as messed up as it felt. The officer asked for the usual ID and wanted to know why I was parked off the road, telling me it was a violation. He played the beam of his flashlight around the inside of my car, but, luckily, not on my face. He never mentioned it. I guess he also hadn't seen the blue Ford, he never said a word about that, either. I explained why I was there by telling him my air conditioning stopped working and I was playing with the controls, trying to get it to run. He dismissed me with a warning not to park off the road in the future. I said I wouldn't. I also silently thanked him for probably saving my life.

By the time I arrived home I had one helluva world-class headache. I gulped some aspirin and took a hot shower, before looking at myself in the mirror. When I did, I knew I'd have a lot of questions to answer tomorrow morning at the office, but with what had happened tonight explaining my battered face was the least of my worries. I fixed a stiff drink, then sat in the dark in my favorite chair and began rethinking the whole crazy mess.

The drink helped me relax – maybe too much, I had a hard time staying awake. My thoughts were rambling...David's death; I still didn't know why, but at least I know who killed him. Lefty and Righty...I wonder who they are and where they're from...can't place that accent. I've gotta be more careful...they're killers, and that son of a bitch Lefty hits like a piledriver – I don't think I've ever been hit that hard. They sure don't impress me as being very smart though, hell, they know where I live...followed me home that first time. Maybe they'll come here tonight...I guess it depends on how badly Lefty is hurt. And me with no gun...never owned one, so if they do come I'll have to rely on my old Louisville Slugger...right here next to my chair ...also know I can't leave for Tampa until something is done about both of them... gotta make sure Suzy and everybody are safe. I put my half-finished drink on the table and was out like a light.

My head was pounding and the repeated ringing went through me like shock waves. Why won't it stop? After I got my eyes half open I realized I had fallen asleep in my chair; the dim light coming through the window telling me it was almost dawn. My legs refused to cooperate and that damn ringing wouldn't stop. Then it did, but started up again almost immediately. It was my cordless phone laying on the table next to my dead drink. I grabbed the phone and grunted something; my mouth and my voice didn't seem to be working very well.

"Is that you, Cole?"

"I think so, who's this?"

"It's Ben. God, you had me worried, and you sound terrible. I let your phone ring at least twenty times, then I hung up and dialed again. I knew you were supposed to be home, so I thought maybe something happened to you. Are you O.K.?"

"I've felt better. But why in hell are you calling at this ungodly hour, the sun's not even up?" My voice was coming back but I didn't think my head was going to make it.

"I called because I have good news. I just heard the cops nailed the two guys in the blue Ford, the one with the Pennsy tags."

"When...where?" This was fantastic news after last night.

"They were arrested in the ER at the hospital in Cherry Hill. One was apparently banged-up in a fight and the other guy took him there. The stolen car is what screwed them. That's about all I know now, but why don't you meet me at the police station in about an hour and we can get the details first-hand. Sam Abromowitz is on duty – he's the one who called me."

I agreed and Ben hung up. After prying myself out of the chair I plodded up to the bathroom. What greeted me in the mirror wasn't pleasant; the left side of my face looked like I was chewing on a tennis ball, and was about nineteen shades of purple. My left eye wouldn't open more than half-way. With a crooked grin on my face I had to admit that maybe all this was worth it, based on what Ben had just told me.

I put coffee on, took a shower, and decided to pass on shaving. I couldn't remember whether Mrs. Tomasello was coming today – when she does she arrives around six – and I couldn't face the prospect of her questions. So, I quickly drank my juice and coffee, grabbed a pair of dark sunglasses, and left the house.

When Ben saw my face he reacted as I knew he would. I promised to explain everything later, but not until I knew what our two friends were being charged with, and how long they'd be out of commission. I asked Ben how he heard about the arrests so quickly. He explained that Sam Abromowitz was an old friend, and was also the contact who had traced the Pennsy tags for him. It was pure coincidence Sam was on duty when the arrests happened.

Sam offered coffee, which we both accepted, took us into a small office, and in classic police jargon explained what he knew of the arrests.

"The injured perp was driven to the hospital by his partner, who made the mistake of parking in the ambulance zone outside the ER main entrance. Officer Jarvis arrived at the ER in his patrol car at 2:10 a.m., delivering a kid who had apparently OD'd on a controlled substance. By this time the injured perp was being X-rayed and his partner was sitting in the waiting room. He was asked to move the car but, instead, stupidly gave Jarvis some smart mouth, then couldn't produce a drivers license or registration. Seeing the Pennsy tag, Jarvis suspected something was wrong and ran the tag. It was immediately confirmed as stolen, so he called for backup. Then Jarvis tried to cuff the guy and he put up quite a fight. Fortunately, Jarvis handled it and was able to force the guy into the back of the patrol car.

"Meanwhile, they finished treating the injured perp; he had broken ribs and a dislocated shoulder. Said he had fallen off a ladder. When we searched the car we found their papers – both are apparently foreign nationals. In the trunk we also found three automatic weapons, two handguns with silencers, boxes of ammunition, and a fancy wooden case of knives. The clincher was a gym bag containing a little more than four pounds of hashish and a shoe box stuffed with nickle bags of coke. In the same gym bag we also found almost twenty thousand in cash. Both individuals were placed under arrest, processed, and are downstairs in the lockup."

"So what happens next, how long can you hold them?" I asked.

"They're both being held on stolen car, weapons, and possession with intent to distribute charges. Later today they'll be transferred to county jail. To answer your question, they're not going to be on the street anytime soon, unless somebody comes up with bail...and that's unlikely considering the charges. Their twenty thousand has been confiscated, and I would guess bail will be a minimum of fifty thousand each."

"You said their papers were found in the car'" Ben said. "What exactly did you find?"

"In the car's glove box we found two passports, visas, a drivers license, about half a dozen credit cards – all with different names – apparently stolen, and receipts for three different motels, all in this area. Here, I'll show you, we just finished inventorying the stuff."

He dumped the contents of a manila envelope on the desk and spread it out for us to see. The first thing I noticed was one of the credit cards. It was issued to David Nesbitt. After my experience last night I knew these guys were David's killers – something Ben didn't – so I pushed the card in front of Ben and feigned surprise.

"Dammit, Ben, look at this, these have to be the guys who killed David!"

Ben picked up the credit card and stared at the name. "I don't understand what's going on, but it sure looks like you're right! Hell, they've been tailing you, and are probably also the ones who broke into your office. Now this. It's unbelievable. I guess they tailed you because they think you have something – whatever the hell it is they're after. Is it possible David was mixed up in narcotics?"

"Absolutely not, Ben, I'd bet my life on it!"

"Wait a minute," Sam said with a puzzled look on his face, "who is David?"

Without mentioning any of my recent involvement, I spent the next few minutes explaining how David Nesbitt was a client from London who came to see me on business, went to Atlantic City to do a little gambling, and was promptly killed. I gave him the details, as I recalled them, and told him what I saw and was told when I identified the body, and of my later conversations with Detective Lt. Al Ronko, if you could call them conversations.

Sam jotted something on a note pad. Finally, he looked up and said, "This is the first I've heard of the Nesbitt homicide. I certainly have no idea why Ronko acted as he did, although homicide investigations sometimes take funny twists. Maybe there is more to Nesbitt's death than he initially thought. And if the evidence we found here is an indicator, maybe he suspects there is some sort of narcotics connection. In any event, I'll have to talk to Ronko as soon as possible, to let him know what happened here and about Nesbitt's credit card. We'll probably end up working this thing together. Before I call though, are you certain this is your friend's credit card...no way it could be another David Nesbitt?"

"Positively," I answered. "It's a corporate card. Look on the front of the card. Below his name is the name of his bank in London. There's no mistake." I then remembered what Ronko had told me about finding credit cards on the bed in David's room. They obviously missed at least one.

"O.K., it looks like you're right," Sam said as he took the card from Ben and studied it. He glanced at both of us and started placing the items back into the envelope. "I don't think either of you can learn anything from the rest of these papers, even the passports. All they gave us were names and photo IDs. The photos match but the names might be aliases. Just for starters we checked state and local, and drew a blank on both perps. So we sent their prints through NCIC, but haven't heard anything yet. We also talked to the FBI in Philly and Interpol in New York. Both said they'd be back to us by late morning. I'm also waiting for a call from Immigration."

Before we left, Sam promised to notify Ben as soon as their IDs were confirmed. He also said the prisoners would still be transferred to the county jail later in the day, but not until he talked to Ronko and the county prosecutor's office about a possible murder charge. If that happened, bail would be out of the question. That was the best news I had heard in some time.

As we walked across the parking lot Ben turned and grabbed my arm, stopped and looked up at me. "O.K., little brother, level with me. A lot of things have happened over the last week or so that individually don't seem to relate. But, string them together as I did when you were talking in there a few minutes ago and there's no way they can't be connected. First, David's murder, then the crazy business with Trimble's bank, you being followed, your office being burglarized – now this bullshit with the two guys in Sam's jail and David's credit card. With all of that, I feel I'm still pounding square pegs in round holes, and do you know why? It's because you're holding out on me – you're not telling me everything. Example, maybe Sam didn't ask about your face because he was being polite...but I won't be – by any chance are you the 'ladder' that sent our boy in there to the hospital?"

"You guessed that right, and I do owe you an explanation, but believe me when I say I don't have all the answers, because I don't. What happened last night may clear up some of the mystery surrounding David's death, but I don't know that it had anything to do with Trimble's bank and what happened years ago. Maybe, maybe not. I do admit to stalling and not telling you everything, but I haven't lied to you – things just happened too fast. I know you're curious about my face... it's not too pretty. As bad as it may look though, after hearing what Sam said, I think I gave more than I got. But, all things considered, I was damn lucky." I told him the rest of what happened last night.

When I finished he looked at me and shook his head. "Jesus, Cole, you were lucky, lucky you're not dead. Why didn't you report it to the police, or at the very least go to the hospital and get checked out? You also could have come to my place."

"No, the hospital wasn't necessary, and as far as the police are concerned, what could they have done at that point? As it happened, things couldn't have worked out better. And, until I know more of what's going on, I don't want to involve you or anybody beyond what I already have. Besides, I wasn't thinking too straight last night."

O.K., but now that these two are in jail what are you going to do next? This may completely change things."

"I'm not making any firm plans until Sam tells us exactly who these two guys are. I still need your help in getting the information from your FBI friend that we discussed yesterday." I was still having trouble making my face work, but I forced a grin and said, " Other than that, you can do me a huge favor by coming to my office and explaining to everybody what happened to my face. Save me a lot of time."

"No thanks, little brother. You can handle that chore yourself. I'd love to be a fly on the wall though...just to see you bobbin' and weavin' around the truth."

Before I left I did make Ben promise to call me as soon as he heard from Sam Abromowitz.

When I arrived at the office Nancy looked up from her desk and stared at my face. Before she could ask the obvious I told her to call Suzy, Joe Mancuso and a few others into my office. When Nancy and the others arrived I explained as briefly as possible what had happened on my way home last night. I also related what Sam Abromowitz had told Ben and me earlier this morning about the arrests at the hospital; the charges, and the suspicion that the two guys in custody were involved in David's death. I finished by saying this should put an end to the recent craziness – purposely avoiding any reference to what had happened over the past twenty some years. The reason for the avoidance was my own indecision about whether this latest incident had any connection whatever with Trimble's bank and the past history of their mysterious client. No matter how I tried to rationalize it, I just couldn't tie the two issues together. Nothing seemed to fit.

Joe Mancuso is a very laid-back, gentle person. He won't even go fishing because he thinks it a cruel sport. So I wasn't surprised when he seemed more upset than anybody. "What the hell is going on, Cole – they break into our building and mess-up everything...you should've seen my office, they follow you and try to kill you, and now you say they probably killed David. I don't get it. Why? Who the hell are these guys?"

"The police don't know yet who they are, but they're working on it. We're not sure, Joe, but apparently they were after something they thought David had, and then thought I had. And I haven't a clue as to what it could be." I really didn't know for certain, but I did know it had to be something I found in David's attaché case.

"O.K. guys, now you know as much as I do. I'll let you know if anything new develops."

Everybody left but Suzy. I was surprised she hadn't said anything up till now. With a somber look on her face she walked over and leaned on the edge of my desk. "Cole, I'm sure you couldn't have done anything to stop what happened last night, but, my God, this is what I've been afraid of. I'm just thankful it wasn't worse. Do you really believe it will end now?"

"I can't be sure. Realistically, I still don't know if there's any connection between what's happened here and Trimble's bank. Oh, and thanks for not bringing that up in front of the others. The fewer people who know about it the better. We won't know if it's over unless, and until, something else happens. I've put my plans for Tampa on hold until I know who these two guys are and whether there are any apparent ties between them and Trimble's client. Right now the whole situation is pretty murky."

"I understand, Cole. Don't worry about the Trimble business getting around the office. Nancy knows about David's attaché case, but that's all. You, Ben and myself are the only ones who know the rest. But, please, whatever you have to do...remember your promise to me – no unnecessary risks. I would also feel better if you had a doctor look at your face."

"I haven't forgotten my promise, and believe me Suzy, all my face needs is time, not a doctor. It actually feels a little better already."

After Suzy went back to her office I spread my copy of the pages from David's leather binder around my desk. I needed to make sense of the coded entries written in the margins of the pages, combinations of numbers and letters. I consider myself pretty good at crossword puzzles and cryptograms, but after more than an hour of trial and error

I knew I wasn't getting anywhere, so I asked Nancy to have lunch sent in.

Food didn't help, mostly because it hurt like hell to chew. After another hour of unproductive doodling I gave up, put David's puzzle back in the file, and switched to office work. By three I realized why I wasn't accomplishing anything, all my concentration was on the clock and my phone – awaiting a call from Ben. He finally called around four and told me he was faxing me info on the two jailbirds. Sam Abromowitz had come through with ID's confirmed by both Interpol and the FBI. According to both agencies, most of the data was furnished by an 'anonymous source' within the CIA.

The fax was three pages long, two for Lefty and one for Righty. It looked like both had long-standing histories in Europe. Although neither had apparently been convicted of anything, the reports suggested it was the result of political connections and intimidation more than their innocence. It was no surprise that Lefty was the boss. His real name is Moussa Muzzadin, a fifty-eight year old Iranian national who entered the country illegally with his partner about eight years ago through Mexico. They were picked up by Immigration at the border, but escaped before being processed. The FBI got involved immediately, but both men disappeared and didn't surface again until yesterday, at the hospital. By the different entries in the reports it seems all of the agencies had files on these guys but, whether it was bureaucratic indifference or just a screw-up, they never found Muzzadin or his partner...the reports were blank after 1989. Maybe it was because the two did such a good job of staying under cover.

Muzzadin's physical description fit the man I knew with the sledge-hammer punch; five-ten, two-twenty, black hair with a swarthy complexion, deep-set brown eyes and bushy, black eyebrows. What I read next did surprise me: Muzzadin was a former member, actually third in command, of the Shah's secret police, the Savak. He headed-up the Shah's execution squad, and earned the nickname 'mad one'. He was also college educated, considered extremely intelligent, and was fluent in four languages, plus all of the dialects of his home country – from Persian and Kurdish through Pashto and Ossetic. When the Shah left Iran, Muzzadin fled to Turkey, where he joined a terrorist group and dropped out of sight. He was later identified as a leader of groups that conducted raids for the Pakistanis. Still later, he was reportedly spotted in Libya and Iraq. But his home base was Turkey, where he apparently recruited his partner Bahram Salemi.

Salemi was born and raised in Turkey. His date of birth was unknown, but he was in his early thirties, six-five and two-sixty. Salemi was bald, with two gold front teeth and a pock-marked complexion. Known to be very strong, he had an IQ approaching moron, but was expert with knives and was considered extremely dangerous. According to the report, Muzzadin was rarely ever seen without Salemi at his side.

Amen. A couple of real nice guys. I now realized just how lucky I was.

CHAPTER SEVEN

Raymond Barnes stormed back and forth in the small motel room, alternately pulling the dirty drapes aside to scan the parking lot and then sipping cold coffee and munching on donuts he had bought at the shop down the highway. He was furious. It was seven in the morning and local news was on TV. As angry as he was, he decided to watch the sports news for the scores of last night's games, so he grabbed the remote and flopped down on the edge of the bed, spilling the rest of his coffee on the blanket. "Screw it," he said aloud, "I'm not waiting around any longer for Muzzadin and his half-wit goon to show up, I'm gettin' out of this flea bag."

What fueled his anger was the thought that maybe Muzzadin had stiffed him, had taken off without him after promising him three grand for his help. Barnes was just about broke and had asked for a grand up front, but Muzzadin refused. Was this why? On the other hand, based on his no-show last night at McQuaid's maybe Muzzadin didn't get what he was after. If that was the case, they probably hadn't taken off yet. Even though Barnes had known Muzzadin and Salemi for only a couple of weeks, he knew their routine and the bar and diner where they hung out. They also had the motel unit next to his. So, if they were still in the area he'd find them, and if Muzzadin tried reneging on their deal he'd regret it. That much he knew for sure.

Barnes had his own car and was supposed to meet Muzzadin at eleven last night on the parking lot at Hammel & McQuaid. Barnes had been there previously to disable the alarm system when the three of them broke into the building, but never found what they were looking for. Muzzadin was supposed to bring this guy McQuaid back to the building last night to get whatever the hell it is he's after – one way or another. If it turned out that what he wanted was locked in a safe – and McQuaid refused to cooperate – it would be Barnes job to open it, something he was really good at. But nobody showed, and he waited until three this morning before giving up and returning to his motel, a little more than four hours ago.

Just as he was about to turn off the TV a news bulletin flashed on the screen, two guys being put into a police cruiser – one with his arm in a sling. He recognized both Muzzadin and Salemi. The announcer said they had been arrested at a local hospital and were being held on stolen car, drug and weapons charges. "Shit," thought Barnes, "I told that asshole to ditch the car and pick-up another. At least switch the plates. He wouldn't listen. Now maybe I'm really out my money. I gotta figure some way to work this out, or cut my losses and take off."

Barnes had no idea where Muzzadin stashed his money. He had seen him flash a money clip more than once, fat with twenties and fifties. But that probably wouldn't cover what he was owed, and he wasn't going to settle for a dime less than three grand. Of course he'd take it all if he found more.

It was probably useless, but he decided the best place to start looking was in Muzzadin's motel room next door. Even though Muzzadin kept it locked, the connecting door between their motel rooms offered little resistance, and in less than five minutes Barnes had tossed the room and found nothing, not even a toothbrush. This confirmed his suspicion that they were going to take off as soon as Muzzadin got what he wanted.

Barnes went back to his room and gathered up his few belongings while trying to decide what to do. He didn't know too much about Muzzadin's and Salemi's background, but he knew they had been in this country illegally for a long time. Barnes was convinced that besides the dough he carried with him Muzzadin had to have big money squirreled away somewhere, he wasn't dumb enough to keep it all with him – maybe a safe deposit box or a locker. He also knew Muzzadin would never voluntarily tell him where the money was and, if the TV report was correct, he wouldn't be getting out of jail any time soon. So the only way he'd get his hands on the money was to spring Muzzadin from jail, and then squeeze him, squeeze him hard. It would take some doing, but he thought he knew a way to make it work.

Raymond Barnes was thirty-one years old, was small and wiry, and wore metal framed glasses. His neat, bookish appearance misled most people, but he had been in scrapes with the law more times than he could remember since being picked up for shoplifting at age ten. Born and raised in the area, he learned how to survive and how to play the justice system. At eighteen he was arrested on car theft charges – he and a buddy were funneling cars to a local chop shop – and spent three months in the county jail, the longest three months of his life. A shyster lawyer took every cent he had, but did manage to get him out of doing any hard time at Riverview. The prospect of more jail time convinced Barnes to at least try turning his life around. He decided the first thing he needed was a change of scenery, so he enlisted in the army.

During his early years in the service Barnes kept out of trouble. He graduated from electronics school and later was selected for training with an elite demolition unit, specializing in long-range wireless detonation of plastic explosives, sometimes days or even weeks after the charges were hidden. Barnes was their best student. By the time he re-enlisted he was considered an expert and had been involved in half a dozen covert operations. Then his life turned around again; his unit was sent to Germany. During his second year there he got bit by the quick-money bug and everything went to hell. Even though he had never gotten involved with drugs, personally or otherwise, an army buddy convinced him there was easy money to be made and set him up with a supply line, small but profitable. He found he could pull in over a thousand a week by pushing the junk just on the base. He tried to keep everything low-key and small scale, but eventually he sold to the wrong guy and got nailed. Barnes tried working his old justice system magic, but the best he could do was a court martial, six months in the stockade and a dishonorable discharge.

Since returning to the States more than four years ago Barnes had moved around a lot. At least he now had some special skills to peddle, and he did, whether penetrating somebody's security system or packaging explosive "take-out menus", as he jokingly called his specialty. What he did wasn't legal, but it was always profitable. Then, about a year ago he messed up a job in New York, messed up bad. Killed the wrong guy and created a lot of heat for the wrong people. Word spread fast among the wise guys and now nobody wanted to use him, regardless of price. So here he was, almost flat broke, screwing around for a lousy three grand, even though common sense told him to take off.

Getting Muzzadin out of jail would be tough, and squeezing him later for the money might be even tougher. Barnes plan was risky, but because he knew they normally didn't keep prisoners in local jails for more than a few hours, and also knew the county system for transferring prisoners, he was sure he could pull it off. First, he had to check his equipment and then make a phone call.

Barnes opened the large duffel bag he had retrieved from the trunk of his car and spread the contents on the bed. He selected what he needed and put these items in a plastic laundry bag, complements of the motel, and returned everything else to his car. He went back inside and wiped the room clean of prints, then stopped at the motel office where he checked out. Before leaving he asked to see their Philadelphia yellow pages. Not wanting the call to go through the motel phone system, when he found what he wanted he got in his car and drove to a diner about a mile down the road where he knew they had pay phones. His call to the police station was answered by a desk clerk who transferred him to the duty sergeant. Barnes had decided to pass himself off as a Philadelphia attorney, a real one out of the phone book

– but one he hoped they didn't know. Using legal terminology gleaned from personal experience, Barnes explained that he had been retained to represent Muzzadin and wanted to come in to review the charges and to see his client. The sergeant cut him off before he could finish. "Don't waste your time, counselor, the prisoners are scheduled to be transferred to the county jail by mid-afternoon. I suggest you call Camden and arrange your meeting through them. They're calling the shots now, sorry."

Barnes thanked him and hung up. This was exactly what he had hoped to hear. A lot of years had gone by, but the system hadn't changed.

Barnes needed a different car to carry out his plan, so he drove to a nearby shopping mall. He concentrated on an area of the parking lot where he noticed a lot of cars with sun reflectors stuck inside their windshields, a good indication of all-day parking by mall employees, and cruised the aisles until he spotted two likely targets. He pulled into an empty slot and waited. When the security truck made its next swing through the area Barnes immediately grabbed his equipment bag, locked his car, and walked cautiously to the two cars he had picked, parked next to each other. In a span of less than three minutes he switched the plates of both cars, broke into the older of the two, and was headed out to the highway. He smiled and said to no one, "Brings back old memories – switching tags was my trademark. It's risky, but it confuses the shit out of everybody and buys me a lot of time. But hell, I guess I've lost some of my finesse; I used to do the whole deal in less than two minutes."

On the way to his destination he bought a newspaper and a container of coffee. When he arrived at the police station he parked on the street about half a block away, where the entire building was in his line of vision. After again checking his equipment on the front seat, he put the opened paper in front of him, sipped his coffee, and waited.

Barnes had to wait less than an hour for the Sheriff's van to arrive. It pulled close to the side of the building and an armed guard and driver got out and went inside. "Good," thought Barnes, "the driver doesn't seem to be armed. That makes it even easier." The van had double rear doors but no windows in the back at all. A few minutes later three shackled prisoners were led through a side door and placed in the rear of the van. It was Muzzadin, Salemi and a black guy. Muzzadin still had his arm in a sling. After padlocking the rear doors the driver and guard got back in the front of the van and backed out of the driveway. Barnes started his car and, keeping a safe distance behind, followed the van through the residential streets. Traffic was light, but it would be at least fifteen minutes before he reached the spot where he'd make his move.

About a mile outside of Camden there were three vacant buildings lining the right side of the highway, in the middle of which was a boarded-up former gas station. As the van neared the station, Barnes pulled close behind, then moved up on the right side. When he was close enough he reached through the open window and shot-out the van's front tire using his silenced Beretta. The van veered to the right and Barnes had to brake hard to avoid being sideswiped, but, as he had planned, the van driver steered into the vacant gas station, with Barnes right behind. The guard opened his door and started to exit, but before either he or the driver knew what had happened Barnes jammed his gun in the guard's gut and forced him back into his seat.

"Unsnap your gun, now! Do it carefully and hand it to me with two fingers. Also the shotgun from the rack, and be quick about it. Screw with me and you're both dead." For emphasis he jammed his gun hard into the roll of fat hanging over the guard's belt. When he had both, he put the guns on the ground and shoved them under the van with his foot. Satisfied that he had all their weapons, Barnes grabbed the guard's handcuffs from his belt and cuffed his left wrist to the steering wheel. In almost the same motion he grabbed the ignition keys and then snatched the radio mike and ripped it from the unit. He then stuck his gun in the driver's face. "All right buddy, where are the keys for the back doors?" The driver pointed to a single key hanging on the dash. "O.K., bring the key, get out your side and walk around the front of the van toward me, very slowly. Like I said, try anything cute and you're both dead."

As soon as he opened one rear door Barnes ordered the driver inside. "No, please don't put me in with them, they'll kill me!"

"That's your problem," Barnes answered. "I can't have you running around out here." With that he grabbed the driver by the back of his collar and shoved him inside the van.

Muzzadin saw Barnes through the open door and as soon as the driver was inside he moved to the opening, with Salemi and the black guy right behind. Before they knew what was happening, Barnes snatched Muzzadin's sling and yanked him through doorway, then slammed the door in Salemi's face and replaced the lock. "Not you, shithead, I just want your boss."

Muzzadin was on the ground, twisting in pain. Even though his arm was in a sling his wrists were chained together. His legs were also manacled at the ankles. "You imbecile," he yelled, "you've injured my shoulder again. And let Bahram out of the truck, now! We need him."

"Not on your life, Muzzy old boy, I don't need him at all, I just need you. Now, get in my car, on the floor in the back, and be quick about it."

Barnes pulled away from the disabled Sheriff's van and the din created by the van driver, who was yelling and banging on the sides of the van. He headed back to the mall, with Muzzadin screaming obscenities at Barnes in his native tongue. Less than two minutes from the van a police cruiser flew past in the opposite direction, its lights flashing. "Hate to disappoint you, officer," Barnes said sarcastically, "but you're going the wrong way." Then he laughed.

When they arrived at the mall Barnes circled the area where he had left his car. Everything looked O.K. Surprisingly, the slot where the stolen car had been parked was still empty. He drove to where his car was parked and jumped out. In less a minute he transferred a protesting Muzzadin to his car's trunk, led by his wrist chains. Slamming the lid shut, Barnes, breathing hard, admitted out loud, "God, you're heavy, and it's a good thing you're hurting – I don't think I could handle you otherwise. And I know I'm a hell of a lot safer with you in there." Throwing the bag of tools on the back seat of his car, Barnes drove the stolen car back to its slot and carefully wiped it clean of his prints.

He had no intention of going back to the motel where they stayed the past few nights. Once Muzzadin's escape hit the news that desk clerk would be on the phone to the cops. He didn't like the place anyway, too many people milling around. For what he had to do now he needed to be isolated as much as possible.

Barnes headed east on Route 70 until he found a motel with units in the rear, facing away from the highway. "I'll only be here one night," he told the desk clerk. "I want a unit in the back where it's quiet. And make it a first floor room, I don't like stairs...have a bad back." The clerk assured him it would be quiet, none of the other units back there were rented yet, and probably wouldn't be.

Barnes backed his car into the parking slot directly in front of his unit. After scanning the area he opened the trunk and led a very angry Muzzadin inside, cursing and fighting every step of the way. "Sit in that chair over there and keep quiet. I'm going to get my stuff out of the car, then I'll see what I can do to get those chains off. And if you want my help, don't try anything cute."

He had no intention of either removing Muzzadin's chains or helping him. To the contrary, when he returned a minute later with his gear he knew exactly what he'd do to make the foreigner cooperate.

Muzzadin slumped uncomfortably in the chair, rubbing his shoulder with his good hand. If he sat still he could relieve the burning ache in his shoulder, but not the jabbing pain from his broken ribs. Every breath was torture. "What game are you playing, Raymond? First, you leave Bahram behind, then you aggravate my injuries. True, you succeeded in freeing me from the police, but why the rough handling... have you forgotten who you are working for?"

"This is no game, Muzzy. The only reason you're here is to tell me about my money, so I didn't need to double my risk by springing your buddy. I only work when I get paid, and I haven't seen a dime yet. And by the way, since I know you were going to take off without paying me, my price is no longer three grand, it's now ten."

Muzzadin tried to get out of his chair, but stopped when Barnes pushed him back and pointed a pistol in his face, the end of the silencer jammed under his nose. "This is a fools errand, Raymond," he said with a forced smile. "Stop and think. My personal belongings and all of my money were in the car the police confiscated. I have nothing. As you say in this country, not even a pot to piss in. But, work with me and we can get more."

"I heard on the news exactly what the cops found in your car. Don't bullshit me, Muzzy, that was chump change. I know you have to have big money stashed somewhere, and I think you're going to tell me where. If you don't, I'm going to make you a cripple, one knee at a time."

With this, Barnes moved his Baretta down to Muzzadin's left knee, and clicked off the safety.

"Wait, wait, don't do anything foolish!" Beads of sweat glistened on Muzzadin's forehead. "Move that gun and maybe we can work out some way to get you your money."

"Not good enough, Muzzy. I need you to tell me something more definite than 'maybe'." Sliding the nine-millimeter between Muzzadin's legs he pulled-off a round, blowing a hole in the edge of the chair and missing his crotch by less than an inch. Muzzadin grabbed himself with both hands and recoiled back in the chair.

"All right, please, no more! I will tell you where more money is located. But we will have to get it together. Bahram and I have a small apartment in New York that we use as our base of operations. There is a key taped under a drawer. It is for a safe deposit box in a bank about two blocks away. The box contains the rest of my money, everything."

"How much?"

"Do not worry. You will get your ten thousand."

"One more time. How much is in the box?" Barnes again pointed the gun at Muzzadin's knee.

Muzzadin knew that to get out of this room alive he had to arouse Barnes's sense of greed, so he lied. "There is about ninety thousand in cash, plus some Mexican and Canadian money."

"Good, good," Barnes said, his eyes wide with excitement. That much money would enable him to take off for South America and buy him a great life-style. And down there he might even parlay it into really big money. "O.K., no point in wasting more time here, we're taking off for New York right now."

"There is not time today," Muzzadin countered, hoping his stall for time would work. "It is almost two hours from here and the bank will be closed."

"Dammit to hell, you're probably right," Barnes said, looking at his watch. "I'm not sitting up all night to watch you, though, so forget any ideas you may have about taking me down. You're going to spend the night tied in that chair. Behave yourself and we'll be out of here first thing in the morning."

Barnes slid the gun under his belt and reached across the bed to retrieve a length of nylon line from his duffle bag. He knew Muzzadin couldn't move fast, at least not without a lot of grunting and groaning.

It was the last mistake Barnes would ever make. By the time he sensed movement behind him the taut chain between Muzzadin's wrists was under his chin and violently twisted, lifting his feet from the floor and snapping his neck.

Muzzadin did groan with pain, and Raymond Barnes died with a gurgling cry on his lips.

CHAPTER EIGHT

I took my copy of David's papers home with me to see if I could make sense of his coded notes. Mrs. Tomasello had left a chicken pot pie and a tomato and onion salad for my dinner. I zapped the pie, grabbed a cold Becks and sat at the kitchen table scanning pages from David's binder while I ate.

The coded entries intrigued me. Flipping through the copies I found only six pages that contained the margin notes. Maybe they meant nothing, but, if so, why had David felt it necessary to create a code? Was he concerned that somebody would see his notebook, or was there a more sinister reason? Each notation consisted of two letters followed by sets of one or two numbers separated by slashes or dashes. The notations were also of different lengths. I grabbed a pencil and paper and copied the sets of numbers and letters. Being a word game nut it struck me that maybe all David did was substitute letters for numbers and vice-versa, about as simplistic as a code could be. It was certainly the easiest way to start; so I made a list of the alphabet and wrote a number next to each letter. The first entry was on the page containing financial data for the ranch Walter had acquired in Montana back in 1972. The hand-written entry read "GB-13/19-20-9-5-2-18-9-19/3/13-19". Using substitution I translated this into "72-M/STIEBRIS/C/MS". The two numbers were obviously the year, and I knew Stiebris was the victim. The first "M" could be the location; Montana, but I didn't know what the "C/MS" stood for. Regardless, David's entries appeared to be so simple it made me wonder why he thought it necessary to be cryptic. Using the same method I converted the other five notations. In each case the translation identified the year, the location and the last name of the person who died or disappeared. Checking these against the notes given to me by Trimble I knew the notations covered all of the deaths and disappearances except Davids. The only puzzle were those last three letters. In the notations for the first four events, in '72, '77, '81 and '83, the last letter was "C". In the last two; '90 and '91, the last letter was "U", but all ended with "MS". Maybe everything but the last letters was meaningless and the code was David's way of creating a smoke screen. I decided to consult my old dog-eared dictionary to see if any words beginning with "C" and "U" jumped out at me.

I was on the third page of "C's" when my phone rang. "Hey little brother," I heard Ben say, "I just had a call from Sam Abromowitz and he gave me some bad news...really bad news – Moussa Muzzadin is on the loose!"

"How? What the hell happened?" I felt a chill run down my spine.

"All Sam told me was that Muzzadin and Salemi were being taken to the county jail when an accomplice forced the sheriff's van off the road and disabled it. The accomplice freed Muzzadin but left Salemi behind. Both took off in the accomplice's car and disappeared."

"Ben, I don't like this one bit. That bastard still wants David's attaché case and I don't think we'll see the last of him until he gets it, or gets caught trying. He's a fanatic, and he knows I have the case. He's also hurt and by now is probably desperate. I'm particularly concerned about Suzy and Julia. I'm sure he knows where they live, and I hope I'm wrong, but he may try using them as leverage to get to me. We've got to get both of them away from here, and quickly. It has to be tonight. Maybe there's someplace better, but the first two places that come to mind are Abigail's in Boston or your place in the Poconos. Your place is closer and that's a plus because we can get them out of here in the next hour or so. I'll get Joe Mancuso to drive them up there, maybe stay with them 'til this mess gets cleared up. What do you think?"

"Well, Abigail's is out; she and the kids are still on vacation on the Cape, so my place is the best choice, at least for now. But why Mancuso? I think you should go with them, get away from here for a few days. You're the one he's really after because, as you just said, he knows you have the attaché case. "

"No, Ben. Between London and Muzzadin I have a ton of work backed up at the office. On top of that I'm still planning to go to Tampa."

"Well, I think you're stupid for assuming a lot of unnecessary risk, but I'm not going to waste time arguing. Get it set up with Joe and Suzanne and I'll bring the keys to the cabin to your place. I'm coming over anyway. No way are you staying alone until this animal is caught. I hope I'm wrong, but you probably haven't seen the last of Muzzadin. I'll leave here as soon as I make one more phone call."

"Ben, I don't need a baby sitter. Drop off the keys and then go home, I don't want you involved in this. I've got a good alarm system, and if all else fails, I've got my trusty baseball bat. I'm as safe here as anywhere. So please listen..."

"No, Cole!" Ben interrupted. "How are you going to stop him if he comes armed? Besides, two pairs of eyes and ears are better than one. I'm staying, period!"

When Ben hung up I called Joe Mancuso. Without going into any detail I told him I needed him to take a business trip, a trip that might last a week, so pack accordingly. When I told him he had to leave tonight, and to stop by my place as soon as possible, he wanted to know why it couldn't wait until tomorrow. I told him I'd explain the urgency when he got to my place. He didn't sound too pleased, and if I was in his place I wouldn't be either, but said he'd come right over.

I then called Suzy and told her what had happened and what I wanted her to do. She balked at leaving me; said she'd bring Julia and stay at my place. When I told her it was all set up with Ben and Joe Mancuso and that it was the best way to protect Julia she finally agreed. She said they'd be ready to leave within the hour.

While I waited for Ben and Joe to arrive I went through the house and checked windows and doors. Everything seemed secure. I also got my Louisville Slugger out of the closet.

A few minutes later Ben arrived with the keys. He also had an overnight bag and his cellular phone. Twenty minutes later Joe arrived. He was obviously upset at being pulled away from his family on such short notice. "Geez, Cole, if you'd told me about this at the office I could have made plans to be away. My wife is pissed at both of us. On top of that I'm about half way through the take-off for that medical complex and the bid is due in ten days."

"Joe, I apologize for the inconvenience, but I only found out about this problem less than an hour ago." I then explained exactly what had happened and what I wanted him to do. His anger turned immediately to concern. "I'll have Nancy call your wife in the morning and explain everything. We just can't tell her where you are. This may be over in two or three days, but if it isn't resolved in a week I'll have to make other plans."

"Cole, before I pick up Suzanne, if it's all right with you, I'll swing past the office and get the plans and the stuff I need for the estimate. I can work on it at the cabin and probably finish it by the time we come home. I'd rather not have anybody else work on it – it's a very complicated job and it's too easy to miss something important. Besides, I hate other people screwing with my work."

"That's fine with me, Joe," smiling at his dedication to his work. He is one in a million. "But two things to keep in mind: first, I don't care how you do it but make sure you're not being followed when you leave Suzy's for the Poconos. Start out by taking a few back roads and make sure nobody is on your tail. Second, don't let Suzy or Julia out of your sight. When they're outside the car or the cabin I want you on them like white on rice. And another thing – don't let either of them con you into doing anything different."

"I understand, and I'll be careful. But...ah...what do we use for money?"

"I've got two hundred in cash for you. That should cover you for a few days. Use your company credit cards whenever you can. I'll wire you more cash if you need it. Oh, by the way, there's a phone in the cabin and I'd like you to call me at the office every day around three. And don't be reluctant to call the local cops if you think something is wrong. Anything you want to add, Ben?"

"Only directions on how to find the cabin. I've drawn a map to show you how to get to the cabin from the turnpike extension. It's about nine miles from the main road and it's pretty secluded. The nearest neighbor is about a quarter mile away, and the closest town is about a mile. The cabin is built on the side of a hill and there's a garage under the cabin. This time of year there won't be many people, so I think you should keep your car in the garage, out of sight. All the utilities are on and there is enough food in the freezer and pantry to last for two or three days. Any questions?"

"No," Joe said. "I know what you want me to do. And don't worry Cole, I'll take good care of Suzanne and Julia."

"I know you will. One final thing before you leave – you should get to the cabin before midnight, so call me here as soon as you arrive. I'd like to know that you're safely there."

"O.K. And I'll be careful not to be followed."

Joe called a few minutes before midnight and said everything had gone smoothly. He was sure nobody had followed them. I thanked him and asked to speak with Suzy. I told her I missed her already and blew her a goodnight kiss. It was a relief to know the three of them were safe.

Ben and I had been sitting at my kitchen table drinking coffee awaiting Joe's call. When I hung up Ben said he was too nervous to sleep and thought he'd spend the night in the living room in my recliner.

"Ben, that's crazy, have a little faith in my alarm system. I'm turning out the lights and going to bed. You have the guest room."

"Well, I'm not sitting here in the dark, so I guess I'll go too. But I doubt if I'll sleep much."

I turned out the lights and we went upstairs. I checked the alarm keypad in my bedroom to make sure the first floor and outdoor motion sensors were on. I don't know if I'm just a stupid optimist or have nerves in all the wrong places, but I was asleep within two minutes of my head hitting the pillow.

I awoke to a loud noise, followed by another. They sounded like gunshots and seemed to come from the front yard. The glowing green numbers on my clock radio said two-twenty. I flew out of bed and looked out my front window. The outdoor floodlights were on and I caught a glimpse of someone running toward the side yard. He was big guy and I didn't recognize him. It wasn't Muzzadin! I threw on some clothes and ran to the back of the house. Before I could open the blind there were three more gunshots. I heard floorboards squeak and when I turned around Ben was standing in the open doorway, looking confused and half asleep. He started to say something as I ran past him and headed downstairs. Half-way down I heard approaching sirens; thank God, somebody had called the cops. Then my alarm horn started blaring; stupid me had tripped it when I came downstairs, so I disarmed it at the front door keypad. I had no idea what was going on, but as I stood inside my locked front door, peering through the small window, a police cruiser with rack lights flashing pulled into my driveway. Then a second cruiser pulled in at the curb. I knew the fast response had nothing to do with my alarm. There were cops all over the place!

I unlocked the front door and stepped out on the porch. Lights were coming on all over the neighborhood. "Please stay inside sir," one of the cops yelled to me. "We'll be in to talk with you as soon as we know everything is secure." Before I could move two unmarked cars pulled nose-in at the curb.

I went back inside in time to meet Ben coming down the stairs, a questioning look on his face. "What happened...is it Muzzadin?"

"I don't know for sure, but I haven't seen this many cops in one place since my last visit to Dunkin Donuts."

I went to the back of the house and looked out the kitchen window. Flashlight beams were bouncing off trees and shrubs. A body was laying on the ground, face down, the upper torso in one of my flower beds. Cops were also in my neighbors' back yards. I figured this was going to take a while so I made a fresh pot of coffee.

Ben and I were on our second cup when somebody knocked on my back door. It was the big guy I had seen running through my side yard. "Sir, I'm Detective Sergeant Fleisher. I was assigned stakeout duty here – I've been here since early last evening. My chief told me part of the story about the perp who escaped from custody yesterday, and how he was after you. I saw his mug shot at the station yesterday, but it was a poor picture. I think he's the corpse in your back yard, but I can't be sure. I understand you've seen the perp up close. It will save us some time if you could confirm his I.D. Do you mind?"

"No, I'll take a look, but before I do I'd appreciate some information. I didn't ask for protection; how come the stakeout? And what led to all the shooting?"

"I don't know who ordered the stakeout, and I'm not permitted to talk about the shooting. You'll have to talk to my chief about both."

I followed Fleisher outside, with Ben right on my heels. My backyard was full of cops, stomping through my garden and shrubs and in and out of my neighbor's yards. Light were everywhere. One guy in plain clothes was taking flash pictures of everything. A body bag was spread on the ground next to the corpse. When they rolled the body on to the black plastic I saw the face. It was Muzzadin, without a doubt. I could never forget that face. He still had wrist and ankle cuffs in place, but the chains had been cut.

Less than an hour later most of the mob scene had dispersed and, with the exception of the crime scene tape, my backyard was back to normal. Ben and I were back at my kitchen table drinking coffee with Sam Abromowitz and Detective Fleisher. It turned out that Sam was the 'chief' Fleisher had referred to earlier. I asked him what had happened.

"Fleisher and I have to get back to the station to write this up," Sam said. "Even though it was a justifiable police shooting there will be an internal investigation and a ton of paperwork. We don't normally discuss an event like this with anybody until the investigation is completed," Sam added, "but under the circumstances we'll try to explain what happened. Just understand that what we say is off the record. After Ben called earlier this evening to ask for police surveillance I assigned Jerry Fleisher to stakeout duty. Jerry, go ahead an explain what happened."

"Sure thing. I was parked across the street, about two doors down, when a car with its lights off pulled in front of your house.

The perp got out and started toward your front door. I radioed for backup and got out of my car and that's when all hell broke loose. Your floodlights came on, and he turned around and headed back to his car. I yelled to him to stop. Instead, he pulled a gun and fired at me. He must have realized that he couldn't get back to his car, so he took off toward the back of your house. He fired at me a second time and I fired back, but missed. My second and third shots brought him down.

I believe you know the rest of it."

"I do." I said. "And thanks for everything you did – including you Ben. But why didn't you tell me you had called the police?"

"Because, knowing you, little brother, you'd have called and canceled the surveillance," Ben replied, a look of smug satisfaction on his face. "You don't like taking advice from your older, smarter brother. Considerably smarter, I might add," he said, breaking into a big grin.

"This time, maybe," I said, trying my damndest to keep a straight face. "But you can't always be wrong, Ben. I think the score is now something like Cole ten and Ben one."

Sam Abromowitz downed the rest of his coffee, pushed his chair back and said they had to leave. He added that somebody would be back after daylight to again check the scene. He'd be in touch if anything new developed.

After they left I locked the doors and went through the house turning out lights. Ben and I then went back to bed. I don't know if Ben slept, but I didn't. I was really wired; a combination of too much coffee and too much adrenaline. I watched the street light pattern on my bedroom ceiling for what seemed like hours, then saw it fade as the sun came up. The thought that kept revolving in my mind was Muzzadin. How and where did he fit in the puzzle? Was he responsible for all the disappearances and killings...or just David's death? And why kill David? Was Muzzadin involved with Tampa? I finally gave up and took a shower.

Ben decided to follow me to the office in his car. We each wanted to talk to Alex Trimble and it was already after noon in London.

Ben had sent Trimble an agreement that would absolve us of any liability, but Trimble hadn't responded. I wanted to find out if Trimble had ever heard of Mousa Muzzadin or Bahram Salemi, and also how he was making out with the liquidation effort.

I caught Trimble just as he was leaving for lunch, but not before the officious Miss Nickleby tried to impress me with her overblown importance as Trimble's first line of defense; his protector. She informed me that he was not accepting any outside calls today. "After all," she said, in a condescending tone, "he's a very busy man and, besides, he's about to leave for a very important business luncheon. I suggest you either leave a message or call back tomorrow."

"I have no intention of calling back, Miss Nickleby. I'm calling from the United States. What I have to say to him may well influence the future of your bank. Timing is of the essence," I didn't lie, but I sure bent the hell out of the truth. "If you want to accept responsibility for that then so be it."

"Oh, dear," she whispered. "Just a moment." After less than a minute Trimble came on the line.

"Alex, this is Cole McQuade. My brother Ben is here with me on the speaker phone. He wants to talk about the agreement he sent you, but first I want to tell you that two men who apparently were responsible for David's death have been apprehended. One is dead and the other is in custody.

There may be one other involved as well, but he's still on the loose. The two we know about are foreign nationals, an Iranian and a Turk, both in this country illegally. I need to know if you have any knowledge of either one."

I then described both Muzzadin and Salemi. Trimble said he had no knowledge of either and couldn't recall seeing anybody in David's company that matched the physical descriptions I had given him, or even being in the bank. "The majority of our customers are business and professional people from the surrounding neighborhood, and they're well known to our staff. I'm sure two characters such as you described would have drawn the attention of our guards, and I would have heard about it. I'm sorry I can't be more helpful."

He wanted to know how Muzzadin and Salemi had been caught and how Muzzadin had been killed. I told him, without going into much detail. He then had questions about how the two were implicated in David's death, which I also answered as briefly as possible. I looked across my desk at Ben who kept pointing to his watch. I told Trimble that Ben wanted to talk to him but, before I put Ben on, I wanted to know how the liquidation effort was proceeding. He said he was pleasantly surprised because it was proceeding very smoothly. He expected everything to be concluded by the end of next week.

Ben jumped in at this point and asked Trimble about the agreement. Trimble said he had no problem with it, but it was currently being reviewed by the bank's solicitor. He expected to have the solicitor's comments within a day or two and would call Ben as soon as the document was returned to him. Ben said he would have to review any requested changes in wording with the solicitor, but wanted the document finalized and signed within the week. Trimble said he would contact his solicitor and have him call Ben direct.

As soon as we ended the call to Trimble I punched in the number for Ben's cabin in the Poconos. Joe answered on the second ring. I explained what had happened during the night and told him that everybody could come home, the danger was past. He said that was great news because they were so worried about me that none of them had slept very well.

Suzy was cooking breakfast for the three of them and they could leave for home as soon as they ate. I asked him to put Suzy on the phone. Before she came on the line I could hear Joe's muffled voice on their end.

"Cole," Suzy said, her voice quivering. "Joe just told me that Muzzadin is dead – and you're O.K., thank God.

I've been so worried about you I couldn't sleep at all last night. Are you sure you're all right?"

"Absolutely, Suzy, I'm fine. Take your time coming home and when you get here I'll explain what happened. The mystery surrounding this crazy situation hasn't changed, but at least we don't have to contend with Muzzadin any longer. We'll discuss it further when you get home. Have a safe trip."

Suzy, Julia and Joe arrived at the office a little after two that afternoon. After I gave them a quick rundown on what had happened to Muzzadin they announced that they were going home for a shower and some sleep. They all looked a bit bedraggled. Joe and Julia left my office but Suzy hesitated, and I knew she was upset. I got up and moved from behind my desk as she closed the office door and came to me, tears glistening in her eyes. She put her arms around me and her head on my chest, quietly sobbing. "Cole, I imagined all kinds of crazy things happening to you last night and I didn't sleep a wink...please hold me...I'm so tired. I apologize for blubbering but I guess the anxiety of the past few weeks has finally caught up with me."

I put my arms around her and kissed the top of her head. "You have nothing to apologize for and every right to be frazzled. Our lives have been turned upside down by things we have no control over. It's also been damn frustrating – all I've been able to do up till now is wait for something to happen, and then react – almost like Pavlov's dog; ring the bell and watch Cole jump. I hate that. Since David's death I feel like I've been sleepwalking through a bad dream, and then the reality of it hits me...and it's damn scary."

She tipped her head back and kissed me and I felt the warm wetness of her tears. "Don't misunderstand, Cole, I believe you've handled things the only way you could...you've tried to protect all of us. And even though I've panicked at some of the things you've done, it was only because I didn't want anything to happen to you...I need you and I want you in my life. After our time together in London I realized how important you are to me, but I wanted to sort things out, to be sure of my feelings. I have, and in case you haven't guessed by now, I want you to know...that I'm deeply in love with you."

"Suzy, nothing could make me happier than sharing the rest of my life with you. Like I told you in London, I think I've been in love with you since the first time I saw you."

"I know I could spend the rest of my life right here in your arms," she said. "I have a great idea," she said, a grin returning to her face. "We're entitled to some fun, so why not come for dinner tonight, and then stay with me – I'll even serve you breakfast in bed."

"Sounds great, but what about Julia?"

"Julia knows how I feel about you, she and I had a long talk when we came home from London. You already know she's crazy about you, and after I told her how I feel about you she hasn't stopped talking about it – or teasing me by asking me when you and I are going to start 'Phase Two', as she puts it. I haven't seen her so happy in years, she's like a five-year old on Christmas Eve. So don't worry about Julia, she's thrilled about everything, and I know she'll understand if you spend the night."

"O.K., sounds great to me," I said. "It'll feel good to totally relax for a change. What time do you want me for dinner? And I'll bring the wine."

"Come over around seven. Oh, one other thing before I leave, and I hate to spoil the mood by bringing this up again, but now that Muzzadin is dead can't you end your involvement?

Just walk away from the whole mess by telling Alex Trimble to do his own investigating – if it's really necessary to do more, and I'm not sure it is. Then we can concentrate on getting our lives and our business back to normal."

"Believe me Suzy, nothing would please me more than to walk away, but my gut reaction is that Muzzadin was only part of the problem. I hope the threat to us is over, but I'd never forgive myself if I ignore my hunch and something happens to any of the people I love. I'm convinced that Muzzadin wasn't involved in this from the beginning. There's no record of him being in this country before 1989 and, even if he was, I doubt if he was in it alone. If he wasn't, are we still in danger? I don't know. And then there's the Tampa organization. Trimble thinks they're innocent bystanders, but they've been involved in this as long as his bank. It's possible they've been pulling the strings since day one. All I know is that I won't be comfortable until I know where they fit in the overall scheme. Do you understand why I'm concerned?"

Suzy stiffened and pulled away from me. She was frowning again. "I hear what you're saying and I don't know if you're right or wrong, but I thought that was the reason Ben is working on the agreement with Trimble; to absolve us of all legal responsibility and sever our ties with Trimble's bank. Won't that protect us and relieve your concern?"

"Maybe, maybe not. Until recently I never considered our past involvement with Trimble's bank as significant. I thought we were simply a consultant providing a relatively minor professional service. Whether I was just naive, or plain stupid, I did seriously underestimate our role.

Our recent involvement with David's death and Muzzadin may have been pure coincidence, but, like it or not, we've been attached at the hip to Trimble's bank for more than three decades – up to our eyeballs in their client's operation. Worst case, that's the way I think Trimble's client views us. So I just don't know if Ben's agreement will serve to erase our names from somebody's hit list, if such a list exists."

"Are you saying that you have to go to Tampa? I just don't know what that's going to accomplish."

"It may not resolve anything, but I've got to see their operation first-hand and talk to their people, particularly this Maria Sippano that Trimble mentioned. Beyond that I'll let my instincts take over. My first impressions are usually pretty accurate."

"How long will you be gone?"

"Probably just overnight. But I'm not going anywhere for a few days. I've got to spend at least two days here in the office catching up on work."

Suzy was still frowning when she left my office. She said she still wasn't totally convinced about the necessity of going to Tampa, but, regardless, the subject of Trimble's bank and Tampa would be off limits tonight – tonight was to be a fun night.

"We can discuss Tampa tomorrow," she said.

And I knew we would.

After the staff left for the day I was working my way through the pile on my desk when Ben called to tell me that his FBI contact, Brian Hamilton had just called him back. "As I suspected, Cole, I felt I was hearing a Bureau sound bite. When I spoke to him earlier I asked him to check with their field office to see if they were involved in the investigation into David's death. He just told me that *officially* their agency is not involved, however, '*other federal agencies are*'. I asked him who. He said he couldn't tell me, but did say that the case has *'international scope'*. When I asked what that meant he said he couldn't elaborate.

"We know that Muzzadin and Salemi were fugitives since 1989, and these 'other federal agencies' have to be either the CIA or Immigration, maybe both. But, little brother, that raises some questions; were they following Muzzadin and his friends before David was killed? If not, how did they get involved so quickly in Atlantic City? And if they were, why didn't they nail Muzzadin before David was killed? I asked these questions of Hamilton and he claimed he had no further information."

"Hold it, Ben! Regardless of what Hamilton said, indirectly he answered my question. If any federal agency is involved in this, either before or after the fact, they had to be behind the Atlantic City police gag order. That's why Ronko suddenly refused to talk to me. Dammit, this presents all kinds of interesting possibilities. Were they after Muzzadin simply because he was an illegal alien, or for bigger and better reasons? It would also be interesting to know if any agency has talked to Sam Abromowitz. Since Muzzadin was killed by the local police, maybe the feds have contacted Sam's department."

"That's a good point," Ben said. "I'll give Sam a call."

For the next hour or so I sat at my desk trying to work, but had little success; I couldn't concentrate. A little voice in my head kept asking the same questions: why were the feds involved?...why didn't they stop Muzzadin?...was David more than an innocent victim? The pile of work in front of me didn't get any smaller, and when I realized I had reviewed the same piece of paper three times I knew it was time to pack it in.

I stopped home, showered and grabbed my personal gear. On my way to Suzy's I picked up a bottle of Valpolicello and a bouquet of daisies. I knew she liked both. Julia greeted me at the door with a big hug and kiss.

"Cole, you shouldn't have, wine and flowers for little ole' me. How sweet!" She gave me the usual high-five, low-five and a shot to my shoulder; I gave her the expected tweak on her nose, and we both laughed.

"Here, young lady, put these in water and stay away from the wine," I said with a chuckle. "Remember your age; you're still a little girl."

"I beg your pardon," she said, pushing her lower lip out in a fake scowl.

"I'll have you know that I am considered a young woman. Older men grovel at my feet. Besides, I'm not little, I'm almost as tall as my mother. So there!"

I couldn't disagree. She was anything but a little girl. I grabbed her by the back of the neck and steered her into the living room. "Nah," I said. "You're still a kid, but call me in five or six years. Then we'll see. In the meantime, let's go find out what your mom is feeding us for dinner."

Dinner was great. We started out with martinis. I had trained Suzy well; she had the glasses and gin in the freezer. McQuaid's perfect martini requires that you pour a little vermouth in a frosted glass, swirl it once or twice and then empty it in the sink. Fill the glass with gin, top it with a plump stuffed olive, then sit back and enjoy.

As she usually does, Julia complained because she was given the option of soda or tomato juice. She had tomato juice with horseradish.

Dinner started with a delicious Caesar salad, followed by capellini pasta with Suzy's famous sauce; fresh shrimp sauti¿½ed in olive oil, with green onions, red and green peppers, garlic, and just enough finely diced jalapeño pepper to let you know it was there. The red wine and warm Italian bread provided a perfect accompaniment. Suzy offset the peppery sauce with an icy lime sherbet for desert.

"Suzy, that was absolutely perfect. Maybe I'll fire Mrs. Tomasello and hire you as my cook."

Suzy laughed. "Play your cards right big guy and you can have us both."

Julia blushed and looked from me to Suzy. "I think it's time for me to find something to do upstairs," she said as she pushed back her chair.

I looked at her with as blank an expression as I could muster and said, "Not so fast, young lady. You're just trying to avoid washing the dishes."

"Nice try, Cole, but we've got an automatic dishwasher for that job. I am glad to hear I matured during dinner though; when you got here I was a little girl, now you refer to me as a 'young lady'. Besides, you don't want me hanging around, I know you want to be alone with my poor defenseless mother."

With that she gave me a shot to my shoulder, laughed, and ran toward the stairs. She can pack a wallop. "Glad to see my strategy worked," I yelled after her, laughing. I looked at Suzy who also thought it was funny. "I hope you're more defenseless than she is," I said, rubbing my shoulder.

"I don't know, Cole, I guess you'll have to wait and see."

After we cleaned up the kitchen and loaded the dishwasher we took our coffee on the sunporch. Dusk was quickly settling into night, and night sounds were carried through the open windows on a gentle breeze. I pulled Suzy close to me on the glider and we sat in the dark sipping our coffee. Neither of us said a word for a long time. "If I didn't enjoy your company as much as I do, this could put me in the land of nod very quickly," I finally mumbled, "particularly after everything we've been through lately."

"I agree," she chuckled, "but don't you dare insult my libido by falling asleep." With this, she got up and put our empty cups on the table and then sat across my lap. Her hands began kneading my neck and shoulders. She then gently touched the side of my face with her fingertips and kissed me on the mouth, the tip of her tongue exploring. "I'm glad to see your face has healed nicely," she said. "The only thing left is a little discoloration under your eye."

"I seem to remember agreeing not to discuss any of the unpleasantness," I countered. "But since you have, maybe you'd like to kiss it and make it better, then we can start over."

When she did, I put my arms around her, kissed her, and began massaging her back and neck. She seemed to melt in my arms.

"Oh, Cole," she sighed. "I'll give you an hour to cut that out...it feels so good...I could stay like this forever."

Five minutes was about all we enjoyed before we heard Julia come down stairs. She asked Suzy if she could go to a late movie with Becky and then spend the night at Becky's house.

"Besides, you guys don't need me hanging around, unless you want a chaperone." she added with a laugh.

Suzy's response was somewhat equivocal. I knew she'd prefer us to be alone, but her motherly instincts wouldn't let go. "I don't know if that's a good idea. After all the trouble of the past few days I'll worry about you. Who will you be with, and how will you get to and from the movie?"

"Mom, what's to worry about? It'll just be Becky and me. And her dad is dropping us off at the movie and will pick us up later. Besides, I knew you'd let me go, so they're on their way here now to get me. I'm all ready to go."

"You assume too much, young lady," Suzy said. "You may go, but I want you to call me when you get home from the movie. Understood? And no gossiping about Cole being here, either."

"Absolutely...mums the word. Whoops, I think they're here, so I gotta run...love you guys." She kissed each of us on the forehead and flew out the door.

"You were trying your damndest to be stern," I said to Suzy. "But I don't think you convinced anybody – certainly not me."

"It's all your fault," she responded as she chuckled and again buried her head in my chest. "You've turned a good mother into a fallen woman and totally destroyed her ability to discipline."

For the next hour we sat quietly, Suzy snuggled against my chest, the sweet scent of her hair filling my nostrils. Thoughts of how she felt about me succeeded in pushing all of the recent turmoil from my mind, and I suddenly realized that I had never been more contented and happy. Part of that contentment was that I was totally sure of how I felt about Suzy. I had had a few relationships in the past, mostly in college, but I had never felt this way about any other woman. All the green lights were flashing: Suzy was a fantastic business partner; she was a special friend; she was beautiful and sexy; she loved me; and I was madly in love with her. What more could a guy ask for? I turned her face toward mine and told her so.

In less than two minutes we had locked the doors, turned out the lights and found ourselves in a triple-x rated scenario in the upstairs shower, together, and then on the bed, and then on the bedroom carpet, and finally, back in the shower. I don't remember thinking much about it in the past, but I know now that mutual love is not only special, it's a helluva lot of fun.

Suzy kept her word. I awoke to a fabulous aroma and had just started out of bed when she walked into the bedroom carrying a tray of pancakes, bacon and coffee. We were both starving and everything was delicious. As we ate more or less in silence, Tampa and all the nasty business we were involved in began to creep back into my consciousness. I didn't want to break the spell by mentioning Tampa, even though I knew Suzy would – sooner or later. To make matters worse, I wouldn't admit it to her, but I was beginning to question my decision to visit Tampa. Was I overestimating the risk of doing nothing? Would Tampa turn out to be an exercise in futility, a waste of time and money, and do nothing but stir up more trouble? And if I did find a lead, was I willing to follow it to a conclusion? How would it all end? Just a string of questions and potential danger that I might be subjecting everybody to while I was running around looking for answers. But then, as it often does when I'm wrestling with a problem, my mind did a one-eighty flip and the face of Muzzadin flashed in my head, reminding me that the killings had started long before he appeared on the scene. So, where was the logic or common denominator behind all of the earlier events and David's death? Were they connected by nothing more than coincidence? Maybe the killer or killers were still out there. More questions. And thinking again about David and the brutal way he died made me angry. I knew I would never be satisfied until I had answers. Maybe I wouldn't find any, but I had to go to Tampa.

As we were finishing our second cup of coffee Suzy reached over and took my empty hand in hers. "A penny for your thoughts. You haven't said a word in ten minutes."

I tried to force the unpleasantness from my mind with a big grin. "I was just thinking what a lucky guy I am. Last night and this morning have been the best times of my life. I guess that's another way of saying I'm hopelessly in love with you."

"Cole, nothing could make me happier than to hear you say that. Until we went to England together I never realized just how empty my existence had been after Walter's death. I love you deeply. And knowing you love me is all I need to make my life complete."

When I arrived at the office an hour later I found Nancy sitting at my desk sorting through the mess I had left the night before.

"Good morning," she said in her usual pleasant tone. I'm sure Nancy has bad days like the rest of us, but you could never tell by her calm expression and pleasant voice.

"Good morning," I replied. "Are you looking for something specific or just clearing a path through the debris?"

"Actually, a little of both. Joe is looking for the list of sub-contractors for the medical complex bid and said he put it in your in-basket yesterday. He was in here earlier but couldn't find it. I offered to look because he's panicking – it's the only copy and he's afraid it's lost. I was trying to organize some of this clutter while I looked, but was just about to give up when you walked in. I don't think I've ever seen your desk this messy."

"Guilty as charged," I said. "But I hope you didn't throw anything away. Most of the papers on the desk are originals from David's attaché case. That stack in front of you are pages from his binder. I have a copy of everything at home that I play around with when I have time. I now know what part of his code means, but the rest still baffles me. And I still don't understand why he felt it necessary to use a code in the first place. When I left for dinner at Suzies yesterday I was more than a little frustrated, so I left everything where you see it and walked out. Oh, by the way, the list Joe is looking for is under my appointment book. You can give it to him and tell him I added a few names that he should invite to bid. I'll take care of the rest of the mess, as you call it, as soon as you get me coffee."

She took Joe's list and left to get the coffee. I looked again at the scribbled notes I had made yesterday. Without attempting to straighten anything, I opened the dictionary to where I had given up looking for significant words beginning with the letter "C". I didn't get far when Nancy returned with my coffee.

"Nancy, before you leave give me the first three words starting with the letter 'C' that pop into your head. And no cheating," I quipped. "You can't look in the dictionary like I did."

"Like duh, you hadda use a dictionary, gee boss, wow! Before I'm accused of doing it try '*cheating*', and then there's '*cash, clothes and cars*'. And then '*clients, cookies, chocolate, cake . . .*'"

"Stop right there! Other than your favorite things in life I think you've hit on something. '*Client*', damn it fits! If David suspected his client was involved in some way in the earlier deaths he simply noted that with the letter 'C'. Thank you Nancy Todd!"

"You're quite welcome, boss," she said with an ear-to-ear grin. "You realize of course that in less than five minutes the entire office staff is going to know that I solved your puzzle. And you, the office cryptogram and crossword guru. Shame!"

"O.K. smarty, you got lucky. But let's see how you do with these other letters. Start with the letter 'U' and then try the combination of 'MS'"

Nancy had started for the door, but she stopped and turned, still grinning. "I don't know about the 'MS'", she said. "I'd have to think about it for a minute or two, but the 'U' should be easy. How about 'unlisted', or better yet 'unknown'?"

"Yeah, Nancy, I think 'unknown' could be right. I don't know where I left my brains, but you're on a roll. Let's hear your ideas on 'MS' – they appear at the end of the listing for the death of Durwood in'90 and Byrnes in '91. Those listings also contain a 'U' that we now agree means 'unknown'. I would assume that 'MS' stands for two words. I don't think it's a place because the state where each death occurred is already identified in the preceding group of numbers and letters."

"They could very well be somebody's initials," Nancy said. "Is there anybody involved in this who has those initials?"

I grabbed the notes I had written yesterday and scanned through the names. "There are a couple of possibilities," I mumbled, still scanning the pages. "I think you're right again, Nancy.

Just for starters we have Muzzadin and Salemi -'MS', and then there's Maria Sippano – another 'MS'."

"Who is Maria Sippano?" Nancy asked.

"She's one of the major players in Tampa. According to Alex Trimble she's also the one David had some sort of relationship with. I don't know if it was romantic or purely business. I don't even know if it's true. But if David's notes are accurate, the mysterious 'MS' was connected in some way with the deaths of Durwood and Byrnes. I still don't know what this all means, or why David was being so cryptic, but at least we have some idea of what he was trying to say, thanks to you."

Nancy was still grinning when she reached the door and turned to look at me. "Don't worry, Cole, I'll go easy on you when I tell everybody about this. Just remember, the next time you have trouble with a crossword clue, I'm as near as your telephone."

I threw a pencil at her, but missed.

This latest information still left all the important questions unanswered. But with Muzzadin dead and Salemi in jail, if we were right there was only one 'MS' left to consider. So I knew I had to go to Tampa and talk with Maria Sippano.

Suzy walked in as I was putting David's papers back in their folders. When I explained what Nancy and I had just found Suzy really surprised me by agreeing that I had to talk with Maria Sippano.

"I still doubt that anything good will come from this, even after you explained your reasoning to me last night," Suzy said.

"Thinking about what you told me of your conversations with Alex Trimble, the people who died all were tied in some way to David's client. And I doubt if any of them had any forewarning of what was coming. They were blindsided; we at least have knowledge of what happened in the past and can try to protect ourselves. Although I'm not completely sure against what. But you've convinced me that we can't risk doing nothing because, as you said, we can't spend the rest of our lives looking over our shoulders. If I were to talk you out of pursuing this and something happened to one of us I'd never forgive myself. All I ask is that you be careful. O.K.?"

"I will, Suzy. If the killing is over I want to be sure it's over permanently. I want all our lives back to normal."

I spent the rest of Tuesday and all of Wednesday finishing a couple of bid packages with Joe and disposing of a multitude of office details that I had ignored far too long. I also wrestled with the question of whether I should go to Tampa unannounced – just walk in off the street, or call and let them know I was coming. I opted for the latter. I didn't want to get there and be told that Maria was on vacation or out of town on business. It also crossed my mind that if we were interpreting David's notes correctly, and he had in fact tied Maria to at least two of the murders, she could be damned dangerous. She might even have ordered David's killing. I'd have to be very careful.

I had no trouble getting through to her on the phone and found her very easy to talk with. I introduced myself and told her I was coming to Tampa to talk with her, or someone in her office, to wrap up some unfinished details on two projects David and I had been working on prior to his death. It wasn't a complete lie. She said David had spoken of me many times and yes, she was the person I should talk with because she handled all of David's transactions personally. I told her I was catching the early flight out of Philly on Thursday and would see her before noon. She agreed to join me for lunch.

CHAPTER NINE

Even though it was the last week of September, Tampa was having a mid-July heat wave; about ten degrees hotter and a lot more humid than it should have been. And not a whisper of a breeze. I rented a car at the airport and headed for the center of town, following the directions Maria had given me. I found her office easily. Finding a parking space was another story. I parked in a small lot about two blocks from her office and worked up a pretty good sweat by the time I reached their building. It was a mid-rise with a bronze glass facade, located about a block off the main drag. According to the building directory 'M. R. Shaw Management Group' occupied all of the second floor. When I stepped off the elevator I found myself in a very unusual reception area. The only lighting in the room came from recessed wallwashing spots illuminating about a dozen framed watercolors. The center of the room was darkened and contained a grouping of large leather arm chairs arranged around two huge glass topped coffee tables, with glass at least two inches thick. A huge bouquet of colorful flowers in a cut crystal vase sat on each table. And everything was symmetrically arranged on the largest oriental rug I had ever seen. The other thing that struck me was something I didn't see; there wasn't a newspaper or magazine in sight. The place looked more like an art museum than a business office reception area.

The woman seated behind the large desk at the far end of the room looked to be on the high side of sixty. She was heavy, had gray streaked dark hair and an olive complexion with dark circles around her eyes. The scowl on her face contributed to my impression that she was the last woman in the world I would want greeting visitors to my company.

"Yes, young man, what can I do for you," she snapped, hardly moving her lips, and not showing even a hint of a smile.

"My name is Cole McQuaid, of Hammel and McQuaid. I have an appointment with Maria Sippano."

"Do you have a business card?" she snapped again.

When I produced one she studied it for a moment and than slipped it under her appointment book.

"All right, wait there and I'll call her."

She obviously didn't want me to sit in the reception area. I guess she was afraid I'd slip one of the watercolors into my brief case.

As most people do when speaking on the phone with someone they've never met, I had formed a mental picture of Maria. I imagined her to be around fifty, dark complexioned, short, and kind of frumpish. Her voice on the phone was low pitched and raspy. So I was more than a little surprised when she came through the door and extended her hand in greeting. Her complexion was dark, and I thought I was in the ballpark on her age, but she was anything but frumpish. She had striking light blue eyes, contrasting her olive skin, and her medium height was accentuated by a slim tailored gray silk pant suit, heels, and dark hair pulled up into a sophisticated hairdo. She looked every inch the career business woman. I remembered Trimble's comment that David had had a 'relationship' with this woman. It now didn't seem quite as far-fetched as I initially thought. I then tried picturing this woman as being responsible for everything that has happened, including David's death, but a little voice in my head said it seemed ridiculous – she was an innocent bystander just like me. Trying to be objective I admitted to myself that her appearance could be deceiving. Another little voice agreed and said she might look innocent but she was a dangerous, conniving bitch, and I had better watch my step. There most likely would be no middle of the road. My problem was I had to find out which extreme fit – and which little voice to listen to.

"Welcome to Tampa, Mr. McQuaid. You arrived a little earlier than I expected. Let's go back to my office and chat before we go to lunch."

"Fine," I said, as I followed her through a maze of cubicles toward the rear of the building.

Her office was located on a corner of the building and contained the usual furniture and amenities of upper management, but with a definite feminine touch. She closed the door and invited me to sit in one of the two leather chairs facing her desk. With its large windows, high ceilings and light colors this room was the direct opposite of the institutional reception area.

"I thought we'd take a few minutes to get acquainted before we go to lunch," she said, after sitting behind her desk. "I hope you like seafood, because I took the liberty of making a reservation at a small cafe a few blocks from here. They're not gourmet, but they have great crab and shrimp dishes."

"That's fine with me," I said. "I love any kind of fish and seafood."

"Good," she said. "Would you care for coffee while we talk?"

"Sure. Black with sugar will be fine."

She picked up her phone, spoke to someone and a few minutes later the coffee arrived. Two styrofoam cups on an ornate silver tray, with equally ornate silver sugar and creamer. I hate plastic cups. Whatever happened to old fashioned china cups, or even mugs?

"Please call me Maria," she said. "I dislike formality. Besides, David told me so much about you I feel I know you."

"And please call me Cole," I responded. "I don't like formality either. But you have me at a disadvantage; your name was mentioned a few times, but neither David nor Trimble told me much about you."

"Well, there's not really much to tell. I joined the company in 1971, when I graduated from Florida State. The company was much smaller then, only ten employees. I was the eleventh. They gave me the title of 'Field Representative', which at the time was another term for glorified gopher. I did everything from putting bid packages together to expediting completion of projects, and of course getting coffee for the others. It was early 1974 when they first let me handle some of the work for David's bank. Since about 1980 I've handled all of David's projects, or, to be more accurate, the clients projects."

"How did your company get started," I interrupted, "and exactly what is it that you do?" Some of the company's history I already knew from my meetings with David and Trimble, but I wanted to hear it from her, just to see if it agreed with their versions. Before she answered I noticed a change in her expression; her smile disappeared and she was shaking her head very slightly from side to side.

"I'll tell you what, let's finish our coffee and leave for café. It's a short walk and we can talk on the way."

The message I got was that she didn't want to talk here. I was curious as to why, but didn't ask. On the other hand, while we finished our coffee I couldn't resist questioning her about the unusual reception area.

"It is a little out of the ordinary," she said. "And it's certainly not my taste. The paintings were done by our receptionist. She was given carte blanche to decorate and light the area as she wished. A few people have said they like it, but most find it a bit severe."

"Cast my vote for severe. . .and a little depressing," I said. "It seems your receptionist has a lot of clout. Is she a shareholder in the company?"

"No, no, nothing like that."

I started to ask what, but Maria put a finger to her lips and shook her head. She noticed I had finished my coffee, so she suggested we leave for lunch.

She didn't say anything until we got out on the sidewalk. "Please forgive me, Cole, for shushing you in my office. I have some concern about office security, which I'll explain a little later. You asked me how the company got started and what it is we do. How we got started is pretty involved so I'll just give you the highlights.

"The company was founded in 1957 by a gentleman named Bryson – Arnold Bryson. I'm told he was quite old when he started the company. He retired in 1969, about two years after Carlton Alverez was brought in. Shortly after he retired Bryson was diagnosed with stomach cancer and moved to a nursing home somewhere in the Northwest. He died there about six months later. Carlton has been our CEO since Bryson retired and has done a fantastic job. Not only has the business prospered under his leadership, but he's well liked by everybody. Well, almost everybody."

"What do you mean, *almost* everybody?"

"I'll get to that in a minute. First let me finish explaining how the business was started. I said that Arnold Bryson founded the company. That's what public records show, and what we tell outsiders, but the truth is the client founded the company. And Arnold Bryson wasn't the first employee of the company, he was the second. The first was the woman who greeted you when you got off the elevator – our sweet receptionist."

"You're kidding me! Pardon me for saying so, but I don't see how that woman could last forty days as a receptionist – much less more than forty years. I may be speaking out of turn, but she impressed me as being very unfriendly, if not flat out rude. She's the last person I'd want welcoming my clients."

"She's certainly not a charmer," Maria said with a chuckle. "But she hasn't always been the receptionist. The first thirty some years she served as private secretary to Bryson and, later, Carlton Alvarez. About ten years ago she fired our receptionist and moved into her job. Her excuse was that she wanted a less demanding job until she was ready to retire. Carlton has tried to terminate her on more than one occasion, but every time he did he'd receive a message from the client telling him to back off. Her name is Irena Kabojian. Most of the staff refer to her as 'Iron-Face Irena'. We know she's served since day one as a mole for the client and, apparently, there's nothing we can do about it. I dislike her immensely, and don't trust her at all. . .and she knows it. I'm also afraid of her.

"Unfortunately, I have no proof, but I suspect Irena is eavesdropping – listening in on my phone calls, or maybe all of my office conversations. On three different occasions during the past few weeks – in fact it started when David was killed – she has made snide comments about things I've said on the phone, conversations I had in my office with the door shut. And they were things she could not have known otherwise. Like I said, she frightens me."

"Could your office be bugged? Did you ever have anybody check it out?"

"No, Cole, I haven't. I don't want to let her know I suspect anything by bringing in an outsider to check, and I wouldn't know what to look for. I don't know if it's just my phone or my entire office, but that's why I shushed you when you were talking. I probably should have waited until we got outside before telling you anything. And by the way, when I said Carlton Alvarez is liked by almost everybody – Irena is the exception. They totally dislike each other. He feels as I do about her, but realizes he can't fire her. She's jealous of him because she fully expected to be appointed CEO when Bryson retired. Shortly after Carlton was made CEO she marched into his office and told him he had better resign, because if he didn't she'd make his life hell on earth. She later admitted to him that she had suggested to the client that Carlton be fired. I'm sure the reason he's still our CEO is because he's super intelligent and has made a ton of money for the client. I think that irritates Irena more than anything. And as you suggested, in addition to her abrasive personality, she presents a terrible image to the public."

We reached the restaurant and found it very crowded. At first glance it looked as though every booth and table were occupied, with another half dozen people standing in the foyer waiting to be seated. I was surprised when we were quickly escorted to an empty table in a small nook at the rear of the room. The hostess greeted Maria by name and treated us as VIP's. We each had seafood chowder that was delicious. She had a deviled crab, which she said was excellent, while I had a shrimp salad platter, which wasn't. The shrimp were rubbery from being overcooked and the lettuce was not fresh and crisp. While we ate we made small talk. I got the impression she didn't want to talk business here in the restaurant, but by the time we asked for iced tea refills the crowd had thinned out considerably. When the dishes were cleared from the table, Maria leaned closer to me and spoke almost in a whisper.

"I've told you how the company was started, now I'll try to answer your question about who we are and what we do. First, we're not a corporation, which I've always thought a little unusual. Our company name is the 'M. R. Shaw Management Group', but in the industry we're usually referred to as 'SMG'. Depending on our workload we carry forty to fifty employees, mostly construction managers, inspectors and bean-counters.

"I'm a VP, and head up a group called 'Property Management and Development'. There are currently twenty-two people in my group, and we handle development and construction of projects for the client. In addition, we manage and are leasing agents for a number of investment properties, mostly apartment units, shopping centers and commercial office buildings, including the one our office is in. The majority of these are owned by the client, but we also handle property for other investors. Our office here in Tampa is our company's only permanent office, although we do maintain field offices in leased trailers at construction sites.

"Aside from what my group does, the rest of the company handles nothing but construction management. Bottom line though, the client's projects my group handles account for almost sixty-percent of our gross revenue. The rest is derived from construction management services we provide for others, including a number of federal and state agencies, on projects such as highway construction, airport expansion, new port facilities, and the like. We've also done work for NASA at the Kennedy Space Center, and commercial development in the Orlando area around Disney World.

"Last year our billable fees for outside projects were just under four million. This year we'll top out a little over five and a half. We keep busy, and as a result we keep growing."

"Very impressive, Maria, and based on those numbers, very profitable as well. Five and a half mil from outside projects, and that represents only forty percent of your gross income – that's damned profitable! I'm curious though, some quick math tells me your total gross is somewhere around thirteen and a half million. Do you really bill the client for the other eight mil? I mean after all, the client owns your company – you work for him. Why would you charge him for your services?"

Maria hesitated, her face expressionless. "About all I can tell you is the client insists on total accountability; no padding of expenses or deductions, no double sets of books. Every hour spent on the client's projects must be billed, and every penny of income must be reported. Based on what I was told many years ago, the client is paranoid about being audited – particularly by the IRS."

"How do you invoice the client, and how does he pay his bills?" I asked.

"We send all billing to a post office box in Miles City, Montana. Payments have always been wired to our bank here in Tampa, originating in different locations in this country and abroad. Most come from Trimble's bank in London and a bank in Milan, Italy. We've also had a few from the Bahamas. Payments are usually received within thirty days of the billing date."

"That's interesting," I said. "The scope of this client's empire seems to broaden with each new development. But, Maria, before you continue there is something I'd like your opinion on. You may think what I'm about to ask is ludicrous, or certainty too late in the game to worry about, but it leads into something I want to discuss with you before I leave. What I need to know is – what is your perception of the role you, Trimble's bank and my company play in this giant monopoly game? Do you have any concern about the legality of this whole business, and whether some night we're going to turn on the late news and see our faces plastered all over the tube? David tried to convince me that everything was on the up-and-up, yet Trimble admitted to me that their bank has been questioned by at least three different law enforcement agencies about the client's account. My concern is that for as long as all of us have been involved in this, we've played an active role in laundering money for one of the mob families, or worse, a major drug cartel – maybe both. It may be forty some years too late to begin worrying about, but I'm concerned that we're all connected at the hip to this crazy client. If the client is involved in anything illegal, particularly something of this magnitude, and gets caught, we're all going down with him. What court or jury is going to believe us? Best case scenario is we'll all lose our businesses. Worst case is we'll lose our businesses and wind up in prison."

"I don't know that I share your fears," she said. "Maybe it's because things have worked so smoothly for so many years I've subconsciously convinced myself that nothing can go wrong. I agree it's a strange and unusual way to do business, but it's worked for a long, long time. We each do our thing, and I guess we do it quite well because it's worked. Your company is retained by Trimble's bank to find whatever type of facility or land the client orders them to acquire. You do all the legwork, do the site studies and resolve any glitches in zoning or permitting and then turn everything over to Trimble. You're out of the loop at that point. Trimble's bank puts together the financial package, and handles all of the purchasing and settlement details – and then they're out of the loop. Then we take over and do our thing, and the job's done. One of us never gets too involved with the other two.

"What I just described may sound a bit simplistic, but that's how the process works about ninety percent of the time. We do acquire and develop some properties for the client on our own, without any involvement with David's bank. But we do that only when specifically ordered by the client to proceed on our own. When we do, the acquisition funds are deposited by the client in our local bank – David's bank is bypassed completely."

"I haven't heard about this before. Do you have any idea why the client would want certain projects handled that way. What's different about them?"

"I'm not sure," she replied, "but I suspect it has more to do with the size of the acquisition than anything else. They're all valued under a half-million dollars."

"Two quick comments, Maria. First, when you said how smoothly everything has worked you neglected to mention the deaths and disappearances interwoven through the clients business transactions – not to mention David's murder. And secondly, to go back to something you said a few minutes ago; I don't recall whether David or Trimble ever said so, but I assumed all along that your company worked exclusively for the client and that all transactions went through Trimble's bank."

"Cole, as far as the deaths are concerned, no one has ever connected the client to any of them. I know there have been accusations, but never one bit of proof. And as far as my company is concerned, we've always done work for outside interests. The client probably wanted it that way to help us build an independent reputation in the construction community."

"Or an attempt to legitimatize a crooked operation," I added.

The smile left her face and I detected a trace of anger in her voice when she spoke, "You have a right to your opinion, but I certainly don't agree with everything you've said. Let's move on."

"Please don't take anything I've said personally. I'm certainly not accusing you of anything illegal. On the contrary, based on what David and Trimble both told me, you're just doing your job – with no more knowledge of the client than we have. And I apologize for beating a dead horse, but I still find it hard to accept that somewhere along the line the clients name hasn't surfaced. There are so many checks and balances, not to mention audits; a never ending string of regulatory agencies, plus real estate taxes, state taxes, and our friends at the IRS. It boggles the mind."

"I understand exactly how you feel, but believe it or not, Cole, it's true. That's not to say there haven't been questions from time to time, and even a few investigations. As you said, Trimble's bank has had them, and we've had them, but nothing came of any of it. As far as I know, every investigation ended in a blind alley. David also questioned me about the client many, many times. It is the main reason I convinced Carlton Alverez to go to London and talk with Trimble. What really disturbs me is David and I worked very closely together for many years, and yet I think he always felt I was hiding something from him. It saddens me to think he went to his grave doubting my word. I really have no idea who this crazy client is, and that's the truth . . .I swear to you on my mother's grave."

On my flight down from Philly I decided that if I thought Sippano was being evasive, or outright lying to me, I'd find some way to break off the discussion and leave. I'd be honest with her to a point, but I wasn't going to divulge what I knew, or even suspected, until I had some assurance that she would do likewise. I don't know if what she's told me today tipped the scales in her favor, but my gut reaction was that she was being honest with me. And she had already told me considerably more than I hoped to learn during my visit here. I felt it was time to lay my cards on the table and see how she responded.

"Maria," I said. "Our mutual friendship with David notwith-standing, you and I are still strangers. When I came here I had no idea where you and your company fit in this puzzle, and I admit I had serious reservations about coming here at all. Too many people have died. I hope future events don't prove me wrong, but after listening to you I believe you're telling the truth. When I promised Trimble I'd try to get to the bottom of this whole mess, I knew I'd need a lot of help and a few good breaks. You've already given me a ton of information, and I think you know even more that will help me, possibly things you may not realize are significant. I just hope I can count on you to trust me and work with me. Are you willing?"

"Absolutely, Cole," she said, looking directly into my eyes. "But before we go any further with this let's head back to my office. I do have some things I must take care of this afternoon."

"I understand, and I apologize for taking so much of your time. I know I'm imposing on you, but I would like to continue our discussion. If you've nothing planned for this evening why don't you join me for dinner? I'm staying over anyway, and we can talk without worrying about who might be listening."

"Thank you, I would enjoy that," she said. "In the meantime I'll stay at the office and get caught up on some of my work. You can pick me up there, say around seven-thirty."

"That's fine. Maybe Ms Congeniality will be gone by then and I can take a look around your office for a bug. I'm no expert, but if there's something obvious I should be able to find it."

"I can assure you that Irena and the entire staff will be gone by then. Parking will be easier too – you should be able to park in front of our building. By the way, since it appears you didn't enjoy your shrimp salad I'll defer to your judgment in selecting a restaurant," she said, the grin returning to her face. "And the only way I'll veto your choice is if you pick one that I know is bad."

What Maria didn't know was that the last time I visited my parents in Ft. Myers I flew to Tampa, rented a car and spent a week meandering my way down the Gulf coast. The first night I stayed in a five-star hotel out on Sand Key in Clearwater Beach. It was a comfortable drive from downtown Tampa, was right on the Gulf and had a fabulous restaurant. I was confident she wouldn't veto my choice.

After paying the check I walked Maria back to her office and then continued the few blocks to where I had parked the rental car. It seemed to be getting hotter by the minute and the inside of the car was like a furnace. I drove for about ten minutes with the windows down and the air conditioner going full blast. I had a confirmed reservation that Nancy had made for me at one of the major motels on the outskirts of the city. Since I had more than five hours to kill, I looked forward to getting out of these clothes and spending some time sitting by their pool, in nothing but swim trunks and sunglasses. Before I could do that though, I had to commit to paper the information Maria had given me; a lot of things were rattling around in my head. I also wanted to do a little snooping into the track record of the M. R. Shaw Management Group.

I stopped at a roadside phone, dialed 411 and got the number of the local Chamber of Commerce. I called and got their address. Fifteen minutes later I was standing at the counter in their front office. The young guy behind the counter couldn't have been more than a year out of high school. I gave him one of my Hammel & McQuaid business cards and told him the client I represented was getting ready to start site work on a design-build shopping center north of the city on Route 41.

"Bidding will be by invitation only. We're from up north, so we need a list of reputable sub-contractors and construction managers. The total project is going to come in somewhere around six million, so we need outfits with experience on major projects. Who can you recommend?"

"Geez," the kid said. "That's sure a big project. Where's it going to be built on 41?"

"Sorry, I can't divulge that," I responded. "We're still negotiating final details with the owner of the land."

"Oh, I see," he said, a little deflated. "I can give you our list of members; they're indexed by type of business. My boss could give you more information on all of them, but he's up in Tallahassee on Chamber business until day after tomorrow. You gonna be around for a few days?"

"No, I'm leaving tomorrow, but I'll be back in a few weeks. I'd like that list you have, though."

He reached under the counter and produced a thin bound booklet, which he proceeded to thumb through. "Tell you what I can do," he said, pulling a yellow highlighter from his shirt pocket. "I'll mark some of the companies that I know are big, and are also solid Chamber members. O.K.?"

"Sure, that might be real helpful."

After he handed me the marked booklet I casually flipped through the pages until I found what I wanted. They were listed under 'Project Managers/Construction Managers' – the M. R. Shaw Management Group, followed by a two paragraph biography of their operation. Out of six companies in that category, their name was the only one he had highlighted. "What do you know about this Shaw outfit?" I asked, showing him the listing.

"They're a solid company, one of the biggest around. They're also involved in a lot of Chamber programs. I know quite a bit about them because my older brother works for them. Like I said, they're solid."

I thanked him and left. Thirty minutes later I had checked in at my motel, and was in my trunks sitting by the pool, working on my second cold brew. I had brought a notebook and pencil and spent the next hour alternately jotting down notes and dozing off. I filled about three pages with notes, including a few more questions I needed to ask, when I realized I had had enough sun. I was somewhere between well-done and burnt, and I had no intention of making my dermatologist any richer than he already was. I decided on a quick swim, but even the pool water was too warm for my taste. I did a few quick laps, toweled myself off and returned to my room.

After I showered and dressed I worked on the notes again. As I reread what I had written, more questions came to mind, so I marked additional notes between the lines and in the margins. By seven o'clock I was confident that I had recorded all the important things Maria told me. Problem was, some of what she said was most likely unrelated to why I came to Tampa. Later, I'm going to have to sort out what to consider – and what to ignore.

Maria was right. When I returned to her office at seven-thirty I had my pick of a half-dozen parking places in front of her building. There were a few parked cars on the street, and even fewer people.

The lobby outer doors were locked. I pushed the small buzzer button two or three times but couldn't hear any sound from inside. I waited and hit the button again two or three times. I was about to give up when I saw a uniformed security guard shuffling down the corridor toward me. He acted more than a little upset, and was mumbling something about it being after hours and he was on his rounds in the basement when I interrupted him. He also refused to let me in until he checked me out with Maria.

When I stepped off the elevator into the second floor reception area I was surprised to see how different the room looked, compared with earlier today. All of the perimeter recessed lighting was off, and each of the two crystal vases of cut flowers was illuminated by a narrow beam spotlight recessed in the floor below the glass table each vase sat on. The rest of the room was dark. Now the room looked more like a florist's display case than a museum. I'm not sure I liked this any better than the museum look, but I had to admit – it was certainly different.

Maria came out to greet me, and motioned for me to follow her back to her office. The entire floor appeared deserted, with only minimal night lighting. It was not too dim to notice that this was a different Maria. The silk pant-suit and upswept hairdo were gone, replaced with a short, black silk dress, black stockings, heels and shoulder length curly hair framing her face. I still found it difficult to accept that David had cheated on his wife, but if he was prone to that sort of thing I could understand him being attracted to Maria. She was one foxy lady.

"I wasn't sure where we were going for dinner, so I went home, showered and changed. Besides, I had to feed Ralph."

"Who's Ralph?" I asked.

"He's my cat – I call him my attack cat," she said, grinning. "One spitting hiss and a swat with his front claws is usually all it takes for him to intimidate another animal. Probably most humans, too. My neighbor's golden retriever is terrified of Ralph, and he's three times bigger. So much for pets; do you still want to check my office for a bug?"

"Sure, but please understand that what I'll be doing is very unscientific – just looking for anything out of the ordinary. Let's start with your phone." I unscrewed the cap from the mouthpiece and, as she suspected, there was a bug. It took about ten minutes to check other places in the room where listening devices could be hidden, but I found nothing. I suggested that the phone bug be left where it was, and Maria agreed. No point in tipping off old Iron-Face that we knew she was listening. Maria would just have to be careful what she said on the phone. It also gave her a golden opportunity to throw out a few red herrings.

On the way to Clearwater Beach we talked about our personal lives. Maria was big on physical conditioning. She said she jogged about two miles every other morning, and worked-out twice a week in the weight room of a gym. No wonder she looked trim and fit. I knew she had to be around fifty, but she could easily pass for twenty years younger.

I hadn't told her where we were going for dinner. As I pulled into the hotel parking lot she tapped me on the shoulder. "Good choice," she said. "I couldn't have done better myself. This place is one of my favorites. But I am curious, how did you find it?"

"It's a long story, and I won't bore you with the details. Suffice it to say, I stumbled across it. I've eaten here two or three times and had excellent food each time."

Because it was a weeknight I hadn't thought to make a reservation. My mistake. The restaurant was crowded. The maitre d' said there would be at least a half-hour wait, so Maria and I adjourned to the bar. I was just about to order a second round of martinis, when we were told our table was ready.

Maria had filet mignon, medium well, while I opted for the Chilean sea bass. We each started with a spicy lobster chowder, followed with a shared salad of crispy greens topped with gorgonzola cheese, sliced pear and a tangy oil dressing. Everything was delicious. We continued our small talk while we ate. I told Maria some of the history of Hammel & McQuaid, and about my relationship with Suzy. After we finished our coffee I ordered brandy and suggested we find a comfortable spot in the lounge to continue Maria's rundown on the strange circumstances surrounding her employer.

"Maria," I said, "Before you continue where you left off this afternoon, I'd like to ask you a question. . . a very personal question. It's really none of my business, and if you tell me to go to hell I'll understand."

"Fair enough," she said. "What's the question?"

"I won't tell you the source, but I've been told that you and David had some sort of 'relationship'. And the inference was that it was personal rather than professional. Is that true?"

She didn't answer for what seemed like an eternity. Her eyes glistened in the light and I realized she was crying softly.

"I'm sorry, Maria, I certainly didn't mean to upset you."

"It's all right, Cole, I planned to tell you anyway – I knew it would come out sooner or later."

She hesitated again, while dabbing her eyes with a tissue. She reached across and took my hand in hers. She was trembling.

"Please do not think less of David," she whispered. "I initiated the affair. . . and David ended it. It all started about four years ago. Actually, with me it started long before that. I. . . fell in love with him shortly after we met.

"He and I spent many hours together in my office working out details on the client's projects. Occasionally we would go out for dinner, usually after we had wrapped up a project. One night we both had a little too much to drink and, when David took me home, I invited him in. The only way to describe what happened is to say that I seduced him. David took me to bed. . . and spent the night. And the next day – and the next night. For all the pleasure it gave me, David seemed overwhelmed with guilt. When he left for England the following day he hardly said a word. I felt miserable; I knew in my heart that our relationship was over. Worse, I worried that I might never see David again. He didn't return to Tampa for almost three months. We had lunch together the first day, and he was very nervous and apologetic. He said he had enjoyed our short time together, but I think he was just being polite. Then he said he was torn between his fascination with me and his love for his wife. He told me that while he positively would do nothing more to jeopardize his marriage, he also couldn't bear to hurt me. He even offered to resign his position at the bank if it would make things easier for me.

"I told him that I would probably always love him, but the last thing I wanted was to turn his life upside down. I also promised to keep everything on a professional basis from that point forward. And I believe I did.

"Even though our personal relationship was buried in the past, I was devastated when David was killed. I still loved him deeply and I desperately wanted to go to England for his funeral. I didn't because I had no idea who might be there, and I was sure if anyone recognized me they would misinterpret my reason for coming. I didn't want to cause his widow any embarrassment. And, just so you don't misinterpret my motive for helping you, the reason I've agreed to tell you all I know is because I'll do anything I can to avenge David's death."

"I'm sorry for what you've been through," I said. "I also considered David a friend. He was probably the most honest individual I've ever dealt with – his word was more important to him than a signed contract. My secretary always referred to him as a 'true English gentleman', and I think he was. How did you hear of his death?"

"Trimble called our office the day after it happened. I can't remember ever being so upset – I must have cried for a week. Please. . . let's change the subject," she said, forcing a smile, "or I'm really going to start blubbering. Do you remember where I left off when we were talking this afternoon?"

"You told me how your company functions and a little about how it got started, although you didn't explain the relationship between Irena and Bryson."

"Yes, I remember now. I believe I told you that the client founded the company, although all public records indicate Arnold Bryson as the founder. I also mentioned that Irena Kabojian preceded Bryson as the first employee of the new company. To say the least it was a very strange beginning."

"How did you find out about Irena and Bryson," I asked.

"I wouldn't know any of this if David and I hadn't done some serious snooping about five years ago. From the first time we met, David questioned me incessantly about my knowledge of the client. I tried to convince him that I really knew nothing, certainly no more than he did. Then something happened at his bank – I'm not sure exactly what – and Trimble insisted that David come here to question Carlton and myself. It was a fool's errand, and I think David finally realized it. He arrived on a Friday, and the evening he arrived we were having a discussion in my office, when it dawned on me that maybe I could appease David and Trimble by offering to show David our dead storage files in the basement. I had never been through the files, but I knew they were there. I told David that if he was willing I would sacrifice my weekend to help him search through the old records. And that's exactly what it took – all day Saturday and all day Sunday. There were more than forty file cabinets in that room, and we knew that to find any information on the early days of the company, if in fact such information existed, we may have to search through dozens of file drawers. Most of the drawers contained nothing but job files on completed projects, and everything was filed alphabetically, not chronologically."

"Did you really expect to find anything in the files, or were you just humoring David?"

"Probably a little of both. You must understand that this happened about a year before our affair, and I was so in love with David I would have done just about anything he asked. But I was also more than a little curious myself about what the files might contain.

"The office was closed for the weekend, but I had a set of keys and knew how to deactivate the security alarm. The basement storage room was hot and smelled musty. And there were spiders and bugs. It certainly wasn't a nice place to spend a weekend, even with someone you loved. We left empty handed after about six hours of searching on Saturday. By late Sunday afternoon we had found nothing, and were both dirty, tired and frustrated. We were about five minutes away from giving up when we got lucky. Behind some old job folders we found four fat manila envelopes, tied together with twine, and that's where the early years of company history were filed.

"The information in the envelopes started with day one, was filed chronologically, and covered the period of time up to our move into our present office. It was almost like a diary, and was kind of odd. There were no accounts receivable or payable, just personnel records, resumes, tax returns, bank statements, and an assortment of memos and letters.

"The original office was located on the other side of Tampa in a strip shopping center. It was small and consisted of two rooms with a storefront vestibule. As the company grew it became too cramped, so ground was purchased and our present building was constructed. The move into our new offices took place about four months before I joined the company in 1971.

"Arnold Bryson was recruited by an employment agency in 1957. He had worked for years at a small CPA firm in Tallahassee, working his way up the ladder from bookkeeper to office manager. The employment agency lured him away by offering to double his salary. They told him he would be President and CEO, and the first employee of a new real estate and construction management company. He would organize the company, hire employees, and run the entire operation. The day before he was to start his new job a messenger delivered a package to his home. It contained specific instructions he was to follow in organizing and running the business. It also contained the address of the new company's rented office in downtown Tampa, a binder of printed business checks and a receipt indicating a deposit of fifty thousand dollars in the new company's checking account. The 'M. R. Shaw Management Group' was off and running."

"Did you find anything indicating why or how Bryson was picked for the job? And why Irena was hired ahead of him?"

"There was nothing indicating what criteria was used to select Bryson, but you can imagine his surprise when he arrived to open the new office the next morning and found Irena Kabojian seated at a desk, reading the paper and drinking coffee. At this point the story got weird. She informed him that the owner, our client, had hired her. . . to represent the owner. She had started about a month earlier and negotiated the lease for the new office, then had the place painted and furnished. All of this was done before Bryson was hired. She also told Bryson that she was to serve as his executive secretary, and what her salary and benefits were to be. And the real kicker was – she had been given authority to make decisions on certain key issues – whether or not he concurred. Beyond that, she wouldn't divulge any information about the client or anything about her past, personal or otherwise. We found all of this in a very angry memorandum Bryson had written for the file. He was angry, but he was also concerned about the very strange relationship he found himself in. He just didn't know what to do."

"How did Bryson know that Irena was telling the truth and not running a scam?" I asked. "Since he never had direct contact with the client, how could Bryson verify anything?"

"In the beginning he couldn't. He even considered resigning, but the lure of big money changed his mind. About three months later he and Irena locked horns over the hiring of a new field engineer. Bryson had just hired the guy when Irena heard about it. She stormed into Bryson's office and demanded that he call the new hire and withdraw the offer. It seems she had her own candidate for the job. She reminded Bryson that she had final say in the hiring of new employees. He disagreed and ordered her out of his office. Words were exchanged and she threatened to have him fired. The next morning he received a call from overseas. The man at the other end spoke in a deep guttural voice, in very broken English, and ordered Bryson to do as Irena insisted. The caller then said that if Bryson refused he would be terminated within twenty-four hours. Bryson asked the caller for identification, at which point the caller related Bryson's employment history, all the way back to graduation from college. Bryson started to protest, but quickly realized he has no choice and agreed to follow orders.

"About a month later Bryson and Irena had a similar run-in. Bryson lost his temper and threatened to fire her. The next morning he again received an overseas phone call, with the same end result. "

"Over the years since Carlton Alvarez took over, he too has had a number of confrontations with Irena, but the end result is always the same. To his credit, Carlton found ways to work around Irena. He keeps her in the dark as much as possible by generally ignoring her. We all go out of our way to hide things from her. When she gets into one of her snits, or gets too demanding, he lets her do her thing, and then hopes for the best. So far it's worked fairly well."

"So the client has had a mole in your company since the beginning," I said. "I wonder if there are others besides Irena?"

"I don't think so," Maria replied. "At least none we're aware of. Irena pokes her nose into every phase of our business, or at least thinks she does, so she has no need for an accomplice."

"Do any of your employees seem friendly with Irena, maybe socialize with her after hours?"

"Hardly. She seems to be universally disliked by everybody in the office. Most of our people have heard the horror stories and are actually afraid of her."

"It raises another interesting question," I said, "Does Irena have a counterpart in Trimble's bank?"

"It's possible," Maria replied, "but not likely. David and I discussed it, and he said he knew every person in his group personally. He said it was inconceivable that they would be of any use to the client, because each of them was only responsible for a small percentage of the work handled by his group. Like I said, it's possible, but I don't think it's even worth considering."

"I guess the reason David never mentioned Irena to me was because he knew it would support my argument that something was radically wrong. And while we're on the subject of moles, I can vouch for everybody at Hammel & McQuaid. We have fewer employees than either you or Trimble, and only a handful of those know anything of our dealings with Trimble's bank. Other than my partner, our attorney and my secretary, none of my people know anything about you and your organization – and certainly nothing about Irena Whatshername. I wouldn't waste our time worrying about my people being involved in any way with your client.

"And, Maria, one other thing you should know; even though our involvement over the years has been very profitable for Hammel & McQuaid, we're now in the process of severing all ties with Trimble's bank. Our attorney is currently working out the details of a legal agreement with Trimble's solicitor. We're doing this for two reasons; mainly to limit our exposure to liability, but also to distance ourselves from all of the violence that has occurred, both past and present. As I mentioned to you earlier, if the client's business turns out to be as illegal as I think it is, the best case scenario is we'll all go belly up. If that happens, regardless of whether anybody goes to jail – and in my opinion most of the key players probably will – a lot of people at Hammel & McQuaid are going to be hurt. It would destroy the business, and I can't allow that to happen. So, if you and Trimble are half as intelligent as I think you are, you both should start looking for ways to cover your ass."

"As I told you earlier, I don't agree with your opinion of the client. Not at all. My god, you seem to forget that this arrangement has succeeded for more than forty years, and made one hell of a lot of money for all of us. Who cares that he doesn't identify himself?"

"I do, for one. And as I told you earlier, Maria, you've failed to mention all of the violence that has occurred. Even if you ignore all of the previous disappearances and killings, how can you justify David being killed. All of the evidence surrounding his death points directly to the client."

"I think his death was an unfortunate coincidence, but I'm not going to argue the point because I can see that we're never going to agree. Why didn't you tell me sooner about breaking off your relationship with Trimble's bank?"

"I had planned to, but I didn't because I was afraid you'd change your mind about talking to me, or helping me. You have to understand that as much as I'd like to walk away from this, I promised Trimble that I'd do my best to unravel the entire mess. On top of that I feel an obligation to David, something I just can't ignore, not to mention a little revenge of my own after almost being wiped out by the same two goons who killed David."

"What are you talking about – I thought David was killed by two men who tried to rob him at the casino? That's what Trimble told us. Why would they come after you?"

"What Trimble told you is exactly what the news media reported, Maria, but there was more to it than a simple robbery. The killers desperately wanted something David had. When they didn't get it they came after me, thinking he might have given it to me."

I spent the next ten minutes telling Maria about Muzzadin and Salemi and how they killed David, their attempt to kill me, and how

Muzzadin ended up dead. She said she wasn't aware of any of it. I asked if she had ever heard of Muzzadin or Salemi before or had seen anyone fitting their description in or around her office building. She said she hadn't. I started to say something else when she grabbed my wrist.

"Cole, wait a minute, describe Muzzadin again."

I did, and before I could finish she pulled her hand back and a look of confusion crossed her face.

"Yes," she almost shouted. "About a month ago I went out to the reception area to pick up a package that had been delivered. I saw a man fitting that description standing at Irena's desk talking to her. I remember thinking it was strange because I had never seen him before, but mostly because it was a very hot day, and he was dressed in dark, heavy clothing. He looked sinister and totally out of place. He was leaning across her desk with his mouth next to her ear, and they were both talking in a whisper. I couldn't hear what was said, but it was obvious they knew each other. Irena was smiling, something she rarely did."

"Are you sure it was him?" I asked.

"Based on the way you just described him it had to be Muzzadin. Yes, I'm sure. . .I know it was him."

"Does this change your opinion on anything?"

"I guess it should, Cole, but right now all I feel is confused and a little frightened. I think I'd like to go home."

I asked the waitress for our check. While we waited a lot of possibilities were popping in and out of my head. If the man Maria saw with Irena was in fact Muzzadin, and there didn't seem to be any doubt in her mind, it tied him to the Tampa organization. Maybe not to Maria or Carlton Alvarez, but at least to Irena. And maybe Irena was the key to everything. Were Irena and Muzzadin working together? Did she order the hit on David, or was Muzzadin acting alone? Regardless, it was the first positive lead I had.

Maria had given me a ton of information on her company's background, probably more than she realized. Certainly more than I ever expected to get. Now came the tough part; sorting it all out. I needed to think, and the best place for that was back in my motel room. Earlier today I had made some tentative decisions about what I was going to do next. Now I don't know. This latest information on Muzzadin and Irena may completely change my plans.

On the way to Maria's place I thanked her for her help, and told her I'd call her if anything further developed. She said to call her at home to avoid Irena's phone bug. She wrote her home number on the back of her business card and handed it to me.

When I pulled up in front of her place I glanced at the card. What I read on the front reminded me of something I meant to ask her earlier.

"Maria, just who the hell is 'M. R. Shaw'? It's probably a dumb question, given everything we've been through, but any chance that he or she is our phantom client?"

"It's certainly not a dumb question, Cole, it's been asked probably a million times – going all the way back to Bryson. Carlton said he questioned Bryson about it shortly after coming to work for the company. Since it was a small business at the time, Carlton thought it strange that the owner never came to the office. Bryson told Carlton that he had never met Shaw, and had no idea if such a person existed. After some discrete checking, that ended up in a blind alley, Carlton concluded that M. R. Shaw was simply a fictitious business name. And we've never seen or heard anything to dispute that."

She invited me in for coffee, but I declined. I had to get back to my motel and do some serious thinking before I hit the sack. I thanked her again and left.

When I got to my room I did as I promised and called Suzy. I blew her a kiss and told her I loved her. She did likewise and asked me what I had learned from Maria. I told her it was too lengthy and complicated to discuss on the phone, but I'd tell her everything when I got back tomorrow. She said there was nothing new at the office – Joe had his usual list of questions on a bid he was putting together – but she was glad I didn't have to stay in Tampa another day. She missed me.

After I hung up I showered, pulled on a pair of shorts, mixed myself a gin and tonic, and turned out the lights. Some years ago I found I did my best thinking in the dark. I spent about an hour mulling over what Maria had told me, sipping my drink, and watching the tiny red light in the ceiling smoke detector blink on and off every few seconds.

No matter how much importance I attached to some of what Maria told me, my thoughts kept returning to Muzzadin's whispered conversation with Irena. What were they conspiring about? Muzzadin had killed David, that was a fact. She was obviously some sort of agent for the client. Did Muzzadin do it on his own, or was he ordered to do it by Irena or the client? If Maria saw Irena and Muzzadin together a month ago, their meeting must have been just before David was killed. The more I thought about it the more I convinced myself that Irena and Muzzadin were working together. And I'd bet money David was the subject of their whispered conversation. Besides, it didn't seem reasonable to me that the client had ordered the hit. David had been doing the client's bidding for years, and was doing everything exactly as he had done since the beginning. Why kill him now? It didn't make sense.

On the other hand, what did Irena, or Muzzadin, or both, have to gain by conspiring against the client? What was their motive? The only obvious answer was money. Lots of money. Whenever the client ordered the purchase of some major entity, David was involved in the transfer of a huge sum of money. Irena would know about this. And if she knew, Muzzadin might also know. Particularly if he and Irena were lovers.

David died because he had something Irena and Muzzadin wanted. When he didn't get it Muzzadin came after me. Whatever it was, if it existed at all, had to be in David's attaché case. That much I knew for sure. But I've been through all the notes and records in the attaché case and, other than David's crazy code, I don't recall seeing anything that Irena and Muzzadin could profit from. After meeting Maria Sippano I was convinced that the 'MS' in David's code had nothing to do with her. So that left only Muzzadin and Salemi. And if that's who David was referring to, it meant he had to know about Muzzadin. If he did, he apparently never said anything to Maria, or Trimble, and certainly not to me. If David knew that Muzzadin was involved in at least two of the earlier deaths, did he also know that Muzzadin would come after him? I can't imagine David knowing, or even suspecting that, and not doing something to protect himself.

I turned on the light and spent the next hour putting on paper what I thought was important. I had some of the answers I came to Tampa to get, but there were still too damn many questions. At midnight I gave up, set my alarm for six o'clock, and went to bed.

After I showered, shaved and dressed the next morning the first thing I did was call Maria at her home. She answered on the second ring.

"Maria, this is Cole. Sorry to bother you so early, but I have another question – one that I couldn't risk asking on your office phone."

"No problem, Cole. You almost missed me though, I was just about to leave to do my running. What's the question?"

"You mentioned that Trimble called your office with the news of David's death. Who took the call – was it Irena, Alvarez, or you?"

"Well, all calls come through Irena. Carlton was out of the office that day and I'm the one who spoke to Trimble. Why?"

"Did you happen to see Irena after you finished talking with Trimble?"

"No I didn't. I was pretty broken up by the news and I stayed in my office trying to compose myself. When I came out about a half hour later, Irena was gone. One of the secretary's told me that Irena had left in a hurry, claiming she had some personal business to attend to, and wouldn't be back until the next day. As I recall, she didn't come back for three or four days."

"Do you happen to have Irena's home address?"

"Yes I do. I have a company directory with addresses and phone numbers. Hold on."

When she returned to the phone she gave me Irena's address and home phone number. I thanked her and told her I'd be in touch soon.

I had breakfast at a restaurant next door to my motel and when I returned to my room I called my parents in Ft. Myers. I usually call them every week or so and visit about twice a year. My mom answered the phone and said my dad had gone fishing. I told her I was in Tampa on business, but couldn't get down to see them because I had to catch a late morning flight back to Philly. She gave me the hurt mother routine, but I told her I loved her and would visit them for three or four days around Thanksgiving. She said she would call Mrs. Tomasello with instructions to make sure I did.

I asked directions at the motel desk, and on my way to the airport I drove past Irena's house. It was a single home in what appeared to be a very affluent suburb. A winding drive lead from the street to a detached three-car garage. Very effective landscaping shielded the main house from the street. It seemed like a hell of a lot of house for a single woman. I'd put a price tag on it of somewhere close to three-quarters of a million. A little too much house for a receptionist.

CHAPTER TEN

It was mid-afternoon when I pulled into the office parking lot. I picked up my phone messages from Nancy and she told me she had a few letters for me to sign, but otherwise nothing much was happening. Joe Mancuso collared me before I reached my office and said he needed to review some numbers with me for the bid he was working on. I told him to give me thirty minutes and I'd see him in his office.

I was flipping through my messages when Suzy walked in, looking prettier than ever, and planted a kiss on the top of my head. She asked about Tampa and I told her it was a worthwhile trip and that I had a lot to tell her.

"How about having dinner with me this evening?" I asked. "We'll try that new place I told you about in Marlton, and we can talk without interruptions and the phone ringing."

"Sounds great. Pick me up around seven?"

"I'll be there, gorgeous."

The phone messages Nancy had given me would have to wait. I had to call Ben first. I got lucky and found him in his office.

"Ben, I just got back from Tampa. I think it was a good trip – I know I found out a lot more than I had hoped to, which I'll tell you about later. In the meantime I need you to do something for me – it's important."

"O.K., little brother, what?"

"I want you to call Hamilton, your FBI buddy, and see if his people can give us any information on. . ."

"Whoa, hold on Cole," Ben interrupted, "Like I told you before, Brian Hamilton made it clear the last time I talked to him that he doesn't want me calling him, regardless of our past association. He's not the Brian Hamilton I used to know. Whether it's ego or something else, he made me feel very uncomfortable when I asked him to look into David's murder and what was going on in Atlantic City. What the hell is so important that you want me to call him again?"

"Ben, I've got to find out everything I can about two individuals in the Tampa organization; the first is the founder of the company, a phantom by the name of 'M. R. Shaw', and the other is one of Shaw's head honchos – an old battle-ax of a woman by the name of Irena Kabojian. I suspect that Shaw, whoever he or she is, is the mysterious client we've indirectly worked for all these years. And the Kabojian woman is wired to Shaw in some way – maybe she is M. R. Shaw. Regardless, I think she's up to her eyeballs in everything that's happened over the years. The real clincher is Irena Kabojian was involved with our dear departed friend, Mousa Muzzadin. They were seen together just before David was killed."

"Who saw them together – because if it's true it really muddies the water – was it somebody you think is reliable?"

"It was Maria Sippano, and contrary to our earlier concern about her, I found her to be not only cooperative, but also very believable. I'm convinced she got sucked up in this just as we did. Aside from her and possibly her boss, Carlton Alvarez, there's something very strange about Shaw's organization, and I'm convinced it revolves around Irena Kabojian. That's why I've got to know more about her background and where and how she fits in the puzzle. She's been involved with the Shaw outfit since the day it was founded, more than forty years ago. There has to be a ton of background information on her – bank accounts, tax records, credit cards, maybe even a pissed-off neighbor or two."

"Well, Cole, you're assuming Hamilton is going to cooperate – and I'm convinced he won't. Regardless, if your right about this woman it might be easier and probably a lot more productive to work through Sam Abromowitz. I think he'd be more willing to cooperate with me. And besides that he's right here in Cherry Hill."

"I don't agree, Ben. And because he's local is exactly why I feel he can't be much help. The more I get involved in this the more I'm convinced we're looking at something international in scope. I don't think a local police force has the resources and connections to get what I need. On top of that, I'm convinced the FBI or the CIA, maybe both, have been involved in this from the beginning.

"The reason I believe that is Hamilton was very evasive when you talked to him the last time, yet he admitted that some government agencies were involved in the Atlantic City investigation. If they weren't, he could just as easily have said they knew nothing about David's murder."

"I don't know Cole, maybe you're right. I still think I'll be spinning wheels, but I'll call him again. Just don't get your hopes up."

"Fair enough. Make sure you tell him that I've already done some investigating and, regardless of what he gives us, I'm going to follow this to the bitter end.

"While I have you on the phone, how are you making out with Trimble's bank? Anything new on our agreement?"

"Yes, Cole, it's resolved. I have a facsimile of the agreement on my desk, and the hard copy is coming airmail. It's not totally what I wanted, but I'm satisfied it gives us the protection we may need."

"That's good to hear. I'd like to meet with you in the next few days to tell you what I found out in Tampa. I think you'll find it very interesting."

"O.K., little brother, how about lunch tomorrow? You buy."

"Fair enough, cheapskate. I'll pick you up at noon. I hope you like McDonald's. And by the way, as soon as you talk to Hamilton let me know what he says. I know it's difficult on the phone, but try to read between the lines of what he says, and whether he still seems evasive."

I spent the rest of the afternoon meeting with Joe Mancuso, reading my mail and returning phone calls. At five-thirty I bailed out, went home, showered, dressed and headed for Suzy's; stopping on the way to buy wine for our dinner – the restaurant was excellent but BYOB – and a Beanie-Baby for Julia. Suzy said it's the latest fad and that Julia is into collecting the stuffed critters in a big way. According to the sales clerk, I should consider myself very lucky; the stuffed animal cost me under ten bucks, but if the company stops making that particular item, it could be worth fifty on the secondary market. Sure. I told her I had an almost new hula hoop in my basement that I'd sell cheap. As I left the store the clerk yelled after me that I should hang on to the hoop – someday it might be worth a fortune. Sure.

The moment we got in my car Suzy started asking questions about Tampa. I told her I didn't want to talk about it until after we finished dinner; I hate discussing a complicated issue like that in bits and pieces.

When the waiter cleared the table and brought coffee Suzy folded her hands on the table and smiled at me. "O.K., love," she said. "You've kept me hanging long enough. I think I've been more than patient, so no more stalling – tell me about Tampa.

For the next half-hour I gave her a verbatim account of my discussions with Maria, Maria's involvement with David, my impression of Irena, Irena's contact with Muzzadin, and my gut reaction to the entire Tampa situation. I also told her about my phone conversation this afternoon with Ben.

When I finished, Suzy reached across and touched my hand. "I have so many questions I don't know where to begin," she said. "So forgive me if I jump around a bit. First though, I'm disappointed with David, but I guess not really surprised by his affair with Maria Sippano. He was a very aristocratic, handsome man and, from the way you described her, she must be a very good looking woman. Probably very lonely as well. Do you think she was completely truthful with you?"

"I do, Suzy. She answered my questions without hesitation. She volunteered a lot of information about her company, well beyond what I expected. For example; she didn't have to elaborate on the roll Irena played from past to present, or, for that matter, tell me about Irena and Muzzadin. And as far as her feelings for David are concerned, I'm no expert but they seemed completely genuine to me."

"She did know you were coming," Suzy replied. "Do you think it's possible that she's a good actress and put on a show just for your benefit?"

"Sure it's possible, but if that's the case why would Maria tell me about Irena and Muzzadin; why admit to an affair with David – she could have easily denied it – why give me all the background on her company? And why arouse my suspicions about their involvement in some huge conspiracy? She could have omitted half of what she told me and sugar-coated the rest. I would have come home as much in the dark as I was when I left here."

Suzy thought for a minute and then tilted her head as though confused. "Are you saying you now have some idea of what's been going on, and who's behind it?"

"There's still lots of gray areas, but I think I have some of the answers. And I have some pretty strong hunches about the rest. On the flight home from Tampa I looked over the notes from my meeting with Maria, and the notes Trimble gave me when we were in London. I also re-read my own notes that I made after David was killed. When I put them all together a few things became very obvious; the most significant being that Muzzadin and Selemi didn't come to this country until 1989, yet the killings and disappearances started back in 1972. According to Ben, their 1989 arrival was confirmed by both the FBI and Immigration. So it's obvious that somebody else was responsible for everything that happened before they came here."

"Do you have any idea who, and what their motive might have been?" Suzy asked.

"Suzy, I'll answer your question with a question. Who profited from those earlier deaths? The only conclusion I can reach is that the client was behind all of them. It's totally unreasonable to attribute four violent deaths to pure coincidence.

"Also consider this; from what David and Trimble told us – and incidentally, Maria Sippano agrees with them – we know the client was paranoid about keeping his or her identity secret. What if the client suspected, for one reason or another, that each of those four people posed a threat to that secret? Even though the four victims apparently had nothing in common with each other, one common denominator did exist – they each had some degree of involvement with the client, and obviously did something to trigger their elimination. Maybe one or more of them found out the client's identity and tried blackmail. Maybe they got pissed-off over something in their business deal with the client and threatened to blow the whistle – who the hell knows. But I believe the perceived threat to the client's identity provided all the motive needed to seal their fate. People have been killed for a hell of a lot less."

"O.K., Cole, I agree with what you just said about motive, but that still doesn't help us identify the client. And besides, now that Muzzadin is dead and Salemi is in jail – and we're severing our relationship with Trimble's bank – do we really care who the client is? Why should you continue risking your life trying to find out?"

"For a couple reasons, Suzy, but please understand; now that Muzzadin and Salemi are out of the picture I don't think I'm risking my life. During the past few weeks I've devoted a lot of time, money, and a giant black eye tracking down this bastard. Now that I'm convinced I'm on to something, my curiosity won't let me quit. Besides, I told Trimble I'd get to the bottom of it. Aside from that, I owe David some kind of final closure. I think he died not knowing any of the answers."

Suzy leaned closer to me across the table and squeezed my hand with both of hers. "Let's get back to my earlier question," she said. "Tell me what you learned in Tampa that provided you with answers – and I believe you said 'some pretty strong hunches'- about who's behind all of this."

"O.K., Suzy, *answers* may have been an exaggeration on my part – *possibilities* may be a more accurate term. I'll concede the point that my conclusion may not appear as rock solid to you as it does to me, because it's based on some of those possibilities, mixed with some imaginative hunches on my part. Regardless, I'm sold on it.

"To begin, the first disappearance, and obvious death, was Stiebris, the real estate salesman. That happened back in 1972, shortly after Walter located that large parcel of land in Montana for Trimble's bank. As I recall it was more than six-thousand acres. The site was immediately developed by Tampa into an upscale thoroughbred horse farm. The owner was also going to experiment with new strains of hybrid cattle. Anyway, at the time it was the most expensive acquisition Walter and Trimble's bank had ever handled for the client. Shortly after construction began, Stiebris started showing up at the project every day, popping up in different places throughout the site. He insisted on taking a lot of pictures and generally made a nuisance of himself. He was warned repeatedly about trespassing. After being escorted off the site a number of times by their security people, he threatened some kind of legal action against the owner. A few days later he disappeared and has never been seen since.

"Now, consider this – according to both David and Alex Trimble, their first dealing with the client occurred in 1953. Was there a reason why no violence occurred until 1972, nineteen years later? I think so, and I'll tell you why. It's one of my hunches, but I believe the Montana ranch was acquired and built – not for some wealthy investor, but as the home and base of operations for our elusive client. I don't know just yet who he is, but I'll bet a months salary that the ranch is where he is."

"My God, Cole, it just dawned on me, if he's the same individual that started this mess back in 1953, he'd have to be ancient by now. Maybe he's dead. But if he's alive, why. . .why would he want to live the life of a recluse all those years, and with all that money? He sounds like another Howard Hughes, only weirder!"

"I agree, Suzy. Unless it's a second generation heir, whoever it is would now have to be in their mid to late seventies. I can think of very few reasons why somebody with that much money would want to hole-up in Montana for the rest of their life. It's been what – twenty-six, twenty-seven years . . . that's a helluva long time. Like I said, I don't know who he is, but logic tells me that unless he's a certifiable lunatic, he's got to be recognizable – some sort of celebrity – somebody with sufficient reason to totally drop out of sight that many years ago. Maybe he's some big-shot mob figure who wanted to disappear, or maybe a Nazi war criminal hiding from everybody. Maybe even some foreign dictator in exile who thinks he's safer in Montana, hiding under an assumed name. Regardless, he is, or was, a famous or infamous public figure, and wealthy enough to make it all happen."

"Well sweetheart you're probably right, but how do we go about identifying this notorious star of the past?

"I have an idea about that, too. It's a long shot, but at the moment I can't come up with anything better. Tomorrow morning I'm going to Philly to the main branch of the Public Library. I called there this afternoon and spoke to a woman in the Newspaper Department. She said they have on microfilm every newspaper published by the major area papers, going all the way back to day one. I told her I was interested in papers published between 1952 and 1953, and also 1971 and 1972. I also explained the type of information I was looking for and she said unless I get lucky it'll take a lot of searching to find what I'm after. Unfortunately, even though they have on film every page of each paper, their film isn't indexed by topic. I have no idea how long it'll take or what I'll find, but I think it's worth a shot. I could certainly use your help; want to come with me? Who knows, maybe we'll get lucky and find a name or two worth pursuing."

"Sure," Suzy answered. "I love looking through old newspapers, particularly the society pages and clothing ads. If we only had a few names for starters we might be able to get the information by calling the papers direct. All newspapers keep biographies on the famous and infamous. Whenever Joe-The-Movie-Star does something newsworthy, like getting busted for DWI, or beating up his wife, it gets added to his file. That's so that when he drops dead of a heart attack at age forty-one it takes no more than a few minutes to write a two-column obituary."

"Suzy," I said with a grin, "Your basic intelligence and worldly knowledge never cease to amaze me. Last night in bed I dredged my brain for any name from that era that I could remember. Part of my problem is that this all started before I was born. I came up with a grand total of two names – and then realized both had something in common. They were dead. So, I have no names to give the lady at the library. . . we're starting from scratch.

"The only clue we have to work with is the person we're looking for would have to be somebody who was in their mid-twenties to mid-thirties in 1953, which kind of rules out my war criminal idea. The candidate would most likely be some sort of national or international figure, and would have accumulated a considerable fortune; one that could be accessed quickly when cash was needed for a new venture. And, if he or she came from outside the country, to relocate and accomplish what they did, they literally had to buy their way into the United States. They needed friends in high places. Maybe those friends included the CIA, or the FBI, or possibly even the White House.

"Think back to a few weeks ago when Ben had that rather cryptic phone conversation with his friend Hamilton in the FBI, and Hamilton's admission that there were 'other agencies' involved in the investigation into David's death. Ask yourself why the CIA or Immigration would be the least bit interested in David Nesbitt, and how or why he was killed, unless they had already been involved in the plot – maybe since day one."

"I don't know, Cole," Suzy said, letting go of my hand. "I know I'm tired of this whole business – it's completely taken over our lives. I think the smartest thing you can do tonight is forget foreign affairs and take this local lady home. I think we both need to concentrate for a few hours on a domestic affair. Sound good?"

"It sounds great, I seem to recall knowing a fallen woman, but I'm not sure I know any local lady."

We both laughed and headed for her place.

It was a little past ten the next morning when Suzy and I walked through the doors of the library. The receptionist at the information desk steered us in the right direction, and after an elevator ride to the second floor we found ourselves in the Newspaper Department. Six hours later, bleary-eyed, we were on our way back to my parked car. Our efforts had uncovered ten names; eight were possibilities, two were a bit of a stretch. There also were a few others that we didn't bother listing, only because they were either in prison or had appeared in public outside the United States within the past couple of weeks.

On the way back to the office Suzy and I went over the list of names. We agreed that the two least likely candidates should be crossed off the list. Both were Nazi war criminals and, if by some quirk of fate they were alive and kicking in 1953, they certainly were not around when the Montana ranch was built in 1972. The youngest of the pair would then have been 97 years old.

The other eight possibilities presented an interesting kaleidoscope of nationalities, ages, character studies and cruel reputations. There was Francois Duvalier, or Papa Doc as he was known, from Haiti; Rafael Trujillo of the Dominican Republic; Pol Pot of Khmer Rouge fame in Cambodia; the Shah of Iran; General Idi Amin from Uganda; Saddam Hussein from Iraq; Muammar Qadhafi of Libya; and Juan Peron from Argentina. If you included Juan's wife Eva our edited list increased to nine names.

By the time we arrived at our office it was almost quitting time for the staff. Suzy went right to her car and left to pick-up Julia. She had promised to take her shopping for some new clothes. When I passed Nancy's desk she handed me about a half-dozen phone messages and my mail. I told her to go home; I wasn't going to return any calls or see anybody until tomorrow morning. I poured myself a cup of coffee and went to my office, shutting the door behind me.

The first thing I did was to write the name of each suspect at the top of a separate sheet of paper. I then added the biographical data that Suzy and I had copied at the library; initially trying to eliminate anything that didn't seem relevant, which I immediately realized was risky because of my limited knowledge of these people. As a result I decided it was safer to include everything we found. I listed their birth dates; their ages in 1953 and 1972; facts about their rise to power; their reported wealth; family information, if any; known enemies; where they were last seen, and by whom; any known health problems, and were they reportedly still alive. And on and on and on. I also knew that even though we had the names of eight notorious people – I had no real evidence identifying any one of them as our mysterious client. Eight sheets of paper filled with names and narrative, all of which could turn out to be total garbage.

I sat there a long time with my eyes closed thinking about what I had just written. No matter how I twisted the facts, I could not fit any of the eight into the mold of our client. Maybe I was totally off base. What if it wasn't one of these eight? What if it was an eccentric but totally honest, tax paying, super-rich industrialist? It was certainly possible. When I opened my eyes I saw that the sun was disappearing below the horizon and my office was dark.

I turned on my desk lamp and spread the eight sheets of paper across my desk. I had stacked all of my earlier notes at the end of the desk, including the notes Trimble had given me, and the notes from my visit to Tampa. I started scanning through Trimble's notes again, but gave up when I realized that I'd found nothing I hadn't seen at least a dozen times before. I was getting absolutely nowhere. My frustration with this crazy puzzle was irritating the hell out of me, and I don't work well or think straight when I'm mad. To make matters worse, my investment of time and money was quickly adding up. Hammel & McQuaid simply couldn't afford much more of this. I'll have to come up with something quickly or drop the whole investigation and walk away. Aside from my annoyance at the prospect of giving up, something else was bothering me. I couldn't put my finger on it, but a nagging little thought was spinning around in the back of my brain. My subconscious was trying to tell me something; a name possibly, or a place – I couldn't tell which. I decided that the best thing to do was to leave the problem here on my desk and go home. It would still be here in the morning.

I got about half way home when I drove past a shopping center. The main store in the row of shops was a K-Mart, or Big-K I think they now call them, with a huge letter 'K' glowing red on the front of the building. The glow seemed to burn a hole through my head like a laser beam, and I immediately knew what my subliminal self was trying so hard to tell me. I made a U-turn at the next jug handle and headed back to my office.

When I reached my desk my feet must have been two feet off the floor. I grabbed my Tampa notes and one of the eight sheets still spread across the desk. Flipping through the notes of my conversation with Maria Sippano I quickly found the two things I was looking for. I then picked up the sheet on which I had written one of the eight biographies just an hour ago. And there it was; it wouldn't have been easier to spot if it was flashing red neon – the name *Kabogian* – smack in the middle of the second paragraph of the biography for the *Shah of Iran*! I slammed my fist on the desk. Damn, how could I have missed something so obvious?

What the biography told me was that years before the Shah was born, his father, Reza Khan, later known as Riza Shah Pahlavi, was the leader of the renegade Cossacks in northern Persia. With little effort Reza Khan and his Cossacks took control of one Persian province after another. In an attempt to gain a strong foothold in the province of Ishfahan, Reza Khan arranged for the marriage of his sister Farrah to a wealthy Ishfahan farmer and land owner by the name of Oram Kabogian. The marriage was a happy one and it greatly benefited Reza Khan. Not long after the marriage Reza marched on Tehran and took over the city. The paragraph concluded by saying that during the ensuing years Farrah bore her husband six children; five daughters and a son. The names of the children were not given, but I'll bet everything I own that the name of one of the daughters was Irena. *Old iron-face!*

The second item contained in the notes from my Tampa trip was Maria's answer to my question about how the client paid Tampa for their services. Maria said that Tampa invoices were sent to a post office box in Miles City, Montana. Payment was always by wire to their bank in Tampa. The money was wired to Tampa from various banks in this country and abroad, including Trimble's bank in London and a bank in Milan, Italy.

I could understand sending invoices to a post office box in New York City, or Chicago, or San Francisco – or even Tampa, but *Miles City, Montana* – it was ludicrous! I got out my road atlas, and when I saw that Miles City had a population of not much more than eight thousand people, and was no more than an hours drive from the Montana ranch Walter had found for the client back in 1972, I knew with certainty that my hunch was right on target. Could it be. . .could it really be that our cunning and phantom client was the *Shah of Iran*? It had to be him – it just flat out had to be! All the pieces of the puzzle suddenly started coming together in my mind; all the things that didn't make sense up to now, inexplicable things that Walter, David and Alex Trimble – not to mention me – couldn't begin to interpret, began to flow together into a brilliant scheme of deception. And all the while the megalomaniac responsible for it all was living on a ranch in Montana, almost under our noses. I was so elated I just had to tell somebody, so I picked up the phone and punched in Suzy's number.

I was staring at the Shah's biography while I waited for Suzy to answer. Before the phone rang twice I was hit with the realization that something was drastically wrong with my conclusion. I quickly hung up the phone and flopped back into my chair. I kept reading and rereading the last paragraph on the piece of paper in my hand. Damn it Cole, you're stupid, I said to myself; how in God's name could the Shah of Iran be the client – he died of cancer back in 1980 – more than eighteen years ago!

I sat at my desk for the next hour trying to reconcile what I knew with what I thought I knew. No matter how I rearranged the facts, everything still pointed to the Shah being our client. But history nullified all of that; the man was dead, and there were probably dozens if not hundreds of witnesses to his death. Could the present resident of the ranch be his son? According to the biography, his son would now be in his late thirties. Was he carrying on his father's legacy? It was certainly possible. Or had somebody else taken over his kingdom in exile? Maybe another relative, or one of the late Shah's associates. While I was thinking I was also doodling on a pad; jotting down dates and the names of people who have been involved in this. I printed the name of the Tampa company in big block letters – THE M. R. SHAW MANAGEMENT GROUP. I printed the name over and over, forward and backward, but nothing new was apparent. It was just a name. I made a list of first names and middle names, beginning with the letters 'M' and 'R', but, again, they were just names – a dozen or more. Then something I hadn't noticed before jumped off the page and smacked me right between the eyes.

Ten minutes later I was convinced that I finally had some of the answers. After another thirty minutes of picking apart and challenging the few conclusions I had reached, I was still convinced I was right. But, unfortunately, there were more than a few questions that remained unanswered, and I knew the only place they could be resolved was Montana.

I really couldn't afford the time for another trip – I was already more than a month behind in my work, but if I didn't go, who would? I saw no point in giving what I had to anybody else; it was too late for that. If I told the local police what I suspect they'd write me off as a nut case. And I couldn't go to the FBI or the CIA. If I was right about their involvement in this from the beginning, I certainly couldn't trust them to help. I might even wind up dead. So, if I want answers, I have to go.

First thing the next morning I called Suzy and Nancy into my office and explained what I had found and what I planned to do. Suzy reacted as I knew she would; turn the whole mess over to the FBI and walk away. She said I was getting involved with people who could destroy us, and she was flat out scared – and probably right. I tried to explain why I couldn't do what she asked, but I don't think I convinced her at all.

I asked Nancy to go to the basement, where our dead files are stored, and pull out everything she could find relating to Walter's 1972 acquisition of the Montana ranch land. Fortunately, our old files are cross-referenced by date as well as alphabetically.

"Also, Nancy," I said. "Check the 1971 and 1972 indexes for any reference to the purchase, and for any mention of David Nesbitt or Trimble's bank. And the same goes for any mention of the Tampa organization."

"I'll gladly do it, Cole, but first I'm going home and change into some old clothes; those files boxes are covered with dust. I'd also like to have a strong back to help move the boxes around – they're pretty heavy."

"I agree, and I'm sorry I didn't think of that. Ask Jimmy or Tom to help."

I then placed a call to Trimble in London. As usual, I had to contend with old imperious Miss Nickleby. She insisted that Mr. Trimble could not be disturbed; he had a busy schedule today and was preparing to leave for a meeting. I told her my name and that I was calling from overseas, and insisted she at least tell him I was on the line. She must have remembered our verbal sparring during our conversations of a few weeks ago, because in less than ten seconds Alex was on the line.

After the usual greeting and small talk about the weather, I gave him a synopsis of what had developed since he and I last spoke, including my trip to Tampa, my interaction with Maria Sippano and Irena Kabojian, and my suspicions about the Shah and the Montana ranch. He really didn't say too much except to express disagreement with my theory on the Shah.

"That's preposterous, Cole. I don't remember when he died, but I know it was a long time ago. Unless it was the hoax of the century, the

Shah is dead. Exactly what makes you think this person in Montana is the Shah?"

"Well, Alex, whether he's now dead or alive, I'm convinced the Shah of Iran was the original owner of the Montana ranch. I can't prove anything yet, but unless it's the coincidence of the century, there's a ton of evidence supporting my suspicion. First, the Kabojian woman in Tampa is Iranian and is apparently a first cousin of the Shah. She's been a major player in this whole scheme since she came to this country in 1953, and I'm sure that year rings a bell with you. Next, there's evidence that Kabojian was the lover of the late Mousa Muzzadin – and you know the story on him. Add to that what Maria Sippano told me; all Tampa invoices to the client for their services are sent to a post office box in a small Montana town, not far from the ranch. And the clincher is something I haven't shared with anybody yet – my spin on the name of the Tampa company. With all of your dealings with them I'm sure you know that their name is the 'M. R. Shaw Management Group.' The problem is – nobody has ever seen Mr. Shaw, or for that matter Mrs. Shaw – if there is such a person. And this goes back to 1953, the year the company was founded. 1953 Alex, another bell ringer!

"Last night I was sitting at my desk thinking about all the possibilities, all the probabilities, and I was doodling on a piece of paper at the same time. I was substituting names for each of the 'M. R.' initials. I was also playing around with the name 'Shaw.' And guess what I came up with? Try changing the name 'Shaw' to 'Shah.' Now plug in 'Mohammed Reza' for the initials 'M. R.' – and what do you have? How about Mohammed Reza Shah, or more commonly, the Shah of Iran! To be completely correct the name Pahlavi must be added to his title, as in Mohammed Reza Shah Pahlavi. The Pahlavi name was handed down to him by his father; it was apparently the place where his father was born.

"For the first time since David was killed I feel I'm on to something. The reason I called you is because I wanted to find out how your liquidation effort is coming, and also to let you know that I'm going to Montana as soon as possible. I'm convinced that everything we've uncovered so far leads to that Montana ranch. If my suspicions are correct, and I can find some proof, all hell could break loose. I have no idea how it'll end, but it's possible that Mr. Shah and his little empire just might find themselves out of business. Maybe worse. And, if I'm also right about how that empire has remained invisible for so many years, there's going to be egg on a lot of faces in two or three Washington agencies."

"Whoa, Cole, let's back up for a moment. If your suspicions are correct, do you have any idea what kind of hornet's nest you'll be walking into? I'd say you're going to be in extreme danger. You could be killed!"

"I know the risk, Alex, but let's suppose I don't go and next month or next year somebody else disappears or is killed, how will you and I feel? If it's somebody close to me I know I couldn't live with myself – not having been this close to a possible solution. I may be getting involved in a modern day David and Goliath battle, but I have to try. Does it really make any difference if the Shah is dead like the history books say? I think not. I don't care if it's his son, or another relative, or some flunky from his Iranian monarchy – I'm convinced it all started with the Shah and still revolves around him or his successor. I've got to find out."

"Well, I guess trying to dissuade you would be futile. Is there anything I can do to help?"

"As a matter of fact there is. It's another reason I called. I'm trying to put together as much information as possible on the purchase of the Montana property back in 1972. I don't know if anything new will surface, but I can't chance overlooking something that might help me. I'm sure your records contain a lot more detail than ours, particularly on the final stages of the purchase. I'd appreciate it if you would look over what you have and E-mail to me anything you think is important."

"I'd be glad to do that. I'll have the file brought up to me immediately. How soon will you leave for Montana?"

"I hope to leave the day after tomorrow, but that depends on a couple of things. I haven't been able to spend enough time in the office recently and completion of two of our projects has fallen behind. The result is we have two very unhappy clients. I also need to decide what I'm going to do in Montana – and how to go about it. I can't afford to waste time, so that's why I need to learn as much as possible about the purchase and what happened in 1972. Any idea how soon you can send me what you have?"

"The time-consuming effort will be sorting through the file. I doubt if I'll find more than a few pages worth considering, but I'll have Margaret our computer technician stay here as long as it takes to scan and send what I do find. You should have everything before the end of the day – your time that is.

"Before I ring off – you asked about our liquidation effort. I'm pleased to say it is about ninety percent complete. We were able to sell most of the notes at a very favorable rate, actually much better than I thought we would. I'm confident that we could now survive any type of hit the client might throw at us. I'm sleeping much better again. I hope your trip to Montana doesn't change that, so please be careful. And please keep me informed about what is going on."

"I'll do that, Alex. And, likewise, if anything major develops at your end while I'm in Montana, please let my partner Suzy know immediately. I'll be checking in with her from time to time."

After I hung up I called our travel agent to check on airline connections between Philly and Montana. When I explained to her where I wanted to go she said she'd check with the airlines and call me back. Fifteen minutes later she called back to tell me that she could get me there, but I'd have to change planes in Chicago, fly to Billings and then get a shuttle flight to Miles City. With layovers the whole trip would take about seven hours. I could pick up a four-wheel drive SUV rental in Miles City, and spend another hour or so getting to my destination. I definitely was not looking forward to this trip, particularly after she gave me my choices of motels and restaurants.

Nancy walked into my office just before lunch, looking a bit dusty and disheveled. The look on her face told me she was anything but her good-natured self. She cradled three manila folders which she plopped on my desk.

"I hope I never have to go in that room again," she said. "Not only is it creepy, but there are spiders – and you know how I hate spiders."

"I'll tell you what Nancy; go wash up and get Suzy and I'll take you both out to lunch."

"You're just trying to bribe me now," she said, doing her best to appear serious. "Ten lunches won't get me in that room again – but since you offered, I'll go get Suzy. And she and I get to pick where we eat, O.K.?"

"Fair enough," I said, laughing. "And I'll tell you what; I won't ask you to go down there again – at least not until tomorrow."

With an infectious grin back on her face she turned and stuck her tongue out at me as she left my office.

While I waited for them I looked through the three files. There were quite a few notes in Walter's handwriting, plus about a dozen letters and memos in the first folder. The second folder contained nothing but photographs marked in red wax pencil to correspond with notations on three large survey prints, yellowed with age, contained in the last folder. I unfolded them carefully because they had started to disintegrate. The surveys covered an area of slightly more than seventy-two hundred acres and contained a lot of scribbled notes in Walter's hand. They also showed the site's topography, reflecting the gently rolling terrain indicated in most of the photographs. The last folder also contained a copy of a geology report covering eight test wells that had been bored in various locations around the property. At first glance it looked like there was plenty of good water. In addition, the Powder River coursed for almost a half-mile through the southeastern corner of the property. I carefully refolded the survey prints and put them in a large envelope. I wrote a note reminding myself to get copies made at the repro company that does our printing. The information on the surveys might prove very helpful in finding my way around the site.

We went to Nancy's favorite place for lunch, which I usually avoid because it's known as Cholesterol City. Nancy had a bacon burger with cheese, fries and an ice cream soda. Suzy and I had soup and a salad – with a diet soda. I love to tease Nancy, so I told a couple of my favorite spider stories while we ate. Nancy cringed between bites of her burger and Suzy finally asked me to stop. I don't think Suzy likes spiders either.

The E-mail from London came through about four o'clock. Alex had kept his word. Other than copies of the sales agreement, deed and settlement papers, plus copies of correspondence between David and Tampa, there wasn't anything I considered helpful. A note from Alex said this was it. When combined with what I had found in Walter's files all I really had was background information. I knew where the property was; its size and terrain, and how much it cost the client – but very little else.

I called Kelly, my travel agent, and told her to go ahead and book my flights for the day after tomorrow, and reserve the SUV for me in Miles City. I also told her to forget the room reservation; I've been burned before with blind reservations, so I'll scout the area for something decent looking and chance finding a vacancy.

I spent most of the afternoon going over bid estimates with Joe and catching up on paperwork. Suzy stuck her head in my office around five and invited me to dinner at her place. The thought of a long evening with Suzy sounded very inviting, but I knew I needed a full day in the office tomorrow, plus another three or four hours tonight. So we compromised – Suzy ordered Chinese and we had a buffet dinner at my desk. I kissed her goodnight around seven and she left for home to fix Julia's dinner. I got home in time to grab a cold beer and watch the late news on TV.

By seven the following morning I was back in my office, and spent the entire day at my desk. I sent Nancy to pick-up my plane tickets and traveler's checks at the travel agency. When she returned she brought me a deli sandwich and a diet soda, which I ate at my desk. It seemed only minutes later when my phone rang and I realized it was after six o'clock and all of the staff had gone home. I picked up the phone and it was Suzy. In a breathless imitation of Marilyn Monroe she invited me to her place for dinner and whatever. I told her dinner sounded great, but I'd take a rain check on the whatever because I had a seven thirty-five flight to catch the following morning. I'm going to have to practice self-discipline, because after a delicious spaghetti dinner Suzy and I enjoyed more than an hour of whatever. I justified my lack of will-power by saying I'd sleep on the plane.

CHAPTER ELEVEN

I was wrong about sleeping on the plane. My definition of sleeping in the air is to be lulled into a semi-conscious stupor by the harmonics of the engines. My eyes are closed and I still hear sounds around me, but it's like a wide black void exists between me and the sound. Sometimes I can open my eyes and be instantly awake. Other times it takes a while for me to climb out of the darkness.

By the time the attendants collected the breakfast trays we had run into quite a bit of turbulence. I refastened my seat belt, put my chin on my chest, and closed my eyes. I had a window seat, and I no sooner closed my eyes when the four year old seated between me and her mother decided to make life miserable for everybody around her. She refused to be restrained by the seat belt – her mother must have re-buckled it at least six times. The kid stood on her seat, jumped on her seat, annoyed the people ahead of us and behind us and, when the attendant told the mother that the child must sit in her seat, with the seat belt buckled, the kid threw a temper tantrum unlike any I have ever seen. For more than a half-hour she kicked her feet, flailed her arms at her mother, and yelled. And I mean loud. What really irked me was the way the mother seemed to accept it as normal behavior. The frustrated attendant tried bribing the kid with a cup of juice and a worn teddy bear, missing one eye that she probably keeps on board for such emergencies. Clutching the teddy bear, the kid finally calmed down and fell asleep more than an hour out of Philly. I suspect the attendant never got her teddy bear back.

The second leg of my flight – without the kid and her mother, who apparently were headed elsewhere – was much quieter, and I actually did cat-nap. When we landed in Billings it was raining hard. Packing light with one carry-on bag, I hadn't brought a raincoat, so by the time I located my commuter flight to Miles City and got on board I was a very wet and unhappy camper.

It was still raining when we landed at the Miles City Municipal Airport, but with a little bobbing and weaving I found the car rental counter without getting any wetter. My SUV was ready and waiting, and the very pleasant clerk asked if I had ever been to Miles City before. When I told her I hadn't even been in Montana before, she handed me a state map, plus a map of Custer County and a pamphlet of local restaurants, motels and hotels. I asked where I could get a good deli sandwich and she recommended a place on the outskirts of the city.

It was almost three in the afternoon at home, but it was two hours earlier here, and I was famished. I made one or two wrong turns but finally found the deli the clerk recommended. My corned-beef on rye was nice and lean and came complete with potato salad, dill pickle and pickled green tomatoes. While I ate I spread out the map of Custer County and tried to find the most direct route to where I had to go. The back of the map showed the counties surrounding Custer. Comparing the two maps it was obvious that Route 59 south was the best choice. But before I left I had some business to attend to here in Miles City. I also wanted to spend the night here; it was about a three hour drive to where I was headed and I didn't have any idea what I'd find when I got there. The thought of arriving in some god-forsaken wilderness after dark didn't appeal to me at all.

My first stop was a post office. The old guy behind the counter was busy waiting on the people ahead of me. He seemed to be on a first-name basis with most of them, and when my turn came he raised an eyebrow and said, "You new here, young fella; don't remember seein' you in here before?"

"As a matter of fact, I am," I replied. "I'm from Kentucky," I lied, "And I breed thoroughbred horses. A friend of mine told me about a big place south of here that has some select stock I may be interested in. I don't know the name of the ranch, but I think it's owned by a guy named Shaw."

"Oh yeh, I know the place. It's called the Diamond 27, and it is big – also damned strange. I don't know first-hand, but the son of a friend of mine worked there as a cook for about six months. Said he probably asked too many questions, 'cause one day they fired him, led him to the main gate and told him to git."

"Do you know anybody who still works there?" I asked.

"No – 'cept for the lady who comes here to pick up their mail. She's in here about twice a week, but I don't really know her. She's a real sourpuss – never smiles. She's also some kinda furriner – black hair, dark eyes and skin; speaks with an accent – hard to understand. She could be an A-rab or somethin'."

"You say she's in here a couple times a week? What do they have – a post-office box?"

"Yep. They have a drawer – a big one. It's full most of the time, too."

"When was she here last, and what time does she usually get here?"

"Let's see, it was two, mebbe three days ago. She'll probably be back again tomorrow, and she's always in and out of here by ten."

"Do you know what kind of car she drives?"

"It's some kinda van – I don't know the make. Say, young fella, you sure ask a lot of danged questions. Why you so interested in their mail?"

"I'm not, really. Like I said, I may do some business with them and I like to know who I'm dealing with. Particularly when they're total strangers."

"Well, like a told ya, I've heard some mighty strange stories about the place, so I'd be real careful."

"I intend to be. And thanks for the information."

I drove around town for almost an hour, just to see what Miles City had to offer. I also wanted to find a place to stay and decent places to eat. I was almost ready to give up when I found a small and very neat looking motel about five minutes drive from Route 59. The owner checked me in and also recommended two places to eat, one a diner and the other a tavern, both within walking distance. I locked my gear in the motel room and took off again in my car.

The car radio was giving the five-day weather forecast, and it didn't sound good. It was the first week of October and the day temperatures had been in the high sixties for five or six days. They said a cold front was going to move through the area tonight, bringing rain and much colder weather. I had no intention of getting soaked again, so I drove to a run-down looking Army and Navy surplus store that I had passed earlier. I bought a few things I thought I might need, including binoculars, a compass, a powerful flashlight, a heavy wool sweater, boots, and a poncho with a hood. I might not look too sharp, but I'd be warm and dry.

I drove back to the motel and decided to take a nap. As I lay on the bed, staring at the ceiling, all of the doubts and questions about my trip here began spinning in my head. My earlier good ideas and planning notwithstanding, what the hell was I doing here? What did I hope to accomplish? Even if I satisfied myself that Shaw was in fact the Shah of Iran, what should I do next? What could I do next? Based on the past violence, if I asked the wrong individuals the wrong questions I could get my head blown off. Maybe I should go home and have my head examined before that happens. No, damn it, I'm here and I'm going to see this through. But what do I do next, and what do I have to work with? The reality of the situation is; all I have to work with is my knowledge of the past and a picture of the Shah taken about a year before he supposedly died – so it's obvious I'm gonna have to play my hand one card at a time. I decided that if I can get a first-hand look at the ranch, and also convince myself that Mr. Shaw is the Shah, I'll go home. I knew that once I get home the tough part will be convincing somebody in authority that I'm right. I also knew that it wouldn't be Ben's FBI friend Hamilton, or, for that matter, anybody else in Washington. I don't trust any of them. I finally dozed off and it was almost six when I awoke. I quickly showered and dressed because I hoped to catch the motel owner before he left for the day – maybe pick his brain to see if he knew anything about the Diamond 27 ranch.

Other than my SUV, the parking lot was deserted. The owner was seated on a stool behind the counter, flipping through pages of a boating magazine, sipping a mug of steaming coffee. He offered me a cup, which I accepted. He put the magazine down and seemed anxious to talk – I guess the poor guy was bored to death; I know I would be. They couldn't pay me enough to sit and watch these four walls for fourteen to sixteen hours a day, as I'm sure he did. I tried making small talk by telling him a little about my phony business. His name was George, and he admitted to being a little older than me and said he had been born and raised in a small town just north of the city. I found him to be very articulate and extremely knowledgeable about Montana and, in particular, Custer County. He and his wife had bought the motel about six years ago. They couldn't survive on what they cleared from the place, so she went back to work as a nurse for a doctor in town. George said he had been a school teacher but had to give it up to run the motel. He also said the motel had been up for sale for almost three years, and he and his wife would accept any fair offer. Problem was, as soon as potential buyers saw the books they were scared off.

I gradually turned the conversation to why I was in Montana, and gave him the same scenario I had used at the post office. Without any prompting he voiced the same views as the old guy at the post office when I mentioned the Diamond 27 Ranch.

"George, have you ever had any personal involvement with anybody from the ranch? Have you ever been to the place?"

"I've driven past the place dozens of times, but I only stopped near the place once, about seven or eight years ago. It was a real scary experience. A friend and I were headed south of the ranch to do some hunting. We were on government property about a mile from the ranch. At dusk we pitched our tent and started to cook supper when a 4-wheel drive pickup with the ranch's name on the doors came barreling into our camp. Two guys in uniform got out and told us we had to leave immediately – we were on private property. They both had uniforms and sidearms. My friend told them we weren't on ranch property, it was government land, and said he had no intention of leaving. One of the two kicked the stakes out of the ground and pulled down our tent. The other kicked dirt on the fire and stomped it out. My buddy shoved the guy and got pistol-whipped for his trouble. I tried pulling the guy off my friend and wound up getting some of the same. They told us they'd be back in a half-hour, and if we were still there we'd be shot as trespassers."

"Were you really trespassing – what happened next?"

"We weren't trespassing, absolutely not! But we were scared, so we gathered up our gear and left. About five minutes later we passed a police patrol car parked on the shoulder. We stopped and told the cop what happened. He took down our names and addresses and said he'd look into it. Before he pulled away he told us to think twice before signing any kind of complaint against the ranch guards or the owner. He said others had tried it and their cases always got thrown out of court. The cop wouldn't come right out and say so, but he hinted that the ranch owner had all the local judges in his hip pocket. The owner always claimed that he had millions tied up in his prize breeding stock and thoroughbreds and couldn't risk one being killed by some off-site hunter. In essence, he didn't give two damns where his property lines were."

We talked for another ten minutes or so, but George knew little more about the Diamond 27. I decided to walk the three blocks to the tavern George recommended earlier. The building had a lot of neon out front and a blinking red neon sign in a large blacked-out front window that proclaimed the place to be Rockies Bar & Grill. The menu posted in the window indicated a diner-size assortment of choices.

A waitress seated me at a small table in the dining room adjoining the bar. The dining room was non-smoking, but the bar wasn't; obvious by the blue-gray haze that permeated the room. The majority of customers were apparently smokers – the bar was packed, but the dining room had about a dozen empty tables. I knew I had made a good choice when I sat down and found a bowl of oyster crackers and a pot of horseradish; something I can easily spoil my appetite with. When the waitress came back I ordered a mug of one of their local draught beers to wash down the extra hot appetizer. When that was gone I ordered a small Caesar salad, chicken pot-pie and another mug of beer. The beer was cold, the salad was so-so – too heavy on the lemon – but the pot-pie was excellent; lots of chicken and veggies under a thick but flaky crust. I topped everything off with apple pie and coffee.

I was just finishing when a young guy in coveralls came in and sat down at a table a few feet away. He ordered a double boilermaker and a bowl of chili. What caught my eye was the logo on the breast pocket of his coveralls; the number 27 in green on a yellow background, contained within a silver diamond outline. Beneath that, in script, was the name 'Jerry'. He seemed extremely agitated. Before his order came he sat with his face buried in his hands. I wasn't sure what kind of reaction I'd get, but I decided to try striking up a conversation with him.

"I see you're from the Diamond 27," I said. "I'm headed there tomorrow to look at some breeding stock I might consider buying. I hear they have the best stock west of the Mississippi." I sure hope Jerry doesn't ask too many questions, because I can't tell a Jersey cow from a Brahma bull.

"I used to be with the Diamond 27," he replied. "But not any more. The bastards fired me this morning." He spoke slowly and deliberately, his voice cold with bitterness.

"I was there going on twelve years. . .started as a stable boy cleaning stalls, and worked my way up to trainer. I trained some of the best thoroughbreds ever to leave the ranch. I figure they netted about twenty million just from stock I raised and trained."

"If that's the case why would they fire you?"

"I'll tell you why. I did what was right and the son-of-a-bitch head trainer canned me for it. I guess I shouldn't be too surprised; he and I never got along anyway. He was always bitching about something. I knew sooner or later we'd lock horns."

"Twelve years is a long time Jerry. If he didn't like you why didn't he fire you sooner?"

"He's only had the job for less than a year. Before they promoted him he was a regular trainer like me. I think his new title went to his head. He doesn't get along with any of the other trainers either. They all think he's arrogant and an ass kisser with the owner."

"So what was this so-called right thing he fired you for?"

"What the hell's the difference. . .I'm out of a job. Got a wife, two kids and a big mortgage. You realize how tough it is to find work around here? I was making damn good money – now I'll probably end up flipping burgers in some fast food joint, and lose my house to boot! I worked my ass off for that ranch and what the hell did it get me – nothing!"

"I'd still like to know what they fired you for."

"I dunno what business it is of yours, but like I said, I did what was right. One of the horses in my stable is the ranch owner's favorite – a beautiful, big white Arabian. His name's Cossack and he's one of the fastest horses on the ranch. The owner, Mr. Shaw, rides him three or four times a week. The last time he had him out, the day before yesterday, he was riding him hard when Cossack stepped in a hole and went down hard. He didn't break anything, but he did twist his right foreleg pretty bad. Mr. Shaw was smart enough to walk Cossack back to the stable. I did what I could to treat and wrap Cossack's leg, but I knew it would take time to heal. . . at least a couple of weeks or so, and that's with the right treatment and a lot of luck.

"Well, this morning the jackass manager comes to me and tells me that Mr. Shaw wants me to get Cossack ready; he wants to ride out and inspect some of his grazing stock. I told the manager no way; riding Cossack now could do permanent damage. The manager left, but was back ten minutes later. He said Mr. Shaw thought I was exaggerating and said to saddle Cossack immediately. I again refused – and you know the rest."

I had a decision to make – and fast. I knew Jerry could be a big help to me, so do I tell him why I'm really here? In view of his situation and present state of mind he just might agree to help. On the other hand, if he blows the whistle on me, thinking maybe it could get his job back, I'd be in deep trouble.

I decided to buy him another drink and try to keep him here as long as possible. It might not be too difficult because I suspected the last thing Jerry wanted to do was go home and face his wife and kids.

After finishing his chili and boilermaker, followed by a second and a third drink, Jerry seemed to mellow. The anger had faded from his voice and he now spoke in a quiet, slurred monotone.

"I'm a damn good trainer. . .probably their best. . .their gonna miss me. . .wait an see. . .you need a good trainer, mister?"

"Only if you're willing to move to Kentucky," I replied, feeling guilty about lying. "But first I need you to look at something."

I took the picture of the Shah out of my pocket and slid it in front of him. "Ever seen this guy before?"

"Hmmm, lemme see," he said, holding the picture up to the light. "Yeh. . .looks a lot like Mr. Shaw, 'cept Shaw has a bushy mustache and longer hair. This guy a relative of Mr. Shaw?"

Before I answered I decided to go for broke. I wasn't sure how it would play out, but with Jerry's knowledge of the ranch he could save me a lot of time, and maybe keep me out of trouble.

"Jerry," I replied, "What they did to you was rotten. Maybe you'd get some satisfaction out of helping me tomorrow."

"What do ya mean, help you? At the ranch? I never wanna see the place again. Besides, I'm gonna have one helluva hangover come tomorrow."

"Let me explain before you say no. To begin with, I'm not a horse breeder from Kentucky, so I'm not here to buy horses. I am an investigator from New Jersey, and my target is your Mr. Shaw. If I'm right, he isn't who you think he is, not by a long shot. He's an international figure who is hiding from his countrymen and the law. He's also a fugitive criminal because he's responsible, either directly or indirectly for the deaths of at least seven people we know of. And, if his reputation is accurate, he also has the blood of God knows how many others on his hands. I won't bother you with all the details unless you agree to help me. What do you say?"

"Whoa, man, you got my head spinning. . . you say old man Shaw is a criminal? Most of the workers at the ranch think he's a pain in the ass, a senile old fart . . . but a criminal – a murderer . . . nah, can't be. Besides, what the hell could I do to help you – like I said, I never wanna see the place again – the bastards screwed me. . .royally. . . I need 'nother drink."

"Jerry, it may be hard to understand, but what I'm telling you is the truth. And it's worth two hundred bucks to me to have your help tomorrow. As far as your hangover is concerned, no more booze tonight, let's switch to coffee."

"Before I decide, tell me watcha want me to do."

"Fair enough. All I want is for you to go with me. You can wait in the SUV while I try getting in the main entrance. I'll use the same line I gave you – I'm there to buy horse flesh. If they don't let me in I'll want you to show me how to get on the property without being seen. You say you worked there for twelve years, so you must know places where you can get in and out without alerting the guards. That's all I need you for. Okay? And by the way, my name's Cole, Cole McQuaid."

"I dunno, Cole, those guards are mean bastards . . . I know at least one's a psycho . . .we could wind up dead. First thing, they're gonna search you and go through your SUV from bumper to bumper . . . won't let you through the gate without a search. So I can't go near the main entrance in your SUV. I know a place where you can drop me off to wait for you. If you don't get past the guards you'll have to come back and pick me up . . . and another thing, two hundred bucks don't cut it. I ain't risking my neck for less than four hundred."

"Three's as far as I'll go, Jerry, take it or leave it."

"I dunno, whole thing sounds kinda crazy to me. . .god knows I need the money. . .wife's gonna be sick when she hears I got canned . . .well, O.K., but I want the money up front. . .and in cash."

"I'll give you half before we leave and the other half when we finish. Be here at Rockies tomorrow morning at seven; I'll pick you up. And you better come dressed for bad weather; it's supposed to turn nasty tomorrow afternoon. And another thing; don't say anything to your wife about getting fired, at least not until after tomorrow. It'll only complicate things for you. Let her think you're going to work as usual."

We each had coffee. I sat and waited while Jerry had a second mug, plus two trips to the men's room. I wanted to get back to my motel, but I decided to wait until I was convinced he was sober enough to drive. I sure didn't want him killing himself driving home.

It was almost eleven when I got back to my room. I had to call Suzy. I was sure she was asleep because it was one in the morning at home, but she fooled me when she answered on the first ring. Turned out she was reading in bed waiting for my call.

"Hi, Suzy, it's me. How's everything at home?"

"Everything's fine. I was waiting for your call. Where are you now?"

"I'm calling from my motel room. Just wanted to let you know everything is O.K. It's good to hear your voice."

"Have you been able to find out anything?"

"Only that I'm more convinced than ever that our guy is who I think he is. But I've got to be totally sure before I come home. I'm going to the ranch tomorrow morning; supposedly to buy some thoroughbreds. If I satisfy myself that I'm right about him, I'll be heading home on the first flight out of here."

"I hope so, Cole. I'm really concerned about what you're doing. Actually I'm terrified. . . can't you get the proof you need without going to the ranch? It seems to me that you'll be walking into a hornet's nest."

"Maybe so, Suzy, but I don't know how to get what I need without doing it myself; I have to be sure. Otherwise, if I blow the whistle on this guy publicly and it turns out I'm wrong, I'll be labeled as some kind of nut. I hope you understand – I've got to go."

"I do understand, but that doesn't lessen my concern . . . it only makes me worry more. Just be careful . . . and promise me you won't try to be a hero. Remember, all you're trying to do is confirm his identity. Let the authorities do the rest. I miss you and need you back here safe and sound. When do you think you'll be home?"

"If everything goes O.K., probably the day after tomorrow. But it'll be late before I get into Philly."

"Will you call me tomorrow night and let me know how things went?"

"I will, but it'll probably be late in the evening, like tonight."

"I don't care what time it is, just call. I need to know you're all right."

I promised her I wouldn't try anything heroic and that I would call, told her I loved her, and hung up. Before I went to bed I got my gear together for tomorrow morning. I decided to play the part of a successful horse breeder and dress accordingly; complete with tweed jacket, snap-brim cap and my scuffed leather briefcase, containing some fictitious papers I had put together yesterday back in my office. All my other gear, including everything I bought here earlier today, plus my 35mm camera and 400mm telephoto lens, I stowed in a duffel bag that I intended leaving with Jerry, when I dropped him off at his hidey-hole. When I finally turned out the light and crawled into bed, I was asleep even before I moved to my favorite sleeping position; it had been a long day.

I was up at six the next morning. I loaded everything into the SUV and headed to a diner about a half-mile from Rockies. It wasn't raining yet, but the wind-driven low clouds looked ominous. And it was much colder than yesterday. I had orange juice, coffee, and a grilled cinnamon bun. By five of seven I was parked in front of Rockies, but there was no sign of Jerry. By quarter after seven I began to doubt that he would show. I got my Montana map out and began plotting my route south. I was just about to pull out and be on my way when Jerry arrived in a battered pickup truck, full of body cancer and minus the front bumper and left headlight. He was wearing camouflaged army fatigues, a baseball cap and hunting boots. He was carrying a large metal thermos and a gym bag.

"G'morning Cole," he mumbled in a raspy voice. "I must be nuts for doin' this. If I didn't need the money I'd tell you to go pound sand. You still gonna go through with it?"

"Absolutely. Throw your bag in the back and lets get going."

I pulled away from the curb and handed Jerry four fifties. "Here's the money; you'll get the rest when we get back here tonight."

"Thanks – I hope I live to spend it."

"Relax, and don't be such a pessimist. All I'm going to do is offer to buy some horses and, if I'm lucky, get a good look at your Mr. Shaw. I certainly don't intend doing anything stupid. And the quicker we get it over with the better I'll like it. How long should it take us to get there?"

"It usually takes me a little over an hour. You can double that in winter, when there's a lot of snow or the roads ice up. It's not cold enough to snow, but that sky out there looks like some heavy weather is on the way. Did you bring any food?"

"No. Are there any decent places to eat where we're headed?"

"Not really. There's a mini-market that makes good sandwiches about five miles down the road. Beyond that there's a couple places with lousy food. But once you get within ten miles of the ranch there ain't nothin'."

We stopped at the mini-market and bought sandwiches, some fruit, canned soda and a cheap styrofoam cooler to keep everything in. The sky ahead of us and to the west was black with storm clouds. We no sooner got back on the road when the rain started, light at first, and then the sky opened and it was like driving through a waterfall. The torrential rain continued for almost thirty miles. Twice I had to stop on the shoulder because the windshield wipers couldn't keep up.

If my 'Plan A' worked, I'd be inside and the storm wouldn't matter. If it didn't, and I had to switch to 'Plan B', my fallback scheme, I'd be slogging across God knows what kind of terrain, exposed to whatever Mother Nature was dishing out.

"Jerry, I need you to describe the ranch to me; particularly the roads in and out, where the main house is located, and the guard situation. I also need to know where you're going to be and where to pick you up."

"O.K. we still have about twenty miles to go. When we get there you'll see a two-lane road angling off to the right. You'll also see a large yellow and black sign the says 'Private Property – No Trespassing'. We're gonna continue past that road about a mile and we'll come to a rutted dirt trail. That's where you'll drop me off. The trail disappears into a grove of trees about five hundred yards in. On the other side of the trees is an electrified fence, and on the other side of the fence is a line shack with bunks and a cook stove for the range hands. The shack is used only in the winter, but it's too early in the year, so nobody should be there. The dirt trail is used to bring in supplies for the range hands. I'll be waitin' in the line shack."

"That's fine, but how the hell are you going to know when I'm ready to leave? You realize I could be in one helluva hurry!"

"Sure, but all you have to do is drive up the trail until you see the shack and then honk your horn. There's space to turn around and we can be off and running. Besides, I don't think you're gonna get in to see Mr. Shaw, so you're gonna have to drive to the line shack to get on ranch property – assumin' that's what you still wanna do after those people scare the crap outa you. I still don't see how comin' back to the line shack is gonna help you see Mr. Shaw."

"It may not, but if you're right and I don't get in the main gate, getting on the ranch at the line shack is my only hope. If that doesn't work, my trip here is a total bust."

"Problem is, Cole, the main house is quite a distance from the line shack, and most of the terrain is open grazing land. Some of it's a little hilly, but the house is surrounded by about two-hundred yards of dead-flat grass. There's a few trees around the house and about a half-dozen outbuildings some distance away, but that's it. There aint many places to hide."

"You said earlier that Shaw likes to ride his horse. Any chance he'll be out riding today? Does he ever come near the line shack?"

"He rides all over. But I don't know if Cossack can be ridden yet. He might ride another horse, but either way I'd say you got a fifty-fifty chance he'll ride today."

"That's better than no chance at all, so I guess we'll have to wait and see what happens."

It was still raining hard when we passed the entrance road to the ranch. When we came to the trail into the line shack I turned in and drove to the small turn-around, with the electric fence just beyond. It seemed a lot more than five-hundred yards from the main road, which was now totally hidden by underbrush on both sides of the trail. The line shack was barely visible, hidden by trees and more underbrush. Jerry took his stuff and my duffel bag, went under the fence wire, and disappeared into the brush. I waited a few minutes to make sure he didn't come back and then drove slowly back to the main road. With heavy rain still coming down I was concerned about churning up the dirt trail. The last thing I needed was to get stuck.

Back on the main road, I headed north to the entrance road into the ranch. I turned in and drove past the sign Jerry told me about; "PRIVATE PROPERTY – NO TRESPASSING" and continued for almost a mile on a well maintained two-lane paved road. The road snaked its way through thick stands of pine, oak and evergreen, then abruptly widened to four lanes, with nose-in parking for about a dozen cars off to the right. A large yellow and black sign said "THE DIAMOND 27 RANCH – ALL VISITORS PARK HERE AND REPORT TO GUARD HOUSE – PARKING BY APPOINTMENT ONLY" I wasn't sure what appointment parking meant, but I parked anyway, checked my appearance one more time in the rear-view mirror, grabbed my briefcase and sprinted the fifty yards or so to the guardhouse. The rain was still heavy.

The guard house was one of the most sophisticated I have ever seen. It was brick, with a metal roof and large windows across the front. You could fit most three-bedroom ranchers inside the place. Behind the building was a tall free-standing communications tower. Electric security gates blocked both the entrance and exit roads. When I opened the side door and walked in there were two uniformed guards seated on an elevated platform behind a chin-high counter. The wall opposite them was lined with television monitors, each showing a different scene. I recognized my SUV on one of the screens. Every few seconds the scenes on the screens would change. Secured to the wall below the monitors was a large display board containing what appeared to be a map of the entire ranch. It was divided into zones, and each zone contained flashing red and green lights. Each green light had a number below it. One glance told me the number visible on the screen of each monitor corresponded with the numbered green light on the display board. When the picture on a monitor changed, a new number appeared; the green light for the previous picture went out and the corresponding red light came on.

These bastards had taken a seventy-two hundred acre property and turned it into a giant outdoor television studio. They obviously had something invaluable to protect – or something major to hide. Maybe both.

"Yes *sir*, and who might you be here to see?" the guard closest to me asked. His tone was what I always labeled chip-on-the-shoulder-sarcasm, like an underling responding to a superior, but with absolutely no sincerity or respect.

"I'd like to speak to someone about purchasing two horses – two thoroughbreds," I responded.

"I repeat *sir*, who are you here to see?" he snapped at me, his voice an irritating monotone.

"I would like to see the ranch owner or, at the very least, the ranch manager. I flew in to Miles City yesterday from my ranch in Kentucky. I was told you have some of the best breeding stock in the country. That's why I'm here."

"And, *sir*, do I understand that you don't have an appointment?"

"No. I didn't think an appointment was necessary."

"Well, you thought wrong, sir. The owner, Mr. Shaw, doesn't see any-body without an appointment. The ranch superintendent, Mr. Carson, is off the ranch today on business. So I guess you're out of luck, *sir*."

The guard was apparently in his early twenties and badly needed a course in public relations, not to mention good manners. It suddenly dawned on me that between this kid and old 'Iron-Face Irena' back in Tampa, the whole organization needed retraining. I seldom lose my temper when dealing with people, but something about this guy really ticked me off. On the other hand, I didn't want to jeopardize my reason for being here, so the little voice in my head flip-flopped about four times in two seconds. My temper won out, and I decided to give him a dose of his own disrespect.

"Wait a minute, *boy*," I snapped back. "I didn't come all the way from Kentucky to be turned around by a gate keeper in a Boy Scout uniform. I suggest you immediately call the owner and tell him I'd like to meet with him. I'll need about fifteen minutes of his time. Better yet, get him on the phone and I'll tell him. You got that?"

"Don't call me boy, *sir* – and this is not a Boy Scout uniform. My name is Karl Seitz – and that's Karl with a 'K'. I'm in charge of security for the ranch, and unless I have specific orders from Mr. Shaw, I'm the one who decides who gets past that security gate. And without an appointment, nobody – and I mean *nobody* does! Also, for your information, each of my men is licensed to carry a gun, and is authorized to use it. Get my drift, *sir*?"

"Damn right – and your security operation here doesn't impress me one little bit. Like I just said; get Mr. Shaw on the phone and let me talk to him."

"I'll call him, but I can guarantee he won't see you. In the meantime fill out this questionnaire." He slid a clipboard across the counter to me.

"I'm not here looking for a job," I replied, glancing at the form. "All I want is to buy two horses."

He glared at me. "Nobody gets on the ranch without first filling out the questionnaire; helps us keep out the triflers and particularly the troublemakers." He leaned closer to me across the counter and glared again. You got a choice, *sir*, either fill out the form or get back in your vehicle and leave."

I grabbed the clipboard and started filling in the information. Seitz watched me write and made no attempt to call Shaw. When I finished I slid the clipboard back to him. He glanced at the form and still made no attempt to call Shaw. "So you're from Kentucky," he said. "You didn't fill out the rest of your address; what part of Kentucky you from?"

I had to think fast. A friend of my father bought a small farm in Kentucky when I was a kid. My folks took the family there one summer for a few days. It's where I learned to ride a horse. "My place is out in the country, about halfway between Louisville and Elizabethtown, three miles off Interstate 65."

"You sure don't talk like any Kentuckian I've ever met. How long you lived there?"

"About four years. I'm originally from New Jersey."

"I knew you weren't from Kentucky. What other information you holding back, sir?"

"You've got all the information you need. Like I said, I want to buy two horses; I'm not trying to sell you or Mr. Shaw anything. Now what the hell's your problem. Either get him on the phone or I'll take my business somewhere else."

He finally picked up the phone and punched-in an extension number. I don't know who answered; I could only hear this end of the conversation, but by the tone of his voice I knew Seitz wasn't talking to Shaw, and I also knew my chances of seeing Shaw were slim to none. Seitz hung up the phone and told me that Shaw was checking a newborn colt in one of his stables, and wasn't available.

"I don't mind waiting," I said. "I have nowhere to go but home, so I think I'll stick around until he returns."

"I think not, *sir*. Strangers make Mr. Shaw very nervous. Our standing orders are to never admit anyone except employees, approved vendors, and people who have made an appointment. And they have to be escorted to their destination on the ranch. In addition, your vehicle is parked illegally – parking is reserved exclusively for persons with appointments. I suggest you leave immediately and call later for an appointment. Understood, *sir*?"

"Perfectly, *boy*." With that I picked-up my briefcase and left. It was still raining hard, and when I got back to my SUV I started the engine and turned on the wipers, but decided to stay parked where I was. I wanted to see what would happen if I tested the Boy Scout's parking ban. Sure enough, about five minutes later a four-wheel drive pickup, with oversized tires and the Diamond 27 logo on the door pulled in beside me. One of the Boy Scout's crew got out and tapped on my window with his nightstick. I cracked the window open and asked what the problem was.

"You are parked illegally. This vehicle must be removed immediately or it will be towed. Do you understand, sir?"

"Sure do, but tell your troop leader that I'll be back. *Understand*?"

He looked puzzled. I didn't wait for a response, but put the SUV in gear and took off. I watched in my rear view mirror to see if he was following me, but when I came to the first bend in the road he was still standing in the same spot, hands on his hips.

Mr. Shaw may have had what he considered good reasons for creating the type of security system I had just witnessed, but the militaristic Green Beret regimen seemed to me like overkill. Maybe he had more to hide and protect than even I imagined. But, if he wasn't who I suspected, he had to be one paranoid nut. Either way, he certainly discouraged visitors, probably friend and foe alike. I decided to take no chances.

I couldn't risk being followed, so when I got to the main highway I purposely turned left and headed toward Miles City, instead of turning right toward where Jerry was holed up in the line shack. There was very little traffic, and I clipped along doing about sixty, while checking my rear view mirror every few seconds. So far there was nothing behind me. I drove three or four miles and was ready to make a U-turn to rejoin Jerry when a small object appeared in my mirror. I stepped on the gas and was doing near eighty, but the object grew larger and larger. It moved close enough to identify as the security pick-up truck, with my friend with the nightstick at the wheel. He was alone.

For the next five miles, regardless of what speed I maintained, he stayed fifty yards behind me. Obviously he wasn't trying to intercept, just follow me wherever I went.

I knew I had to shake this guy or I'd never be able to go back to meet Jerry. When I spotted a gas station some distance ahead of me I decided to try something, but I knew it would work only if my pursuer was as dumb as I thought he was. I pushed my speed up to eighty again and he stayed right on my tail. As I approached the first ramp into the station I stood on the brake pedal, fish-tailed off to the shoulder, turned in and skidded to a stop in front of the first set of pumps. My friend in the pickup couldn't stop fast enough and continued past the station. He kept going and disappeared over the crest of a small hill. I figured he would pull off onto the shoulder and wait for me.

I had the attendant fill the tank while I borrowed the key to the men's room. The station had two service bays. The overhead doors to the bays were closed and each door had one small window, which, fortunately looked too dirty to see through. I asked the attendant if he could give me a quick lube and oil change. Three minutes later the SUV was up on a lift and I was peering out through the dirty window in the closed garage door.

Sure enough, not five minutes later the guard in the pickup truck pulled into the station and stopped in front of a gas pump. I slipped the attendant a twenty and told him that if the guy in the pickup truck asked about me he was to say I got gas and then left in a big hurry, heading south.

I watched as the pickup tore out of the station and turned south toward the ranch. When the attendant returned to the service bay he said the driver of the pickup truck did ask about me, and when he told the guy which way I headed, the driver yelled something about me being too smart for my own good, and he'd make me pay for causing him so much trouble. The attendant looked terrified. When I paid him for the service he looked at me, shaking his head. "Mister, that guy was plenty mad. I wouldn't mess with anybody from the Diamond 27; they're a bunch of mean dudes. If you're on your way back to Miles City I'd get there fast. Know what I mean?"

I said I did, and thanked him for his help. I gave the pickup truck another five minutes and then took off south; the last thing I needed was to overtake the pickup, so I held my speed down to fifty. When I passed the road leading into the ranch I breathed a sigh of relief when I saw no pickup truck or other signs of life. So far so good.

The rutted trail into the line shack was also devoid of any signs of life. The rain had slackened a little as I moved through the twisting path and into the turnaround. I backed off the turnaround into the high grass and underbrush; high and thick enough to almost completely hide the SUV. When I stepped out I saw Jerry waiting for me on the other side of the fence. He said I was gone so long he thought something bad had happened. I assured him it hadn't; things didn't work out the way I had hoped they would, but I knew my situation could be a lot worse.

The rain was now mixed with sleet, and the wind was getting stronger. It had also swung around and was now blowing out of the north, and it seemed to be getting colder by the minute. The line shack was warm inside – Jerry had built a fire in the Franklin stove. My clothes were still damp from the earlier soaking, so the heat felt good. But after seeing the TV surveillance system in the guard house a red flag went up – would smoke coming from the chimney show up on one of their monitors? I sure hope not. The shack was a large, single room, with bunks along the back wall, a table and chairs, and a metal cabinet containing canned foods and bottled water. There were kerosene lanterns, but no electric and no plumbing. So I guess we do what the bears do.

There was a window in the front wall next to the only door. The other three walls were windowless – Jerry said that was done to keep the shack as warm as possible in the winter, when outdoor temperatures dropped into the single digits and stayed there for days at a time, with nighttime temperatures well below zero.

"How far is it to the main ranch house?" I asked.

"I'd say a mile and a half, maybe two," Jerry answered. "If you look out the window you can see we're at the bottom end of a narrow valley. It's mostly grazing land. There are some wooded areas, but most of the ranch is rolling grassland. Not much difference in elevation from high to low. The ranch house is beyond the far end of the valley and quite a ways off to the right."

"I expected to see a lot of rock and mountains. Of course where I come from, anything higher than a mole hill is considered the Alps."

"Well, Cole," Jerry chuckled, "There aint no Alps around here. You gotta go west, past Billings out through the Butte area before you run into any real mountains."

"Is this the only line shack on the ranch?"

"Yep, the only one. They built it here because the wranglers chase most of the strays into the valley. Storms out here develop real fast – we get line squalls in the summer and lots of snow in the winter, sometimes with little or no warning, so this is where the guys head if they know they can't make it back to the pens and the bunkhouses. This place has been a life-saver for a lot of ranch-hands, particularly in the winter. Blizzards out in this country are usually a real bitch – snow's horizontal – with a white-out so blinding you can't see your horse's head. It's easy to get lost and freeze to death. And speaking of snow – we might see some today. I don't like the look of that sky, or the way the temperature's dropping."

Jerry was looking at a thermometer mounted outside the window. "It's reading about thirty degrees," he said. "When we left Miles City this morning it was forty-eight."

I started toward the window when Jerry let out a yell. "I'll be damned," he said. "Gimme your binoculars, quick! That looks like Cossack coming out of a ravine, four – maybe five hundred yards up the valley."

He grabbed the glasses from me and stared through then for what seemed an eternity. "Yep," he said, handing the glasses to me, "that's

Cossack all right, and that's Mr. Shaw riding him. He's got two other guys on horses with him. Shit, Cole, looks like they're heading toward us. How the hell could they know we're here?"

"You think they're coming here?" I asked, knowing the answer before I asked the question.

"'Fraid so, Cole, why else would they be heading into a dead-end valley?"

"I know you were trying to be helpful, but I think the smoky fire you built told them somebody is here."

"Yeah, you're probably right – It was stupid of me! Dammit, I knew I'd regret coming with you – I knew it!"

"Take it easy Jerry, they're still some distance away. Grab your stuff and we'll make a break for the SUV."

As bad as I wanted to run, I first had to look at the infamous Mr. Shaw. I grabbed the binoculars from Jerry and moved to the window. When I focused on the white stallion and the rider, I saw an older man with gray-white hair protruding below the brim of a large, dark green cowboy hat. He also had a gray-white close-cropped beard, not full enough to hide a chiseled nose and sharp, angular features. He wore light colored boots, dark pants and a bright yellow poncho. I tried superimposing my mental images of the dozens of pictures of the Shah of Iran that I had recently poured over – pictures from the 40's right up to the time he supposedly died – and his biography that I had practically memorized. The more I looked at this figure on a horse, the more I became convinced that I was looking at the late Mohammed Reza Pahlavi Aryamehr Shahanshah of Iran. My God, this is absolutely incredible! As strong as my suspicions have been, I can't believe my eyes. It quickly dawned on me that nobody else was going to believe me either. The Shah alive! Sure, and so is John F. Kennedy. I can hear it now – what the hell you been smokin' Cole McQuaid! The fantasy of this situation is one thing, but the reality of the image in my binoculars is undeniable.

"Cole, for God's sake we gotta get outa here now! I think the other two guys are armed – and they're gonna be on us real quick."

I grabbed my stuff and we were out the door in ten seconds flat. Once outside I looked back at the three riders. They were still about two hundred yards away, but now they were coming at a full gallop.

We threw our stuff in the back of the SUV and I gunned it through the rutted trail toward the main highway. We hadn't gone more than a couple hundred yards when dead ahead of us the security pickup truck was blocking our path. They had picked a spot where trees on both sides of the trail made it impossible to get past them. The same guard who had tailed me earlier today was leaning against the front fender of his truck with a shotgun cradled in his arms. His boss, Karl Seitz, stood a few feet away. He also had a shotgun, but his was pointed straight at us.

I braked to a stop about ten feet from the pickup and rolled down the window. Seitz walked toward us and tapped the front fender of the SUV with the barrel of his shotgun.

"Out of the vehicle, both of you. Now!" he yelled. "And keep your hands in sight. You're both under arrest for criminal trespass and breaking and entering. If you don't mind my saying so sir, you're both in deep trouble"

Jerry and I got out and Jerry immediately started toward Seitz, his hand raised above his head and his face flushed with anger.

"Seitz," Jerry said, almost shouting. "You're dead wrong. McQuaid here wants to buy some horses. You wouldn't let him in to see Mr. Shaw so I brought him out here hoping to see some grazing stock in the valley. I figured that maybe if I helped McQuaid get the horses he's after it might change the bosses mind and help me get my old job back."

I give Jerry credit, he's a fast thinker. But he didn't impress Seitz.

"Jerry, you're a lousy liar. Your past employment here don't cut no ice with me; you got fired because you don't know how to obey orders. But you better obey mine or you're gonna get your head blown off – so stop right there and keep your hands where I can see 'em. Up. And Mr. McQuaid, sir, get over here beside Jerry, and keep your hands in sight too. Now, damn it. Move!"

While Seitz covered us with his shotgun, the other guard cuffed our hands behind our backs. According to the patch on his breast pocket his name is Russell Jenkins. Jenkin's pickup truck was a crew cab; he opened the passenger door and shoved us into the back seat. Jenkins drove the pickup, while Seitz drove my SUV.

Five minutes later we drove through the raised gates at the security headquarters building. Jenkins led Jerry and me to a room at the rear of the building and put us in separate steel-barred cells on opposite sides of a wide aisle. From what I could see there were about six cells. I couldn't see any windows in the room and the single door we came through looked to be heavy steel. I'd bet that most police departments in South Jersey have no more than two or three cells; and here in the middle of nowhere they've got a half dozen. Something is really wrong with this whole picture. It's like the Shah has established his own country – more accurately a monarchy – here in Montana, and I don't understand how he gets away with it. It's like we were in some small, third-world country. Where the hell is the local law?

After locking each of us in our cell Jenkins left the room. The temperature in the room was on the high side of eighty, and I was sweating. Jenkins hadn't removed the cuffs, so I couldn't take off my jacket or sweater. I figured the room was being monitored; I could see one camera on the ceiling of the aisle. There were probably others. I also had no doubt the cells were bugged for sound, so I'd have to play the game accordingly. I was concerned about what Jerry might say, and when I looked across he was pacing his small cell, mumbling something under his breath.

"You know these people, Jerry," I said. "Why are they overreacting like this – all I wanted to do was buy two horses." I motioned up to the ceiling mounted camera, but I don't think Jerry got my message.

"I don't know why, Cole. But I don't mind telling you I'm scared. These bastards are crazy and there's no telling what they'll do. I'm just sorry as hell that I let you talk me into bringing you out here. I must have been nuts!"

I tried mouthing words to him to shut up, while alternately nodding my head up and down, then staring and pointing a finger at the ceiling. All I got in return was Jerry staring through the bars at me, his expression telling me he thought I was nuts.

I was thinking about what I could say next when the door to the room opened and Jenkins walked in carrying two small brown paper bags. He slid one bag through the bars of my cell and sat it on the floor, then told me to back up against the bars so he could unlock my cuffs. After he did he repeated the same procedure with Jerry.

"There's food in the bags, but eat slow, guys," he said. "It's mid-afternoon, so this is lunch and dinner. There won't be any more food today." He stood in the aisle with his arms folded and watched us, a self-satisfied smirk on his face.

I guess the reality of my situation was beginning to sink in. I was a prisoner; probably miles from any kind of help, and the prospect of getting out of here was beginning to look mighty dim. These bastards could cause me to disappear off the face of the earth, and nobody would know where or how it happened.

The names of the earlier victims who had disappeared without a trace flashed through my head; Stiebris in particular. He was the first, and it happened here on this ranch. Maybe the poor guy is buried under the floor I'm standing on.

I needed to think; there has to be some way out of this mess. For lack of anything better at the moment I decided to try the old television cop show line.

"Jenkins," I said. "Regardless of what you think I'm guilty of, I'm entitled to call my lawyer. And I want to do just that – right now!"

Jenkins turned to face me and laughed. "McQuaid, you'd better understand something. You trespassed on private property, posted private property I might add, and then you broke into one of our buildings. So we'll decide who you can call, and when. And that applies to you too, Jerry. I suggest you both shut up and eat your food. Captain Sietz and maybe even Mr. Shaw will be in to talk to you a little later. Beyond that, all I can suggest is don't make any long range plans." He chuckled and the smirk faded, instantly replaced with a sadistic grin. I guess he thought he was funny. With that, he turned and walked out, locking the big door behind him.

I scanned the walls and ceiling of my cell and didn't see anything resembling a camera or a peep hole, so I moved to the back of the cell where I knew the corridor camera couldn't see me. I waived my arms until I caught Jerry's attention and then put a finger across my lips. With my other hand I pointed toward the corridor ceiling and the video camera.

Jerry finally caught on and nodded agreement. I spent the next few minutes silently mouthing words to Jerry, hoping he'd understand what I didn't want him to say. He nodded again. All I can do now is play it by ear, cross my fingers, and hope for the best.

I sat on the edge of the bunk and opened the brown bag. I didn't realize how hungry I was; it had been a long time since breakfast. The bag yielded a ham sandwich on rather dry looking rye bread, an overripe apple, a can of warm cola, and a small plastic packet of mustard. Wow, how lucky can a guy get? Then it dawned on me that I better start worrying about saving my ass, not the quality of jailhouse food. It wasn't the worst food I've ever had, but I'd have trouble giving it half a star.

When I finished the sandwich I laid on the bunk staring at the ceiling. I had to come up with some kind of plan to get out of here. With all the security and technology in this place breaking out would be next to impossible. First, I was behind bars in a locked room. I had no weapon. Beyond that I'd probably be outnumbered five to one. The only conclusion I could reach was that I'd have to find some way to outthink or outsmart them – and, based on what I've seen so far, that's going to be next to impossible – even with a helluva lot of luck. These guys seem to be not only tough, but very smart.

I've never been in a situation like this before; I knew that one wrong move and I'd be dead. To make matters worse I glanced across and saw Jerry pacing his cell. I got him into this and I'd have to do everything I could to get him out.

The only positive thing that's happened since I got here is that I accomplished what I set out to do. What I saw earlier at the line shack convinced me I was right; Mr. M. R. Shaw is in fact the 'late' Shah of Iran – without a shadow of doubt. As unbelievable as I knew this was, I also knew that even if I get out of here my job would only be half done – it won't be easy, but I'll have to find somebody who believes me. And that somebody will have to have the clout to do something about it.

I laid there staring at the ceiling for more than an hour, discarding one idea after another. Just as I sat up on the bunk the door to the cell room opened and Karl Seitz swaggered in.

"All right, McQuaid," he said. "Were going for a little walk. Mr. Shaw wants to see you in his office. Walk over to the bars and turn away from me. I've gotta cuff you."

I saw no reason to argue – looks like I'd get to see the Shah up close – so I did as he ordered. After the cuffs were in place Seitz looked up at the corridor video camera and gave some sort of hand signal, then unlocked my cell door.

Seitz got behind me, holding on to the chain between my cuffs, and steered me outside the cell room. After a few left and right turns we were in a blind corridor, with a door at the far end that turned out to be an elevator.

"I'm confused," I said. "A one-story building with an elevator? What do you have, a penthouse sandwiched between here and the roof?"

"We're not going up, McQuaid, we're going down. Just be patient."

There were no indicator buttons inside the elevator, but it seemed like we dropped at least two floors before the doors reopened. When we stepped out of the elevator we walked across a carpeted corridor and stepped onto a wide conveyor belt that was flush with the floor. This is unbelievable; an underground tunnel with a moving sidewalk! The conveyor extended to my left as far as I could see. The tunnel appeared to be solid concrete and had indirect lighting on both sides, and the air seemed dry and warm. I didn't say a word, but the more I saw of this place the more concerned I became about my chances of getting out alive.

After traveling for two or three minutes the conveyor ended at a blank wall similar to where we got on. On the left was another elevator. On the right was a guard watching us through a large glass window. This place has security like a Federal Reserve bank.

After another short elevator ride, this time heading up, we stepped out into a small carpeted room, empty except for a rather nondescript female seated behind a small desk.

"Good afternoon, Captain Seitz, you are expected. Mr. Shaw is in his office. Go right through."

"Thank you, Miss Kinnard," Seitz responded.

The single door opposite the elevator slid silently open and, with Seitz still behind me, we continued our journey. We passed through a room containing a lot of leather chairs and heavy oak lamp tables. There were no windows; the walls were lined from floor to ceiling with loaded bookshelves. After passing through another carpeted corridor we entered a small, beautifully furnished room – obviously some kind of reception area – with a real knockout redhead seated behind an executive desk. There were large heavy looking oak doors on three walls of the room.

The redhead greeted Seitz and told us both to take a seat; Mr. Shaw was on the phone. A few minutes later a light flashed on her desk. She picked up her phone and listened for about ten seconds. When she returned the phone to its cradle, she told us that Mr. Shaw would see us now.

The Shah's private office was even more opulent than the reception area. He was standing behind his desk when we walked in. As I had seen back at the line shack, he had long gray and white streaked hair and a close-cropped gray and white beard. He also wore very dark tinted glasses, which I thought a bit unusual since there was nothing but artificial light. Compared with the pictures of him that I had studied before coming here he was the right height, but had put on some weight; particularly his face. I still had no doubt about his true identity – I'd stake my life on it. It then dawned on me that maybe I have done just that!

"Karl," the Shah said, "please remove Mr. McQuaid's handcuffs. You may also leave us alone."

He spoke excellent English, but with a trace of accent that I couldn't quite identify. I couldn't take my eyes off of him.

"Are you sure, sir?" Seitz replied. "I don't trust this guy at all."

"Do not worry Karl, I believe Mr. McQuaid is intelligent enough to realize that any attempt to escape our hospitality would be futile."

"Yes, sir, but if you don't mind I'll wait in the library."

"Suit yourself Karl."

The Shah motioned for me to sit in a large chair across from his desk. He continued to stand motionless, watching Karl leaving the office and closing the door behind him. It wasn't until I sat down that he began pacing the length of his desk. I was curious as to why he wanted Karl to leave the office. Something odd was going on.

"McQuaid," he said in a rather raspy voice. "I do not intend to waste my valuable time playing your game of charades. I know who you are and I also know why you are here. We both know that you are not here to buy horses. That said, let me ask why you are pursuing this asinine attempt to harass and embarrass me? You have nothing to gain and much to lose. Who is behind this and what do they hope to accomplish?"

His voice surprised me. He spoke slowly in a very controlled manner, with just a hint of that elusive accent. After many months of effort on my part and so many years of speculation by others – it seemed almost anticlimactic to see the mysterious 'client' in the flesh, and to hear his voice. Was this really the end of the trail? Could it be this simple? But how the hell does he know so much about me? It was a question I couldn't answer. I quickly decided that the safest path for me was to continue playing dumb, but before I could speak he stopped pacing and pointed a finger at me.

"McQuaid," he said, his voice trembling, "I'll be totally frank. Based on what my people tell me, you have a baseless suspicion that I am the late Shah of Iran. Your premise is totally ludicrous.

"Mr. Shaw," I responded. "I have no idea what you are talking about. I'm not working with or for anybody other than myself. I'm truly here for no reason other than to purchase two thoroughbreds for my stable. Why is that being construed as harassment?" Before he could answer I continued.

"I met Jerry in a bar last night and he told me your head trainer had fired him. He also said he thought you liked him because he trained and cared for your personal horse. Since I had been told by others in town that you and your ranch are very inaccessible, I thought Jerry might help me get in to see you. I think he agreed to help me because he thought if he brought you some business you might give him his old job back. So, again, I am only here to buy . . ."

The Shah stopped pacing and extended both hands in the air. "Mr. McQuaid," he snapped angrily, "Do not insult my intelligence with more of your lies. Would you like me to tell you all about your recent visit to my Tampa office? A visit that had nothing to do with buying horses. You were prying into my affairs. And if you think I am bluffing I'll gladly show you a video tape that covers much of your comings and goings while you were there."

He really caught me off guard. I had spent a lot of time in Tampa with Rita, and she seemed so open and above board I couldn't believe she was a stooge of the Shah. Other than Irena I didn't have a clue who could have filmed me. Regardless, I knew for sure that I had to see the film; for no reason other than to see who was – and who wasn't in it.

"O.K.," I responded, feigning anger. "I think you are bluffing, so show me the damn film!"

"Very well, Mr. McQuaid, but you are simply stalling for time. It will change nothing."

I knew it wouldn't, but I had to buy time any way I could. I still had no idea how to get out of here.

He sat on the edge of his desk, and with a hand-held remote opened a section of wall revealing a large screen TV. The video tape lasted about ten minutes. There was no mistaking my image on the screen. There were segments of me coming into the building, talking with Irena in the reception area, and others of me entering and leaving Rita's office. But none inside her office. There were shots of me in the corridors and even in the men's toilet room. But there was nothing of Rita and me beyond the walls of the office building, or at the restaurants where we had lunch and dinner, and later that evening when I dropped her off at her home. It was little consolation to realize what I was watching was obviously edited tape from security cameras. But it told me nothing about who in the Tampa office sent it to the Shah. I also realized that given the predicament I was in it really didn't matter.

The Shah had dimmed the lights in the room before starting the film and the room was still semi-dark. I knew that whatever I was going to do – I had better do it damn quick, because if the Shah called Seitz back into his office I was a dead man. I didn't know how it would play out, but I had to make my move now!

The Shah still sat on the edge of his desk, about six feet from me. The cuffs Seitz had taken off me were sitting on the desk in front of me. I said a prayer under my breath and jumped out of the chair. Before he knew what was happening I slammed into him and knocked him backwards on the desk. His head hit the desk hard, but he was still conscious and began wildly swinging one arm at me. With his other arm he reached down and slid open a desk drawer, his hand flailing in search of something. I saw it first – a Colt .45 pistol. My hand reached it just ahead of his. I had no time to see if it was loaded because the Shah was pounding my chest. I also had no time to think about what I was doing – I was moving on adrenaline and survival instinct! I glanced at the gun and flipped the safety off and quickly jammed the muzzle under his chin. Suddenly he became motionless, wide eyes staring up at me and his body rigid.

"I implore you Mr. McQuaid, move the gun – please . . .it has a hair trigger so please, please listen to me. It will fire with the least amount of pressure on the trigger. I will not resist, so please move the gun!"

I moved back so he could sit up, but kept the gun pointed at his head.

"Stand up and don't touch anything on the desk – do it slow," I said, not recognizing my own voice. I didn't see any alarm button, but I figured there had to be one. When his feet touched the floor I backed away and with my free hand grabbed the handcuffs still lying on the desk.

"Move away from your desk and get against the wall – facing it. And don't even think about yelling for help, 'cause if you do I'll kill you! I've got nothing to lose at this point."

I stayed behind him, with the gun jammed between his shoulder blades. With one hand I managed to cuff his hands behind his back, then turned him to face me.

"We're gonna walk over to the door. I'll open it a crack and you're gonna tell the redhead to get Seitz from the library and bring him in here. And remember – say the wrong thing and you're dead, and she'll also be dead before she can get out of her chair."

I was trying my damndest to sound threatening, but my voice still wasn't cooperating; not only did it sound squeaky but it was breaking up.

I held tight to the chain between the cuffs and put my foot close enough to the door so he could open it no more than an inch or two. I stayed out of sight with the gun pointed at his left ear.

"Cathy," he said quietly, "please go to the library and get Karl. Tell him to come directly to my office."

When she said she would I quickly closed the door. I didn't want the Shah anywhere near his desk, so I turned one of the visitor's chairs to face the door and pushed him into it, holding the back of his collar with one hand and with the other keeping the gun against the back of his head. I had no idea how Seitz would react when he walks in on this, but I knew my only chance of getting out of here was to use the Shah as a shield.

It seemed no more than a few seconds before the door swung open and Seitz stepped through. He froze when he saw me with the gun. His sidearm was holstered on his right side and, as he reached to unsnap the strap, the Shah screamed at him.

"Don't Karl, don't. He will kill me. Come in and shut the. . ."

Karl didn't listen. A microsecond of hesitation on my part allowed him to pull the gun from its holster and swing it up toward me. I have never in my life fired a gun at a human being, but in that same microsecond I knew that if I didn't I would be dead. I wasn't even sure if my gun was loaded, but I squeezed the trigger once, twice, and almost in slow motion watched the slugs tear into Karl's torso, flinging him back against the door frame. He fell in a heap and landed on his back; his gun spinning across the carpet. The noise from my gun was deafening, and was followed by screams from outside the door.

Through the open door I could see Cathy the redhead. She was hugging herself and screaming at the top of her lungs. I pulled the Shah out of his chair and pushed him through the doorway to where Cathy was standing.

"Cathy! Stop screaming now! If you do I won't hurt you. . .I promise. . .otherwise I'll have to stop you."

I waved the gun in her face and her screaming turned into uncontrollable sobbing; she was hysterical. I told the Shah to lay on the floor, face down, until I figured out what to do with Cathy. I couldn't leave her here to sound an alarm, and I certainly didn't want to take her with me.

There was a door with a key lock in the wall behind her desk. I opened it and found a small storage room lined with shelving filled with office supplies. She was still blubbering when I led her by the arm into the room and told her to sit on the floor and keep quiet.

"You've got light and plenty of air to breathe in here. Behave yourself and I'll let somebody know you're here," I said. I shut and locked the door and dropped the key on her desk.

I looked into the Shah's office to where Seitz's body lay. He hadn't moved. I checked the side of his neck for a pulse and felt none. He was dead. Since I wasn't sure how many shots were left in the Shah's gun I grabbed Seitz's pistol from the floor, slid the safety on, and pushed it into the waistband of my pants. It was a plainer version of the Shah's Colt.45, and I figured it would have a full clip. I didn't know how much firepower I'd need to get out of here, but I wanted to even the odds as much as possible.

I grabbed the chain between the Shah's handcuffs and told him to get on his feet. I had no idea where I was in this labyrinth of rooms and corridors. My head was spinning with questions about what to do next; fear that I was doomed; remorse because I had just killed somebody, even though I knew it was self defense, and poor Jerry, probably still in his cell in the guardhouse. I wanted to get away from this place as fast as I could, but I couldn't leave without Jerry. Besides, unless they've moved it, my SUV is parked right outside the guardhouse. That seemed to be the most direct way out of here. But it would also be the way I'd run into who knows how many armed guards. Nothing is easy!

"Mr. Shaw," I said. "You're going to lead me back to the main guardhouse. But we're not going the same way Seitz brought me to your office. I'm not going to risk being ambushed in one of your underground tunnels – with no place to hide. I'm sure you know another way to get there, so you're coming with me. Consider yourself my hostage and shield – I'll be behind you all the way. And the gun is gonna be right between your shoulder blades until we're out of here. Understand? You saw what I did to Seitz. Give me any trouble and I'll do the same to you."

The Shah looked at me through steely dark eyes. "Mr. McQuaid," he said. "I do not want to die. But, regardless, you're not going to kill me, because if you do you will lose your shield, and if that happens you won't make it to the front gate."

"You may be right," I responded, "but don't test me. I may not get out of here alive, but I guarantee you won't either. Now, show me another way back to the guard house."

"We will have to go by car," he replied. "The tunnel you came through is the only way to get there underground and out of sight."

He led me through what appeared to be underground living quarters to yet another elevator. We saw nobody on the way. After another short ascent the elevator doors opened and we stepped out into a short hallway between what appeared to be a kitchen on one end and a living room on the other. As we entered the living room, a woman seated at a desk at the far end of the room jumped to her feet.

"Mr. Shaw, what is going on? Why are you. . ."

Before she could finish I pointed the gun at her and ordered her to move from behind the desk and sit in one of the upholstered chairs.

"Do as he says, Cindy," the Shah said. "and do not be frightened."

The Shah turned to me and actually forced a smile. "Mr. McQuaid, in order to get my car one of us will have to call the garage. Do you really want to risk that?"

I answered by leading him to her desk, where I picked a cordless phone off its cradle and dropped it in Cindy's lap. "Call," I said. "Make it short and sweet. Tell them to bring the car immediately. And no funny stuff."

I watched her punch in a number and then tell whoever answered that Mr. Shaw's car was to be brought to the main house immediately. I took the phone from her and laid it on the desk. I noticed a wide doorway behind her desk, leading to a room that seemed to be enclosed with nothing but windows.

"What's out there?" I asked.

"It is a sun room and my public office," the Shah answered. "I conduct all ranch business there, meeting vendors and other visitors."

Looking through the expanse of windows I could see the weather was getting worse. I could see the snow and hear the sleet pinging against the windows. The macadam road leading to the house was wet, but the grass areas were already white with snow. The sky was dark gray, with low black clouds scudding along in a swirling strong wind – if I didn't know how cold it was, I'd expect to see flashes of lightning. Given my predicament, I wasn't sure whether this weather was good or bad for me. Then something caught my eye at the far end of the sun room near the high ceiling. It was a security camera panning the room. The realization then hit me that I wasn't going to surprise anybody; I was heading into an ambush at the guard house. With the multitude of monitors I saw earlier, how many other cameras had picked me up since I took the Shah hostage and shot Seitz? They had to know what was going on.

So it was a coin toss. Do I try to leave through the guard house, or find some other way off the ranch. Either way, my odds of getting out of here alive seemed to be shrinking by the minute – even with my hostage.

As I watched through the sun room windows a car materialized out of the swirling snow, heading toward us. Suddenly, beyond and to the right of the car, a plane heading away from us descended, it's lights blinking in the dark stormy sky. It appeared to touch down and then disappear into a white wall of snow. It's probably a wild long-shot, but maybe there is another way out of here!

When the car driver walked through the front door he headed directly to Cindy's desk, brushing snow from his leather jacket. "Geez,

Cindy, where does Mr. Shaw want to go in this lousy weather? It's brutal out there."

I stepped through the sun room doorway with the Shah in front of me and pointed my gun directly at the driver.

"I'll answer your question," I said, "just as soon as we're all in the car."

I figured security probably knew by now exactly where I was and what I was up to, so I decided to leave Cindy behind. She'd be excess baggage I'd have to keep my eyes on. I told her to sit on the floor in the corner and not to move.

The car was a big sedan. I told the driver to get behind the wheel, as I put the Shah in the front passenger seat. I got directly behind the Shah and kept the muzzle of my gun pressed against the back of his head.

"What's your name, driver?" I asked.

"My name is Angelo," he responded. "I don't know what your problem is mister, but where are we supposed to be going?" He turned his head and looked at me, moving his head from side to side almost imperceptibly, like he was trying to tell me something.

"He wants you to drive off the ranch through the main gate," the Shah interjected.

"No!" I said. "I've changed my mind. Sorry if it disappoints you *Mister Shaw*, but I'm not driving into a turkey shoot at the front gate. Angelo, I want you to drive to the airstrip. Find the plane that just landed. And let's not waste time faking any detours. Understand?"

"Yeah, I do." Angelo answered. "But I don't think the plane's gonna help you get out of here – I'm surprised Paul even landed here in this weather, much less try to take off again."

"Who's plane is it, Angelo? You obviously know the pilot."

The Shah turned his head slightly. "McQuaid," he said. "The plane is mine, and Paul Miller is my pilot. He just brought Alex Carson, my ranch manager, back from a business trip to Chicago. And like Angelo said, Paul will never agree to take off in this weather. You're on a fool's errand McQuaid."

"We'll see about that," I said.

A few minutes later we stopped in front of a small hanger. A Learjet was parked in front of the closed hanger doors and was being refueled from a small tank truck. The truck driver was standing at the rear of the truck, hands in his pockets, looking very cold. No one else was visible. Snow was now accumulating on the blacktop, so the temperature was still dropping.

"Angelo," I said. "Pull up as close as you can to that small door at the end of the hanger." There were lights on in a window next to the door and I could see a shadow moving around inside. I crossed my fingers and hoped it was the pilot.

With Angelo and the Shah in front of me we walked into the room. It was a small office and there were two guys inside. One was seated at a desk doing paperwork; I assumed he was the pilot. The other guy was in a chair with an open briefcase on his lap. The room was quite warm but I was shaking with cold. Or maybe it was just nerves. Both scrambled to stand up when they saw the Shah and me behind him with a gun.

"What the hell's going on!" the guy getting out of his chair yelled, spilling the contents of his briefcase on the floor. "Who are you?" he said, looking at me.

"Who I am doesn't matter," I said. "Are you Alex Carson?"

The Shah again turned to look at me, his eyes cold as ice. "McQuaid, gun or no gun you are trying my patience. What difference does it make who's who? Yes, this is Alex and that guy is my pilot, Paul. Now, do whatever you're going to do, but do it quickly! I am becoming very agitated and physically tired."

My hastily formed plan was to have the pilot fly the Shah and me out of here. The Shah was my only bargaining chip, so I had to keep him as a hostage. But now I had four people to watch and, with this lousy weather, every minute I waste further decreases the chances of getting that plane off the ground. Then I remembered poor Jerry, probably still locked in his cell back at the guard house, and my spirits really plummeted. I couldn't desert Jerry. Out of desperation more than anything I turned to Angelo.

"Take the car, Angelo, and go to the guard house. Tell whoever is on duty that Mr. Shaw wants you to bring their prisoner, Jerry, here immediately. And, again, Angelo, no tricks! You've got exactly fifteen minutes to get back here with Jerry. Take longer than that or come back with somebody other than Jerry and Mr. Shaw dies. Understood? Now go!"

Angelo said he understood and headed for the door. As he opened the door he turned toward me and nodded his head ever so slightly, an almost undetectable grin on his face. It was like he was trying to give me some sort of signal. Problem was, I didn't know whether to be relieved or alarmed. One way or the other, it probably wouldn't make much difference – I was smack in the middle of a pretty scary situation.

I didn't think Alex or Paul would be carrying a gun. I checked them anyway and found nothing. I told both to sit on the floor with their backs against the wall. I pushed the Shah into the desk chair and stood an arm's length away, nervously looking out the window for the return of Angelo.

He was back in less then fifteen, but my heart sank when I saw two people exit the rear door of the car. I could feel my heart pounding in my chest. The first was Jerry, still handcuffed. Right behind him was Russell Jenkins, Karl Seitz's sadistic second-in-command. I stepped behind the Shah and held the gun to his right ear. Things were getting more complicated by the minute, and I knew somebody was going to get hurt – maybe die. I just hoped it wasn't me.

Angelo came through the door first, followed by Jerry, then Jenkins. When Jenkins saw me he stopped in the open doorway and pulled Jerry toward him. Before I could blink, Jenkins gun was jammed under Jerry's chin.

"What the hell's going on here?" Jenkins yelled. "Are you all right Mr. Shaw?"

"Not really, Russell, I think that's obvious."

Angelo had stepped to one side, his head moving from Jenkins to me and back again. "Angelo," I said. "I told you to bring Jerry here – nobody else – what happened?"

"I had no choice McQuaid," he said. "When I got to the guard house Jenkins was at the front counter on the phone. He was having an argument with whoever was on the other end of the line. I told him Mr. Shaw wanted me to bring Jerry here. After he slammed the phone down he said something funny was going on and he'd bring Jerry here personally. He said he wouldn't let Jerry out of his sight."

The Shah stiffened. "Russell," the Shah said. "Who was on the phone and what did they want?"

"It was the state Attorney General's office, sir. They wanted to notify us that the Highway Patrol was on the way here from their field office in Miles City. They were coming to investigate a missing person's report. I tried to convince the guy on the phone that we could handle that type of investigation ourselves."

"And just who is missing, Russell?" the Shah asked.

"The bastard holding a gun on you – McQuaid! He must have friends in high places to get the Attorney General's office involved."

Russell's nervousness was showing. He had a twitch in his right eye and he kept shifting his weight from one foot to the other. He also looked as white as the snow outside.

"Russell," the Shah said, cold anger in his voice. "Why didn't you refer them to the Sheriff's office, as we always do in situations like this; you know we have friends there! My standing order has always been to keep the Highway Patrol off the ranch. Why didn't you do that?"

"I tried, Mr. Shaw, but the guy wouldn't listen to me. I really think. . ."

"Russell," the Shah interrupted, almost shouting. "Your job is to follow orders, not to think! You've made two serious mistakes. First, you didn't respond to the emergency that developed in my compound a short while ago. With so many security cameras, how could you not know what was going on? I was taken prisoner by Mr. McQuaid here, who also shot and killed Karl. And you saw none of that?"

"Karl is dead?" Russell yelled, moving his gun from Jerry to me. "On my mother's grave, Mr. Shaw, I didn't know any of that happened. I was in the cell room checking on our prisoner and then went to the front desk to answer the phone when the Attorney General's office called. I'm sorry, but I wasn't paying attention to the monitors. I guess I was too preoccupied with the phone call. . ."

"Unacceptable, Russell, totally unacceptable," the Shah interrupted. "I will not be interrogated by anyone from the Attorney General's office, and I don't want them snooping around my property. You could have prevented that if you had handled the phone call intelligently. By not doing that you have made it necessary for me to take drastic action – something I've hoped I'd never have to do. I've dreaded this moment for years."

"Please, Mr. Shaw, let me go back to the guard house. I can prevent them from coming on the ranch."

"And just how do you propose doing that, Russell? You'd compound disobedience with stupidity. The Highway Patrol is only following orders from their boss, the Attorney General. What will you do, Russell, kill them? Within hours we'd have an army of law enforcement people crawling all over my ranch."

The Shah turned his head and looked at me, anger still contorting his features. "Mr. McQuaid," he said. "You hold the trump card here. At least for the moment. If you kill me, Russell will surely kill you, unless you're willing to shoot through your hostage friend to kill Russell first. Most of the people in this room could be dead in a matter of minutes. On the other hand, all you really want to do is leave the ranch with your friend, alive and healthy. Am I correct?"

"That about sums it up, Mr. Shaw," I answered. "So what do you have in mind?"

"I would like to suggest a compromise, Mr. McQuaid."

"I'm listening, Mr. Shaw."

"My offer is this:" he said. "First, Russell will give his gun to you, along with his prisoner, Jerry. You will then remove my handcuffs and escort Paul, my pilot, and myself to my plane. Russell also will accompany me as my bodyguard – less his weapon of course. And one other person will join me on the plane – someone you have not met; Inez, my personal assistant. Alex, please call her now on the speaker phone and tell her to dress warm and meet us at the plane. She'll have to drive here in the van."

"Whoa, Mr. Shaw, just hold on," I said. "If I agree to this – and I don't know that I will, she's to park behind the plane and get on board immediately."

The Shah shrugged his shoulders. "That's fine, McQuaid. Tell her that Alex." Turning to face Alex, the Shah continued, "You will stay here, Alex. I want you to meet the Highway Patrol when then arrive. Tell them anything you want, but do your best to keep them off the ranch. You probably will not succeed, and that is exactly why I cannot be here. I will not be interrogated by those people. I will call you tomorrow for your report and to give you further instructions.

"Angelo, as soon as we take off you are to drive Alex, McQuaid and Jerry to the guard house. Alex, you will wait there for the Highway Patrol. McQuaid, I trust that you and Jerry will leave the ranch immediately. I ask that you not be here when the Highway Patrol arrives. Now, does everybody understand what I want them to do? McQuaid, do you accept my compromise?"

Before I could speak, Paul, the pilot, stood up and began shaking his head. "Mr. Shaw," he said. "It will be suicide to attempt a flight out of here tonight in this weather. Visibility is getting worse by the minute. Please reconsider!"

"It is risky, I agree," the Shah said. "But I'm confident you can do it. I've seen you fly in worse weather. McQuaid, you haven't answered me! Time is critical here!"

"I accept," I said. "As long as everything is done in the sequence you just outlined. Alex, get this Inez on the phone now and tell her she has exactly ten minutes to get here or the plane leaves without her. And Russell, remove Jerry's handcuffs and give him your gun, handle first. Jerry, as soon as you have his gun I want you to search Russell for other weapons – and be careful – I don't trust him at all!"

Turning back to the Shah, I said, "Why are you so concerned about a visit by the Highway Patrol. If you're the legitimate businessman you claim to be, what do you have to hide? Seems to me you're totally overreacting."

"Let me be the judge of that, McQuaid. The Attorney General, in fact the entire Montana Department of Justice, have tried for years to find cause to search my property. I do have an informant in their midst who has told me that they have even tried fabricating evidence that I'm the leader of a religious cult here on the ranch who advocates the violent overthrow of the government. Ludicrous, absolutely ludicrous! Now it appears they are using your disappearance as an excuse to snoop around my property. They will undoubtedly show up with a search warrant and who knows what else, but I will not play their game! I will not answer their questions! Beyond that, McQuaid, it is none of your business, and you're wasting my valuable time. Russell, give your weapon to Jerry – do it now!"

A lot happened in the next few minutes. I ordered Alex to call the Inez woman, and on the speaker phone heard exactly what was said. Nothing sounded out of the ordinary to me. Jerry found no other weapons on Russell. We waited a little more than ten minutes for Inez to show up. I was watching out the office window when she did. She parked her van off to one side and walked toward then plane. She was carrying a small suitcase and stopped and stood beside the plane's closed passenger door. Based on the description I got from the old guy at the post office, this was probably the woman who picked-up the Shah's mail on a regular basis. From what I could see in the diminished outdoor lighting she was almost masculine in appearance, with long dark hair and an olive complexion. I got a quick glimpse of her face when she turned in the light. She had a sour expression that looked chiseled in stone – a strong resemblance to old *Iron-Face Irena* in Tampa. I wondered if her last name is also Kabojian.

As I herded the Shah, Russell and Paul out the door, Jerry kept repeating over and over 'Thank you dear Jesus, thank you, thank you, thank you! He had obviously convinced himself that he'd never live to see daylight tomorrow.

Angelo followed my group out the door and he walked directly to the car. I didn't think too much of it until I saw him unlock and open the trunk. Red lights began flashing in my head. What did all of those odd facial expressions he directed at me during the past hour or so mean? What the hell is he up to? I was in the open with no place to hide. I had two choices; either go after Angelo or get this group on the plane fast. I yelled for Paul to hurry it up, and when he opened the plane door I practically pushed the three of them on board. Through the open door I could see the mysterious Inez, already on board. And there was Inez glaring at me – *without doubt I knew she was Irena's sister.* As soon as Paul closed and secured the door I turned and walked toward Angelo's car, trying all the while to keep the car between us. I kept my gun pointed straight ahead. Angelo was yelling something to me but I couldn't hear him above the howling wind. As I approached the front of the car, Angelo was closing the trunk lid, and held an automatic pistol in his right hand. In his left hand he held an open wallet, displaying some sort of gold emblem, all the while yelling that he was on my side – he was the law – please put my gun away. Now I was really confused. He lowered his gun until it was pointed at the ground, but held his gold shield at eye level for me to see. I continued walking toward him and kept my gun raised and pointed at his head.

"McQuaid, don't do anything stupid," he said. "I don't have time to explain now, but my name is not Angelo and my job as the Shah's chauffeur is nothing more than a cover. I work for the United States government and for your own protection I'm asking you not to interfere with what I have do to. Please get behind me and stay out of my way."

I don't know why, but I did what he asked. I slipped my gun under my belt and walked around the car and stood behind him. He never took his eyes off the plane. I looked around but couldn't see Jerry; I hoped he was still in the hanger office keeping his eyes on Alex.

Paul had started the plane's engines. The cabin and running lights were barely visible in the blowing snow. The plane's landing lights were also on. I could see the wing and tail controls moving, so I guess Paul was trying to dislodge the accumulating snow. The lights on both sides on the runway were on when we first got here and were still lit. I didn't know whether Paul would have any problem taking off; I also didn't know what Angelo, or what ever the hell his name is, was going to do next.

I was still standing behind Angelo when the plane started taxiing the short distance to the end of the runway, where it turned into the wind and braked to a stop. Angelo yelled for me to stay where I was and began moving toward the plane at a fast trot. He was about a hundred feet from the plane when it started moving, engine noise screaming above the wind. The plane was accelerating quickly. Angelo stopped, planted his feet, brought his gun up to waist level and began firing. He was spraying the length of the plane with automatic gunfire, emptying one clip and quickly inserting another. The plane was gaining speed rapidly when Angelo began firing again. Just as the plane seemed to become airborne the right wing dipped and struck the runway with a shower of sparks. The tail lifted high in the air and, nose down, the plane cartwheeled once before erupting into a giant fireball and skidded off the runway, leaving a wake of flaming wreckage.

Angelo stood and watched the flames. I guess when he was satisfied that no one survived he turned and walked back to me.

"My god, Angelo," I said. "Was it necessary to do that? I can't believe I just witnessed four people dying like that. Do you know who Mr. Shaw really is – or was?"

"Yes I do, McQuaid," he answered. "I was simply following orders, and there's no time now to explain any more than that. We've got to get back to the hanger office fast. Let's go!"

When we entered the office Jerry was sitting in a chair with his back to the wall. He had Russell's gun pointed at Alex, who was standing with his face pressed against the window. The distant burning wreckage was visible through the window. Alex was white as a ghost and his whole body was trembling. He looked like he could be having some kind of seizure.

"Alex, get hold of yourself," Angelo yelled. "We're leaving right now for the main house, and you're coming with us. I need you to open the safe in Mr. Shaw's office. Cooperate and you won't get hurt. Let's go!"

When we arrived at the main house I remembered locking Cathy in a closet. I told Angelo I wasn't sure where the closet is.

"Don't worry McQuaid," he said. "I want you and Jerry to wait in the car. Alex, I want you to come with me. I need some files out of Shaw's office and some other things from his safe. You're to stay here after I leave. Find Cathy and then contact the rest of the staff. Tell them if they want to live they better gather up their personal belongings and get off the ranch fast. Unless you want to see more dead bodies you'd better convince them to move fast, cause all hell's gonna break loose here in just about ninety minutes. You can then leave too, if you want to live. Now let's go!"

In less than ten minutes Angelo came through the front door carrying a cardboard box. He put it on the seat next to him and we took off for the guard house.

"Angelo," I said. "Who are you and who do you work for? Are you CIA, FBI, or what?"

"You'll find out soon enough exactly what this is all about, McQuaid," he responded. "I assure you I'm not employed by either of those agencies, but I do work for the federal government – the executive branch and the Attorney General. We know all about you and what you've been up to the past few months. After you get home we'll be in touch and I'm sure we'll answer a lot of your questions. In the meantime keep your mouth shut.

"When we get to the guard house I want you and Jerry to get in your SUV and take off. As soon as I take care of a few things I'll be right behind you. First, I've got to turn the Highway Patrol around. So, McQuaid, drop Jerry off in Miles City and get your ass home as fast as you can. And, again, a warning to both of you – don't say anything to anybody about what happened here today. If you do, you could be in big, big trouble. Besides, you'll have a tough time getting anybody to believe you. Understand?"

We both said we did. Jerry began mumbling something under his breath. I think he was scared out of his wits! Ten minutes later we were speeding north on Route 59 toward Miles City. Neither of us said much. I kept my eyes glued to the road ahead and never looked back. All I wanted to see was home sweet home!

CHAPTER TWELVE

Instead of the seven hours it took me to get to Montana, the trip home seemed like seventy hours. A few minutes out of Chicago the events of the past couple days caught up with me. The flight was not particularly crowded and the seat next to me was empty. I was bone tired, so I spread out as best I could, put my chin on my chest and dozed off. I was just tumbling into darkness when the image of the fireball enveloping the Shah's jet flashed in front of me. I awoke with a start, shivering – a feeling of ice water coursing through my veins. I sat there rigid, eyes wide open, thinking about the people that had died and, even scarier, the number of times I could have been killed. I had been very, very lucky! I forced myself to think about the happy prospect of going home.

Before leaving Miles City I called Suzy to tell her when my flight was due in Philly; I needed a ride home from the airport. She said she and Ben would meet my plane. Between bouts of sniffling and blowing her nose she said this was the happiest day of her life, because she loved me and she knew I loved her, and I was alive and well! She had convinced herself that I'd never return from Montana. I didn't tell her, but yesterday I'd shared those sentiments.

The lights of Philadelphia never looked so beautiful – I was home at last. Suzy was waiting in the terminal and she had brought Ben along with her. After lots of kisses and hugs from Suzy, which I returned, and hugs and backslapping from Ben, which I also returned, we found Ben's car and headed for home. On the way they must have asked me a million questions. I gave them a synopsis of everything that happened, but I didn't mention killing Karl Seitz. I also didn't mention Angelo, or what he did to the Shah's plane. I did tell them that I had seen and spoken with the notorious M. R. Shaw, in fact had spent some time in his company and, without any doubt whatsoever, became totally convinced he was the former Shah of Iran. I also told them the Shah is now really dead, at least to my satisfaction, because I had witnessed his death first hand. Ben wanted to know if I had killed him. I told him no. He also wanted all the details and asked me to meet with him as soon as we reached my office. It was almost six o'clock and Suzy insisted I come to her place for a home cooked dinner. I politely refused both.

"Thanks guys," I said. "Just drop me at my place. I'm gonna take a long hot shower, have a peanut butter sandwich, washed down with about four fingers of Southern Comfort, and go to bed. I may sleep for a week, so expect me at the office when I get there.

"I do have a question, Ben," I added. "I was told somebody labeled me a 'missing person' with the Montana Attorney General's office. They dispatched the Highway Patrol to the Shah's ranch looking for me. That set off a whole chain of events – which I won't go into now. Any idea who contacted the A.G.'s office with that phony tale? Could his initials have been Benjamin McQuaid?"

"Of course it was me, Cole. Suzy called me very, very upset. She knew where you were supposed to be and, even though it was hours before you were supposed to call her, she had a premonition that you were in great danger. I initially refused to do it, but she kept badgering me – must have called me four or five times. I gave in when I remembered that I went through law school with one of the Montana A.G.'s assistants. I called her. I guess you know the rest."

"O.K., Ben." I said. "The way things played out I guess it helped save my life."

I didn't make it to the office until almost noon the next day. After I had showered and dressed Mrs. Tomasello made me a huge breakfast of eggs, bacon, her special home-fries and wheat toast with honey. Between that and about twelve hours sleep I felt almost human again. When I sat down at my desk I realized it was a lot less cluttered than when I left; good old efficient Nancy at work. All she left for me was a small pile of mail, a few letters to sign and about a half-dozen calls to return. I finished all of it in less than an hour and was on my way to Joe Mancuso's office when Suzy stopped me.

"Cole," she said. "I don't want to know all the gruesome details, but I think you should tell me what happened in Montana. I've planned a real nice dinner for this evening – one of your favorites – and it'll just be you and me; Julia's baby sitting. I need to be with you and I am curious about how you knew it was the Shah. Please don't say no!"

"Dinner sounds great Suzy. I want to be with you, too. As far as Montana is concerned it was one crazy trip. Parts of it seem to be nothing but a bad dream, a real scary nightmare. Why don't we go home together after the office closes. I'll help you fix dinner and we can talk then."

"I'm looking forward to tonight," she said. "Do you think the whole unbelievable mess with the Shah and all the killing is finally over?"

"I really do, Suzy. There may be some loose ends to tie up – like what's going to be done with the Montana ranch, and will the Tampa office continue to exist – things like that. Also, since his bank is sitting on a big pile of the late Shah's money, I imagine Alex Trimble will be involved in some way, too. Which reminds me, it's probably too late today, but first thing tomorrow I've got to call Alex."

About an hour later I was sitting in Joe's office going over some estimates with him when Nancy beeped me and said I had a call on line two from a guy named Angelo. He said it was important that he talk with me. I told her I'd take the call in my office. I only knew one Angelo and I'd assumed I'd never hear from him again. The sound of his name brought a flood of bad memories.

"Cole McQuaid," I said, when I picked up the phone. "What can I do for you?" I asked.

"Cole, this is Angelo. Do you recognize my Montana accent?" he asked.

"You don't have a Montana accent, and I only know one Angelo, so what do you want?"

"There are a few things we have to tidy up before we can close the book on Montana," he said. "We need to talk – and by 'we' I'm referring to you, me and my boss. We must meet with you personally. Before you object, let me emphasize three things; first, this is a national security matter – we represent the executive branch of the government – so this meeting will take place, forcefully if necessary; second, we are all on the same side so you will be in no danger; and third, as an accommodation to you we will meet in Philadelphia – instead of our headquarters – tomorrow afternoon at two o'clock. I will give you the address of a condominium in the Society Hill section of the city. One other thing; you must come alone. Will you cooperate?"

"I sure as hell don't want to, but you've made it sound like I really have no choice. I just want to put everything that's happened behind me and get on with my life. Is this meeting really necessary? Can't we do what you want on the phone?"

"I'm sorry Cole, but that's not possible. As I said, this is a national security matter. We must also discuss the shooting death of Karl Seitz. You were responsible for that – regardless of justification – and I'm sure you don't want your involvement to become public, *if you know what I mean*. So, you'll be there tomorrow? If you've got a pencil and paper I'll give you the address. Are you familiar with Society Hill?"

I assured him I was, and wrote down the address he gave me.

"Remember Cole, two o'clock sharp – please don't be late – and make sure you come alone. And no wires, you'll be thoroughly checked when you enter the building."

After we hung up I sat at my desk for a while trying to figure out what information I had that could be so important to Angelo and his boss. Hell, Angelo worked on the ranch. He probably knows everything that's happened there since the day he arrived.

I decided not to mention tomorrow's meeting in Philly to Suzy. I didn't understand why they wanted to talk to me and I knew Suzy wouldn't either. She's had more than her share of worry about me.

Dinner at Suzy's was delicious as usual. I made the salad and cooked the blackened salmon, while she did the garlic mashed potatoes and green beans. I opened a chilled bottle of dry white wine that nicely complimented the salmon. After a relaxing leisurely dinner we took our coffee into the living room and spent the next hour discussing my odyssey in Montana. I told her everything except the part about Angelo riddling the Shah's plane with gunfire. I lead her to believe the crash was caused by the weather. I also didn't mention the call from Angelo today and the meeting in Philly tomorrow.

"I've heard enough, Cole," she said. "It's very depressing and I'm sure you went through hell. I'm so thankful you're safely home – please stay here tonight, I need you close to me."

We left the front light on for Julia and went to bed early. I don't know if I disappointed Suzy, but I was asleep almost as soon as my head hit the pillow. With Suzy's naked body entwined in mine I slept better than I had in quite a while.

I was in the office the next morning by eight. The first thing I did was call Alex in London. I was surprised to hear him say that Tampa had called him yesterday and told him that a tragedy had occurred in the organization and he was to cease all financial dealings for the client until further notice. They refused to give him any further information.

I started to give him a rundown of my Montana trip, when it crossed my mind that maybe I shouldn't say too much on the phone. Trying to be cryptic I said that my earlier guess about the client's identity was right on the money. Before I could say any more Alex interrupted.

"Cole, please – I don't think it prudent to discuss this matter on the telephone. I'm extremely interested in what happened, but we must find another way to converse. Just answer one question: Will it be possible for us to discuss future business directly with the client?"

"No, Alex, it won't." Alex was quiet for so long I thought our connection was broken.

"Alex," I almost yelled. "Are you still on the line?"

"Yes, Cole, I'm still here. I find what you just told me very distressing – an enigma; good from the standpoint of morality, but probably ending the likelihood of any future dealings with the client. Please let me ramble on for a few minutes – since David's death you probably have been closer to this situation than anybody, myself included. If there is anything left to salvage – and at this point there may not be – do I need to take action quickly to protect the bank's interests? But, before I can make that decision, I need the benefit of your advice and the information you obtained during your recent trip. I believe we must meet in complete privacy, away from any prying eyes or ears. How soon can you come the London again? And please Cole, this time I insist on paying your expenses. We cannot impose on you further."

My initial reaction to his request was to refuse, but the more I thought about it the more it made sense. There were a lot of loose ends that did need to be tied down – and I still wasn't convinced that Alex didn't have a mole working under cover in his bank.

"I can't give you an answer right now Alex, but I agree that we need to talk. I'll get back to you tomorrow and let you know when I can come. Oh, and by the way; I agree, this trip will be on your dime."

I had another thought rattling around in my head that I'd been kicking around for weeks now. Maybe another trip to England would provide the opportunity for me to resolve that issue too.

When I drove to Philly that afternoon I had no trouble finding the address Angelo had given me. I did have to drive around the neighborhood for almost fifteen minutes trying to find a parking place. Life in the big city. I used the brass door knocker to announce my presence and a big guy in jeans and a plaid shirt let me in. He told me to remove my jacket and kept me in the foyer while he patted me down for a weapon and a wire. Satisfied that I had neither, he lead me up a flight of stairs to a mezzanine level and then through to a rear room furnished like a family room. The room had nothing but artificial lighting because there were no windows or skylights. A man I had never met sat at one end of a large leather sofa. Angelo sat opposite him in an overstuffed chair. Angelo spoke first. "Cole," he said. "This is

George – we don't use last names. George is my director and he has some questions for you. Please sit down."

"That's fine," I said. "But I won't answer any questions until you tell me who you are and who you work for. Are you FBI, CIA or what? And, Angelo, what the hell were you doing working as a chauffeur at the Montana ranch?"

George stood up and moved in front of me, looking down. "Mr. McQuaid," he said. "We normally do not divulge any information about our personnel or our activities – except on a need to know basis. Therefore, we may answer your questions, or we may not; and I will decide whether we do or don't. Just remember that you are here as an accommodation to us, and your full cooperation with us is required . . . and will be given – as I believe you will come to understand in the next few minutes.

"It is reasonable to say that we know everything about you, and you know absolutely nothing about us. We are not FBI and we are not CIA. And we do not answer to either of those agencies. We are a small group who reports only to the executive branch of the government. We are known as ES, which stands for 'Executive Solutions'. We deal solely with anti-terrorist issues, communication and liaison with friendly and unfriendly dictatorships and, on occasion, elimination of individuals deemed dangerous to the interests of our government.

"To be more specific, we have monitored the Shah and the activities on the Montana property since it became his permanent home in the late 70's. At that time the Shah had very powerful friends in this country, and the CIA was given carte blanche to covertly assist him during his reign in any way they deemed appropriate, up to and including elimination of anyone who got in his way. The CIA agent responsible for all of this was a senior operative by the name of Rexton, who ultimately served for decades as the Shah's advisor and liaison. They formed a very strong friendship, so strong in fact that Rexton's superiors suspected him of manipulating the Shah to suit his own purposes. Much later, when the Shah's political problems began to escalate, Rexton tried to convince his superiors to bring the Shah to this country. But political sentiment in this country was also changing and Rexton was told that his proposal was rejected and he was being transferred back to CIA headquarters. The Shah, in effect, was going to be hung out to dry. But this did not deter Rexton. He immediately resigned from the CIA and went back to Tehran. Shortly after, the Shah wound up on the ranch in Montana – and Rexton wound up a very rich man."

"Wait a minute," I interrupted. "How did you get all this information, and if the Shah wasn't welcome here how did he get away with it all these years? It doesn't make sense!"

"Mr. McQuaid, I've given you this background only to convince you that we know the entire history of this situation, including your involvement during the past few months. We have operated for many years with instructions to do whatever is necessary to keep the Shah's presence in this country from the public. He was to be eliminated immediately if it appeared that he was attempting to permanently flee the ranch. Angelo was our eyes and ears at the ranch, and did exactly what he had been instructed to do when it appeared the Shah was attempting to leave. If the Shah succeeded in going elsewhere and his existence became known, the impact on Washington, both past and present, would be devastating. That is all I will tell you."

"O.K. George, I understand your concern, but why am I here? I had hoped this whole crazy affair was ended. I want nothing more than to run my business and live my life, and that picture doesn't included any further involvement with you guys. Understand?"

"Exactly, Mr. McQuaid. The purpose of this meeting is to impress on you the extreme importance of total silence on your part with regard to the late Shah. As far as you're concerned it never happened; it was nothing more than a bad dream. And if you refuse to cooperate, we'll have our psychiatrist attest to your delusional behavior and then be forced to assist the authorities in prosecuting you for the unwarranted murder of Karl Seitz, a security guard working for M. R. Shaw, when he caught you rifling Mr. Shaw's desk, and later causing the crash of Mr. Shaw's private plane, killing four more people. These pictures will help prove our charges."

With that he handed me a manila envelope containing about a dozen eight by ten black and white glossy prints. I was in every one. They obviously had been made from security camera film. Most appeared to be legitimate, but a few had been doctored to make me look like a nut on a killing rampage.

"So, George, all I have to do is keep my mouth shut about the Shah and these pictures will go away? What are you going to do about silencing all of the other people who must have had knowledge of the Shah's existence?"

"You let me worry about that Mr. McQuaid. Other than you, nobody had direct knowledge or any reason to suspect that M. R. Shaw was in fact the Shah. Certainly none of the people working for him at the ranch or in the Tampa office did. Have I made my point Mr. McQuaid; will you cooperate with us?"

"Absolutely, George," I answered. "As I just said, I have my own priorities in life, my own agenda, and they don't include Shaw, Shah, Tampa, you, or anything sounding even remotely like a government agency. So, you have nothing to fear from me. Understood? Now, if you don't mind, I'm leaving – and I know where the door is."

"Thank you for meeting with us Mr. McQuaid – and for you cooperation. Follow my instructions and you will not see us or hear from us again. Goodbye."

Angelo wouldn't look at me as I walked past him on my way to the door.

EPILOGUE

When I got back to my car I got in and sat there for almost half an hour thinking about what I had just heard. It boggles my mind to know there is yet another agency operating somewhere in the netherworld of power politics – in this case a covert group who apparently has more power than the CIA and FBI combined. Who is watching who? Who is pulling the strings. I guess Big Brother is watching – but I'll be damned if I'm going to spend the rest of my life looking over my shoulder.

Before heading for the bridge, I drove to jeweler's row on Sansom Street, parked in a public garage and walked two blocks to my favorite jewelry store. I had bought a number of things from them in the past, including a custom made gold ring containing a 1911 quarter-eagle gold coin my grandmother, Shirley Catlett, had given me when I was born. I had a pretty good idea what I wanted and after scanning their showcases for a few minutes I found it. I also had a pretty good idea of her ring size, so I waited while they sized and polished it. I then selected two embossed wedding bands – one to fit me. I haven't felt this excited about anything since I kissed Suzy for the first time in London.

On my way back to the office I thought again about what George had said. If I went to London to see Alex again, was George going to know? And would he consider it a breech of our agreement? I couldn't risk that, so one thing was certain; if I go to England it has to be for some reason other than to meet with Alex. I'll have to be very careful.

The first thing I did when I got back to my office was call my travel agent. Knowing that I was being very presumptuous, I told her to book two tickets to London on the Saturday night British Airways flight out of Philly. It was now late afternoon on Monday and I had a lot of arrangements to make. I was about to make another phone call when reality set in. Was I was really assuming too much here? I'd better slow down and call Suzy.

When she walked into my office I was suddenly overcome with a bad case of the jitters. My stomach was really doing flip-flops.

I started by explaining that I had to go to England again to meet with Trimble. It was necessary because there were still details to finalize before we closed the book on the Shah. Before I could continue she interrupted -

"Cole, I thought this whole crazy business with the Shah was finished. Haven't you sacrificed enough of yourself? When is it going to end?"

"Whoa, Suzy, don't get upset. Meeting with Trimble is not the main reason I'm going to England. I'm really going to enjoy my honeymoon

– with my new bride. I love her very much, and I think she loves me. But, I guess to put things in the proper order I first have to ask her to marry me. Will you, Suzy?"

She walked around my desk, didn't say a word, sat on my lap and burst into tears. After she composed herself she kissed me. "Cole, I do love you. My only question is why did you wait so long to ask? Of course I'll marry you! And Julia will be thrilled!"

I took the engagement ring I had just bought out of the box and slipped it on her finger. She looked at it and again burst into tears.

"It's beautiful Cole. Do you really want to get married before we go to England? Is there time?"

"We leave for England Saturday evening, so we've got five days to do everything. If I can arrange it, would you want to be married Friday in my church? I'm going to call now to find out about the license."

"Friday is fine, Cole, but I've got a million things to do. First, I have to call Julia, I can't wait to tell her."

Early Tuesday morning I called Trimble and told him Suzy and I would be arriving Sunday morning in London. I told him I wouldn't come to his bank – and I'd explain why when we met – but I'd call when Suzy and I got to our hotel to set up a place where he and I could meet. He started to object, but I told him that's the way it had to be. I cautioned him not to mention my visit to anyone. I also told him that Suzy and I were being married on Friday and he offered his congratulations.

The next few days were a blur. We got the license just in time to comply with the three day wait. The minister agreed to marry us Friday evening at seven. On Thursday my mom and dad flew up from Florida, and on Friday morning my sister Abigail, her husband and kids came down from Boston. Ben was my best man and Julia was the maid of honor. Everything went off without a hitch. After the ceremony everybody went to one of Suzy's favorite restaurants for a reception dinner. Suzy and I spent the night in one of Philadelphia's better hotels, the name of which I kept from everybody. We spent most of the night enjoying each other.

The flight to London was smooth and uneventful. I had tried to get reservations at the Dukes Hotel, but they were booked solid. On the advice of my travel agent I settled for a four-star hotel in the St. James district. It turned out to be quite nice, and was directly across from a small park. After we got settled in and had a late breakfast I called

Trimble at his home. He said he knew the hotel we were in and offered to meet me in the park at two that afternoon. It sounded like the best place for he and I to talk privately.

Suzy decided to stay in our room. When I walked out the front door of the hotel I saw Trimble across the street waiting for me. He was carrying a small package. When we greeted and shook hands it struck me that he was much more relaxed than the last time we met. We walked in he park for a while making small talk. He asked about Suzy and the wedding and said he had a wedding gift for us. After we found a bench and sat down he handed me the package and told me to open it. "I don't know what your plans are after today, but what you'll find in the package may make your stay here with your new wife more enjoyable. At least my wife and I hope so."

The package contained a map, two envelopes and a number of color pictures of a quaint little cottage, surrounded by beautiful roses in full bloom and a landscape of colorful flowers, all overlooking an expanse of rocky beach and blue water. I was puzzled.

"Have you made definite plans for your stay here?"

"Well Alex, yes and no. We have Brit Rail passes and planned on taking a number of trips by rail, using our hotel here in London as a base. We're going to take the overnight train to Edinburgh, stay a few days and then sort of wind our way back to London by train. What are these pictures of?"

"That is our summer home near St. Austell on the Cornwall coast. It is where my wife and I are going to retire in a year or so. She and I want you and your bride to honeymoon in the cottage as long as you like."

"Alex, that is a beautiful gesture. I know Suzy will love it. Is the cottage reasonably close to a rail station?"

"Yes, it's a fairly short drive to the station. If you'll open that small envelope you will find two keys. One is to the cottage front door; the other is to a car parked in the garage behind the cottage. It is not a fancy automobile, we use it just to do shopping and to go to and from the train station. You are welcome to use it while you are here. The map in the package covers the counties of Devon and Cornwall."

"What's in this other envelope," I asked.

"Ahh. We've saved the best for last. But before you open it let me explain. You have expended a great deal of time, effort and your personal finances during the past few months to assist in resolving our problem with our notorious client. Further, as a result of your recommendation we have recouped all but a very small percentage of invested client funds. Our cash reserves are now considerable, and regardless of what happens we stand to make a substantial profit, even if we do no further business with the client. The bank is very grateful for your services and we hope the bank draft in that envelope is adequate compensation for your efforts."

I opened the envelope and glanced inside. The amount was in the low six figures. I almost fell off the bench.

"Alex, my god, this is too much. I only expected you to compensate me for this visit. Really, this is not necessary."

"Nonsense, you have earned every penny of it. It represents a very small percentage of what you have saved us. Now, I asked you to come here to report on your trip to Montana. I did so because in reading between the lines of what you said on the telephone after you returned, it appears obvious that something drastic happened. Since that conversation with you I have had two rather cryptic calls from Tampa insisting that we cease all financial transactions for the client until further notice. When I questioned why, they said some procedural changes were being made. Poppycock! So, Cole, what did happen in Montana?"

I gave him a detailed verbatim report of what I had experienced in Montana, from the time I left Miles City until I returned. I left out nothing. He must have said 'Oh my god' at least twenty times. When I finished, he apologized for putting me through such hell. I tried to make him understand that I went to Montana as much for myself as for anybody else. We sat on the bench for another five minutes without a word being spoken. He seemed to be very upset. Finally, he turned to me and asked if I still wanted to use his summer cottage. I knew Suzy would love it, so I said yes. We stood and shook hands. Alex thanked me again and walked off in the opposite direction from which we came.

Suzy did love the cottage. She also loved the beach, the view of the sea, the sunny days and chilly dark nights. We sat in the sand and watched the sunset, then warmed our bodies in front of the fireplace. For two weeks we walked and talked and drove on the wrong side of the road to small towns where we explored quaint shops and listened to friendly people speak with a strange accent. We even took the train to Edinburgh. But most important of all we were together. And that made it perfect.